Forty Times a Killer!

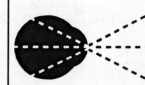 This Large Print Book carries the
Seal of Approval of N.A.V.H.

BAD MEN OF THE WEST

FORTY TIMES A KILLER!

WILLIAM W. JOHNSTONE
WITH J.A. JOHNSTONE

WHEELER PUBLISHING
A part of Gale, Cengage Learning

GALE
CENGAGE Learning·

Farmington Hills, Mich • San Francisco • New York • Waterville, Maine
Meriden, Conn • Mason, Ohio • Chicago

GALE
CENGAGE Learning·

Following the death of William W. Johnstone, the Johnstone family is working with a carefully selected writer to organize and complete Mr. Johnstone's outlines and many unfinished manuscripts to create additional novels in all of his series like The Last Gunfighter, Mountain Man, and Eagles, among others. This novel was inspired by Mr. Johnstone's superb storytelling.
Wheeler Publishing Large Print Western.
The text of this Large Print edition is unabridged.
Other aspects of the book may vary from the original edition.
Set in 16 pt. Plantin.

LIBRARY OF CONGRESS CATALOGING-IN-PUBLICATION DATA

Johnstone, William W.
    Forty times a killer! / by William W. Johnstone with J. A. Johnstone. — Large print edition.
        pages ; cm. — (Bad men of the west series) (Wheeler Publishing large print western)
        ISBN 978-1-4104-7184-0 (softcover) — ISBN 1-4104-7184-5 (softcover)
        1. Hardin, John Wesley, 1853–1895—Fiction. 2. Outlaws—Fiction. 3. Large type books. I. Johnstone, J. A. II. Title.
    PS3560.O415F67 2014
    813'.54—dc23   2014016569

Published in 2014 by arrangement with Pinnacle Books, an imprint of Kensington Publishing Corp.

Printed in the United States of America
2 3 4 5 6   18 17 16 15 14

FORTY TIMES A KILLER!

CHAPTER ONE:
DEATH IN THE STREET

"John Wesley Hardin! I'm calling you out, John Wesley!"

My friend turned to me and his left eyebrow arched the way it always did when his face asked a question.

"All right. I'll take a look," I said, laying aside my copy of Mr. Dickens' *The Life and Adventures of Martin Chuzzlewit,* partially set, as you know, on our very own western frontier.

I rose from the table and limped to the saloon's batwing doors, more a tangle of broken and missing slats than door. I guess so many heads were rammed through those batwings that nobody took the trouble to repair them any longer.

Three men wearing slickers and big Texas mustaches stood in the dusty street. All were armed with heavy Colt revolvers carried high on the waist, horseman-style. They glanced at me, dismissed me as something beneath their notice, and continued their wait.

I told John Wesley what I saw and he said, "Ask them what the hell they want."

"They're calling you out, Wes. That's what they want."

"I know it, Little Bit. But ask them anyhow." Wes stood at the bar, playing with a little calico kitten, the warm schooner of beer at his elbow growing warmer in the east Texas heat.

The railroad clock on the wall ticked slow seconds into the quiet and the bartender cleared his throat and whispered to the saloon's only other customer, "James, this won't do."

The gray-haired man nodded. "A bad business." He stared through the window. "Those men are pistol fighters."

He was not ragged, as most of us Texans were that late summer of 1870. His clothes were well worn, but clean, and spoke of a good wife at home. He might have been a one-loop rancher or a farmer, but he could have been anything.

I stepped outside into the street, if you could call it that.

The settlement of Honest Deal was a collection of a few raw timber buildings sprawled hit or miss along the bank of the west fork of the San Jacinto River, a sun-scorched, wind-blown scrub town waiting desperately for a railroad spur or even a stage line to give it purpose and a future.

I blinked in the sudden bright light, then took the measure of the three men. They were big, hard-eyed fellows. The oldest of them had an arrogant look to him, as though he hailed from a place where he was the cock o' the walk.

That one would take a heap of killing, I figured. They all would.

I swallowed hard. "Mr. Hardin's compliments, and he wishes to know what business you have with him."

"Unfinished business," the oldest man said.

Another, tall and blond and close enough in looks and arrogance to be his son, said, "Gimp, get back in there and tell Hardin to come out. If he ain't in the street in one minute, we'll come in after him."

The man's use of the word *gimp* surprised me. I thought the steel brace on my left leg covered by my wool pants was unnoticeable. Unless I walked, of course. I'd only taken a step into the street, so I could only assume that the tall man was very observant.

Wes was like that, observant. All revolver

fighters were back in those days. They had to be.

Measuring him, it seemed to me that the younger man was also one to step around, unless you were mighty gun slick.

"I'll tell Mr. Hardin what you said." I smiled at the three men. I had good teeth when I was younger, the only part of my crooked, stunted body that was good, so I smiled a lot. Showing them off, you understand.

I figured I knew why those three men didn't want to come into the saloon after Wes unless they had to. The place was small, little bigger than a railroad boxcar, and gloomy, lit by smoking, smelly, kerosene lamps. Only Yankee carpetbaggers could afford the whale oil that burned brighter without smoke or stink. If shooting started inside, the concussion of the guns would extinguish the lamps and four men would have to get to their work in semidarkness and at point-blank range.

Against a deadly pistol fighter like Wes, those three fellows were well aware that no one would walk out of the saloon alive. They wanted badly to kill Wes, but outside where they would have room to maneuver and take cover if necessary.

I can't say as I blamed them. A demon

with ol' Sammy's revolver was Wes, fast and accurate on the draw and shoot.

That's one of the reasons I idolized him. I'd never met his like before . . . or since.

Well, I turned to go back into the saloon and tell him what the three gentlemen outside wanted, but I'd taken only one clumping step when Wes stepped around the corner of the saloon, a smile on his face and a .44 1860 Army model Colt in each hand.

All his life, Wes favored those old cap-and-ball pistols, and he would often say that they were both wife and child to him.

He wore black pants held up by suspenders and a vest of the same color over a collarless white shirt. Shoulder holsters book-ended his manly chest and he sported a silver signet ring on the little finger of his left hand, the hallmark of the frontier gambler.

"You fellows wish to speak with me?" he said, making the slight bow that he considered the stamp of a well-bred Southern gentleman.

Well, the three men had been caught flatfooted and they knew it.

The oldest of them was the first to recover. He pushed his slicker away from his gun and said, "You know why we're here,

11

Hardin."

"Damn right you do," the blond man said.

They were on the prod, those two, and right then I knew there would be no stepping back from this, not for Wes, not for anybody.

"I'm afraid you have the advantage over me," Wes said. "I've never seen you gentlemen before in my life."

"You know us, damn you," the older man said.

"We're here for my brother Sonny," the blond man said.

Wes smiled again, showing his teeth.

Lord-a-mercy, but that was a bad sign. John Wesley was never a smiling man . . . unless he planned to kill somebody.

"I've never heard the name Sonny, nor can I attach it to a remembered face," he said. "How do you spell it, with an *O* or a *U*?"

"You're pleased to make a joke." This from the man who hadn't spoken before, a lean, hawk-faced man whose careful eyes had never left Wes, reading him and coming to a decision about him.

He was a gun, that one. He'd be mighty sudden and would know some fancy moves.

"I made a good joke?" Wes asked. "Then how come I don't hear you gentlemen laughing?" His Colts were hanging loose at his sides as though he had all the time in the world.

"You go to hell." The hawk-faced man went for his gun.

Years later, I was told that the lean man was probably a ranny by the name of Hugh Byrd who had a vague reputation in Texas as a draw-fighter.

Word was that he'd killed Mason Lark up El Paso way. You recall Lark, the Denver bounty hunter with the Ute wife? Back then nobody considered Lark a bargain and even John Wesley once remarked that the man was fast on the draw and a proven man killer.

Well, for reasons best known only to himself, Byrd — if that really was his name — decided to commit suicide the day he drew down on Wes.

His gun hadn't cleared leather when two .44 bullets clipped half-moons from the tobacco tag that hung over the pocket of his shirt and tore great wounds in his chest.

I didn't watch him fall. My eyes were on the other two.

The blond man got off a shot at Wes, but he'd hurried the draw and the slug kicked up a startled exclamation point of dirt an inch in front of the toe of Wes's right boot.

The towhead knew he'd made a bad mistake. His face horrified, he took a step back and raised his revolver to correct his aim.

But the young man's hurried shot had been the kind of blunder you can't make in a gunfight . . . and Wes made him pay for it. His bucking Colts hammering with tremendous speed and accuracy, he slammed three or four bullets into the man's upper chest and belly.

Gagging on his own blood, the yellow-haired fellow dropped to his knees.

Wes ignored him. He swung on the older man who hadn't made a move for his gun. His reactions slower than the others, the fight had gone too fast for him and there was no way he was going to play catch-up.

He tossed his Colt away and raised his hands to waist level. "I'm out of it, John Wesley. Now you've killed both my sons and I want to live long enough to grieve for them."

The man was not scared or afraid to die, but I knew living would be hard for him, each passing day another little death. Blood had drained from his features and I looked into the gray, blue-shadowed face of a corpse.

"No, mister, you're in it," Wes said, smiling. "There ain't a way out. You brought it, and now you pay the piper." He raised his Colt, took careful aim and shot the old man between the eyes.

The blond man was clinging to life, coughing up black blood. He turned his head as the older man fell into the dirt beside him. "Pa!" He reached out and put his hand on his father's chest. His mouth was a shocked, scarlet O. "Are you kilt dead, Pa?"

"Yeah, he's kilt dead," Wes said. "Now go join him in hell."

The Colt roared again . . . and then only the desert wind made a sound.

I reckon the whole population of the town, maybe a dozen men and a couple women, young'uns clutching at their skirts, stood in the street and stared at the three sprawled bodies. The faces of the men and women were expressionless. They looked like so many painted dolls as they tried to come to grips with the violence and sudden death that had come into their midst.

"This won't do," the bartender said. "This is a job for the law." He glanced hopefully around the crowd, but nobody had listened to him.

Fat blowflies had already formed a black, crawling crust on the gory faces of the dead

15

and I fancied I already got a whiff of the stench of decay.

The bartender, who seemed to have appointed himself spokesman for the whole town, looked at Wes. "Who were they, mister?"

"Damned if I know."

The bartender made it official. He reached into his vest pocket and took out a lawman's star that he pinned to his chest. The star looked as though it had been cut from the bottom of a bean can. "I heard one of them say they were here for Sonny," the bartender-sheriff said. "You ever hear of him?"

Wes shook his head. "No, I don't reckon I have. Unless his name was spelled with a *U*."

"You ever hear of a man named Sunny, with a *U*?"

"No. I don't reckon I have." With every eye on him, Wes made one of those grandstand plays that helped make him famous. He spun those big Colts and they were still spinning when he dropped them into their holsters. "Sheriff, a man in my line of business makes a lot of enemies. Hell, I can't keep track of all the men who want to kill me."

"And what is your business?" the sheriff said.

"I'm a shootist," Wes said.

Me, I looked into John Wesley's eyes then. There was no meanness, no blue, luminous light I've seen in a man's eyes when he takes pleasure in a killing . . . but there was something else.

Wes looked around the crowd, his gaze moving from face to stunned face, and his eyes were bright, questioning. *Look at me! Look at me everybody. Have you ever seen my like before?*

Right then, John Wesley was Narcissus at the pool, the man who fell madly in love with his own reflection.

And the people around him, as soon as the gunshots stopped ringing in their ears, fed his vanity.

All of a sudden, men were slapping him on the back, shaking his hand, telling him he'd done good. The women looked at him from under lowered eyelashes and wondered what it would be like to take a gladiator to bed.

Even the sheriff stepped off the distance between Wes and the dead men and grinned at the crowd. "Ten paces, by God. And three men hurled into eternity in the space of a moment!"

This drew a cheer, and Wes bowed and grinned and basked in the adulation.

He was but seventeen years old and he'd killed eleven white men.

The newspapers had made him a named gunfighter, up there with the likes of Longley and Hickok, and he'd have to live with it.

And me, I thought, *But in the end they'll kill you, Wes. One day the folks will forget all about you and that will be your death.*

Chapter Two:
The Dark Star

"I got an idea, Little Bit," John Wesley said. "Hell, it's a notion that can make us both rich."

"Wes," I said, laying Mr. Dickens on my lap, my thumb marking the page I'd been reading by firelight, "does your brain ever stop?"

Wes grinned, glanced at the full moon riding high above the pines, and pointed. "No, I'm like him up there, always shining. And when I get an idea, I shine even brighter."

We'd left Honest Deal at first light that morning, heading west for the town of Longview over to Harrison County where Wes had kin. I was all used up. The dog days of summer were on us and the day had been blistering hot and as humid as one of those steam baths that some city folks seem to enjoy.

The night was no better, just darker.

My leg in its iron cage hurt like hell and all I wanted was to read a couple chapters of Martin Chuzzlewit and then find my blankets.

But Wes, who had a bee in his bonnet, wouldn't let it go. His shirt was dark with arcs of sweat under his arms, and his teeth glinted white in the moonlight. "Well, don't you want to hear it?"

"Hear what?" I asked.

"Don't mess with me, Little Bit. I told you I have a great idea."

I sighed, found a pine needle that I used to mark my page, and closed the book. "I'm all ears," I said, looking at Wes through the gloom.

"All right, but first answer me this. Do you agree that I'm a man destined for great things?"

I nodded. "I'd say that. You're a fine shootist, Wes. The best that ever was."

"I know, but I'm much more than that."

"So, tell me your idea."

"Listen up. My idea is to star in a show. My own show."

"You mean like a medicine show?" I smiled at him. "Dr. Hardin's Healing Balm."

"Hell no. Bigger than that and better." Wes raised his hands and made a long banner shape in the air. "John Wesley Hardin's Wild West Show."

His face aglow, he said, "Well, what do you think? Isn't it great, huh?"

"I don't know what to think. I've never heard of such a thing."

"A . . . what's the word? . . . *spectacular* show, Little Bit. With me as the hero and you as . . . as . . . well, I'll think of something."

"On stage in a theater, Wes? Is that what you think?"

"Maybe. But probably outside in an arena. We'll have drovers and cavalry and Indians and outlaws and cattle herds and stagecoaches and . . . hell, the possibilities are endless." Wes leaned closer to me and the shifting firelight stained the right side of his eager, handsome face. "I'll be the fearless frontiersman who saves the fair maiden from the savages or captures the rustlers singlehanded, stuff like that."

"Sounds expensive, Wes. I mean, paying all those hands and —"

"Damn it, Little Bit, that kind of thinking is the reason you're not destined for greatness. I'll get rich backers, see? They'll bankroll the show for a cut of the profits."

Wes smiled at me. "Hell, we got three hundred dollars for the horses and traps of

21

them dead men back at Honest Deal, so we already got seed money." He read the doubt in my face and said, "It can't fail. Nobody's ever had an idea like mine and nobody else is going to think of it. Man, I'll make a killing and a fortune."

He again made a banner of his hands and grinned. "John Wesley Hardin's Wild West Show! Damn, I like the sound o' that." He let out a rebel yell that echoed like the howl of a wolf in the silence. "Little Bit, it's gonna be great!"

Around me, the pines were black, and they leaned into one another as though they were exchanging ominous secrets. I felt uneasy, like a flock of geese had just flown over my grave. "What do I do, Wes?"

"Do? Do where?"

"In the show, Wes. What do I do in your Wild West Show?"

Wes's eyes roamed over me and I was well aware of what he saw . . . a tiny, stunted runt with a thin, white face, boot-button brown eyes, and a steel brace on his twisted twig of a left leg.

I wasn't formed by nature to play any kind of western hero.

John Wesley was never one to get stumped by a question, but he scowled, his thick black brows drawn together in thought.

Then his face cleared and he smiled. "You read books, Little Bit, don't you?"

I nodded and held up my copy of Mr. Dickens.

"Then there's your answer." Wes clapped his hands. "You'll be my bookkeeper! And" — he beamed as he delivered what he obviously believed was the snapper — "a full partner in the business!"

I said nothing.

"What's wrong? I thought you'd be happy with that proposition."

"I am, I really am."

"Then why do you look so down in the mouth you could eat oats out of a churn?"

"Because the thought just came to me that before you can do anything, Wes, you'll have to square yourself with the law."

John Wesley sighed, a dramatic intake of breath coupled with a frustrated yelp that he did often. "Little Bit, are you talking about Mage again?"

"Well, Mage for starters, but there are others."

"Mage was your friend, wasn't he?"

"Not really. We were together a lot because he wanted to learn how to read and do his ciphers."

"Negroes are too stupid to learn to read," Wes said. "Hell, everybody knows that."

"He was doing all right. He liked Sir Walter Scott."

"He wasn't doing all right in my book," Wes said, his face tight. "Mage was an uppity black man who needed killing."

I smiled to take the sting out of a conversation that was veering into dangerous territory. When Wes got angry bad things happened.

"Ah, you were just sore because he beat you at rasslin'," I said.

"Yeah, but I bloodied his nose, didn't I?"

I nodded. "You done good, Wes. Mage was twice as big as you."

"And ugly with it."

Wes was silent for a while. A breeze spoke in the pines and a lace of mist frosted by moonlight drifted between their slender trunks. I fancied that the ghosts of dead Comanches were wandering the woods.

"You know what he said, don't you?" Wes asked.

"Let's drop it. It isn't that important."

"You know what he said?"

I shook my head. I didn't feel good that night. My leg hurt and the salt pork and cornpone we'd eaten for dinner wasn't sitting right with me.

"He said that no white boy could draw his blood and live. Then he said that no bird ever flew so high that could not be brought to the ground. He was talking about a shooting, Little Bit. He planned to put a ball in my back."

"Mage shouldn't have said that."

"Damn right he shouldn't. And he shouldn't have tried to pull me off my horse, either."

I made no comment on that last and Wes said, "All I did was shoot him the hell off'n me."

I felt his angry blue eyes burn into my face.

"You would've done the same."

"I guess so. If I could shoot a revolver, I might have done the same."

"Everybody in Texas knew it was a justified killing. Everybody except the damned Yankees."

"That's why you should make it right with them, Wes," I said.

"Damned if I will. Since when did the killing of an uppity black man become a crime?"

"Since the Yankees won the war."

Wes spat into the fire. "Damn Yankees. I hate their guts."

"A lot of Texas folks think like you, Wes."

"And how do you feel, Little Bit? Until

real recent, I never pegged you as a Yankee-lover."

"Wes, my pa died at Gettysburg, remember. How do you think I feel?"

"Yeah, you're right. I forgot about that. You got no reason to cotton to Yankees, either." Wes grinned at me, his good humor restored. "I'll pour us some coffee, and before we turn in, we'll get back to talking about my Wild West Show for a spell." He frowned. "Damn it. We'll have no Yankees in it, unless we need folks to shovel hoss shit. Agreed?"

"Anything you say, Wes. Anything you say."

CHAPTER THREE:
"I DON'T ENJOY KILLING"

I saw John Wesley Hardin being born, I was with him when he died, and in between I was proud to call him my friend. He was everything I wanted to be and couldn't.

Wes was tall and slim and straight and moved with the elegance of a panther. He'd a fine singing voice and the very sight of him when he stepped into a room set the ladies' hearts aflutter. Many men admired him, others hated him, but all feared him and the wondrous things he could do with revolvers.

Like England's hunchbacked king, I was delivered misshapen from my mother's womb. My frail body did not grow as a man's should, and even in the full bloom of my youth, if you'd be pleased to call it that, I never weighed more than eighty pounds or reached a height of five feet.

Do you wonder then that I admired Wes so, and badly wanted to be like him? He was my noble knight errant who sallied forth to right wrongs, and I his lowly squire.

I think I know the answer to that question.

And why I pledged to stay at his side to the death.

As I told you earlier, we were headed for Longview to visit with Wes's kin for a spell, but he wanted to linger where we were for a day longer.

"This is a pleasant spot and we can talk about my idea some more. Sometimes it's good to just set back and relax."

I had no objections. I felt ill and my leg continued to give me trouble.

The day passed pleasantly enough. I sat under a tree and read my book and Wes caught a bright yellow butterfly at the base of a live oak. He said it meant good luck.

But when he opened his hands to let the butterfly go, it could no longer fly and fluttered to earth, a broken thing.

Wes said not to worry, that it was still good luck. But he seemed upset about the crippled butterfly and didn't try to catch another one.

The long day finally lifted its ragged skirts and tiptoed away, leaving us to darkness and the Texas stars.

Wes built up the fire and put the coffee on to boil. Using his Barlow knife, he shaved slices of salt pork into the pan and said there would be enough cornpone for supper with some leftover for tomorrow's breakfast.

I was pleased about that. It was good cornpone, made with buttermilk and eggs, and I was right partial to it back in those days.

After supper we talked about the Wild West Show, then, as young men do, about women. After a while, I said I was tired and it was about time I sought my blankets.

I stretched out and tried to ignore the pain gnawing at my leg.

Night birds fluttered in and out of the pines making a rustling noise and a puzzled owl asked its question of the night. A pair of hunting coyotes yipped back and forth in the distance and then fell silent.

I closed my eyes and entered that gray, misty realm between wakefulness and sleep . . . then jolted back to consciousness when a shout rang through the hallowed quiet.

"Hello the camp!"

I sat upright and saw that Wes was already on his feet. He wasn't wearing his guns, but stood tense and alert, his eyes reaching into the darkness.

Even as a teenager, John Wesley's voice was a soft baritone, but to my surprise he pitched it near an octave higher and broke it a little as he called out, "Come on in. There's coffee on the bile."

I wondered at that, but didn't dwell on it because the darkness parted and two men rode into the clearing.

Men made a living any way they could in Texas when Wes and I were young, and those two strangers looked as though they were no exception. They were hard-faced men, lean as wolves. I'd seen enough of their kind to figure that they were on the scout.

Astride mouse-colored mustangs that couldn't have gone more than eight hundred pounds, they wore belted revolvers and carried Springfield rifles across their saddle horns. As for clothing, their duds were any kind of rags they could patch together. The effect, coupled with their dirty, bare feet, was neither pleasant nor reassuring.

But the Springfields were clean and gleamed with a sheen of oil.

Whoever those men were, they were not pilgrims.

One of the riders, bearded and grim, was a man who'd long since lost the habit of smiling. "You got grub?"

"No, sir," Wes said, using that strange, boy's voice. "Sorry, but we're all out."

The man's eyes moved to our horses. "Where did you get them mounts?"

Wes didn't hesitate. "We stole them, sir. But we're taking them back to Longview to square ourselves with the law."

The man turned to his companion. "Lem, how much you figure the paint is worth?"

"Two hundred in any man's money," the man called Lem said. He looked at Wes. "You stole a lot of horse there, boy."

Wes nodded. "I know, sir. And that's why we're taking him back to his rightful owner."

"Who is his rightful owner?" Lem asked.

"We don't rightly know," I said. "But we aim to find out, like."

"Well, you don't have to worry about that, sonny," Lem said. "We'll take the paint off your hands, and the buckskin as well. Ain't that so, Dave?"

The bearded man nodded. "Sure thing. Pleased to do it. And, being decent folks, we'll set things right with the law for you."

"We'll do it ourselves," Wes said . . . in his normal voice.

And those two white trash idiots didn't notice the change! They sat their ponies and heard what they wanted to hear, saw what

31

they wanted to see.

What they heard was the scared voice of a half-grown boy, and what they saw was a pair of raw kids, one of them a crippled, sickly-looking runt.

Beyond that they saw nothing . . . an oversight that would prove their downfall.

It was a lethal mistake, and they made it.

They'd underestimated John Wesley Hardin, and as I said earlier, you couldn't make mistakes around Wes. Not if you wanted to go on living, you couldn't.

"Lem, go git them horses and saddles," Dave said. "Now, you boys just set and take it easy while Uncle Lem does what I told him."

"Leave the horses the hell alone," Wes said.

Lem was halfway out of the saddle, but something in Wes's tone froze him in place. He looked at Dave.

"Go do what I told you, Lem," the bearded man said. Then to Wes, "Boy, I had it in my head to let you live, since you're a good-looking kid and could come with us, make yourself useful, like. But my mind's pretty close to a-changing, so don't push me."

Lem dismounted and then, rifle in hand,

he grinned at Wes and walked toward the horses.

"I told you, leave the horses be." Wes stood very still, his face like stone.

I swallowed hard, my brain racing. *Wes, where the hell are your guns?*

"Boy, step aside," Dave said. "Or I'll drop you right where you stand."

"And you go to hell," Wes said.

Dave nodded as though he'd expected that kind of reaction. "You lose, boy." He smiled. "Sorry and all that."

He brought up his rifle and John Wesley shot him.

Drawing from the waistband behind his back, Wes's ball hit the Springfield's trigger guard, clipped off Dave's shooting finger, then ranged upward and crashed into the bearded man's chin.

His eyes wide and frantic, Dave reeled in the saddle, spitting blood, bone and teeth.

Wes ignored him. The man was done.

Wes and Lem fired at the same instant.

Unnerved by the unexpected turn of events, Lem, shooting from the hip, was too slow, too wide and too low. Wes's bullet hit him between the eyes and he fell all in a heap like a puppet that just had its strings cut.

Never one to waste powder and ball, Wes

didn't fire again.

But something happened that shocked me to the core.

Despite his horrific wound, his face a nightmare of blood and bone, the man called Dave swung his horse around and kicked it into the darkness.

Wes let out a triumphant yell and ran after him, holding his Colt high.

They vanished into the murk and I was left alone in silence.

In the moonlight, gun smoke laced around the clearing like a woman's wispy dress wafting in a breeze. The man on the ground lay still in death and made no sound.

A slow minute passed . . . then another. . . .

A shot! Somewhere out there in the dark.

Uneasy, I picked up a heavy stick that lay by the fire and hefted it in my hand. Small and weak as I was, there was little enough I could do to defend myself, but the gesture made me feel better.

"Hello the camp!" It was John Wesley's voice, followed by a shout of triumphant glee.

The black shades of the night parted and he walked into the clearing, leading the dead man's mustang.

I say dead man, because even without ask-

34

ing I knew that must have been Dave's fate.

"You should've seen it, Little Bit," Wes said, his face alight. "Twenty yards in darkness through trees! One shot! I blew the man's brains out." He laughed and clapped his hands. "If he had any."

Without waiting for my response, he said, "Now we got a couple more ponies to sell and two Springfield rifles. Their Colts are shot out and one has a loose cylinder, so I'll hold on to those." His face split in a wide grin. "What do you reckon, Little Bit, am I destined for great things or ain't I?"

I didn't answer that, at least not directly. "John Wesley, the killing has to stop."

He was genuinely puzzled and toed the dead man with his boot. "You talking about these two?"

"No, I guess not. I mean, the killing in general. You have to think about the Wild West show."

"These men needed killing, right?"

I nodded. "Yeah, I guess it was them or us." I was still holding onto the stick and tossed it away. "Maybe you could've let the other one die in his own time and at a place of his choosing. I say *maybe* you could. I'm not pointing fingers, Wes."

"Name one man I killed who didn't need killing, Little Bit. Damn it, name just one.

And don't say Mage. He was a black man and don't count."

He waited maybe a full second then said, "See, you can't name a one."

"Wes, there are some who say you pushed the fight with Ben Bradley."

"He cheated me at cards and then called me a coward. A man who deals from the bottom of the deck and calls another man yellow needs killing. At least in Texas he does."

"I was there, Wes. You kept right on pumping balls into him after he said, 'Oh Lordy, don't shoot me anymore.' I remember that. Why did you do it?"

"Because in a gunfight you keep shooting till the other man falls. And because only a man who's lowdown asks for mercy in the middle of a shooting scrape, especially after he's gotten his work in."

I was silent.

Wes said, "Well, did Ben Bradley need killing?"

I sighed. "Yeah, Wes. I guess he did at that."

"Then what's your problem?" Wes's face was dark with anger. "Come on, cripple boy, spit it out."

"Don't enjoy it, Wes. That's all. Just . . . just don't enjoy it."

36

Wes was taken aback and it was a while before he spoke again. "You really think I like killing men?" he finally asked.

"I don't know, Wes."

"Come on, answer me. Do you?"

"Maybe you do."

"And maybe I was born under a dark star. You ever think of that?"

Above the tree canopy the stars looked like diamonds strewn across black velvet. I pointed to the sky. "Which star?"

"It doesn't matter, Little Bit. Whichever one you choose will be dark. There ain't no shining star up there for John Wesley Hardin."

Depression was a black dog that stalked Wes all his life and I recognized the signs. The flat, toneless voice and the way his head hung as though it had suddenly become too heavy for his neck.

In later years, depression, coming on sudden, would drive him to alcohol and sometimes to kill.

It was late and I was exhausted, but I tried to lift his mood. "Your Wild West show is a bright star, Wes."

I thought his silence meant that he was considering that, but this was not the case.

"I don't kill men because I enjoy it. I kill other men because they want to kill me."

He stared at me with lusterless eyes. "I just happen to be real good at it."

"Get some sleep, Wes," I said.

He nodded to the body. "I'll drag that away first."

"Somewhere far. You ever hear wild hogs eating a man? It isn't pleasant."

Wes was startled. "How would you know that?"

Tired as I was, I didn't feel like telling a story, but I figured it might haul the black dog off Wes, so I bit the bullet, as they say. "Remember back to Trinity County when we were younkers?"

"Yeah?" Wes said it slow, making the word a question.

"Remember Miles Simpson, lived out by McCurry's sawmill?"

"Half-scalped Simpson? Had a wife that would have dressed out at around four hundred pounds and the three simple sons?"

"Yes, that's him. He always claimed that the Kiowa half-scalped him, but it was a band saw that done it."

"And he got et by a hog?"

"Let me tell the story. Well one summer, I was about eight years old, going on nine, and you had just learned to toddle around —"

"I was a baby," Wes said.

38

"Right. That's what you were, just a baby."
I hoped he wouldn't interrupt again otherwise the story would take all night to tell.

"Well, anyhoo, Ma sent me over to the Simpson place for the summer. She figured roughhousing with the boys might strengthen me and help my leg. Mrs. Simpson was a good cook and Ma said her grub would put weight on me."

"What did she cook?" With the resilience of youth, Wes was climbing out from under the black dog, and that pleased me.

"Oh pies and beef stew, stuff like that. And sausage. She made that herself and fried it in hog fat."

"I like peach pie," Wes said. "And apple, if it's got raisins in it."

"Yeah, me too."

"And plenty of cinnamon."

"She made pies like that." Then quickly, before he could interrupt again, I went on. "I was there the whole month of June, then on the second of July, the day after my ninth birthday, the cabin got hit by a band of Lipan Apaches that had crossed the Rio Grande and come up from Mexico."

"Damned murdering savages," Wes said.

"The youngest of the Simpson boys fell dead in the first volley. His name was Reuben or maybe Rufus, I can't recollect which.

39

The others, myself included, made it back into the cabin, though Mrs. Simpson's butt got burned by a musket ball as she was coming through the door."

"Big target."

"Yeah, I guess it was."

"Hold on just a minute." Wes grabbed the dead man by the ankles and dragged him into the brush. When he came back he said, "Then what happened?"

"Well, Mr. Simpson and his surviving sons held off the Apaches until dark when all went quiet. But they were afraid to go out for the dead boy's body on account of how the savages might be lying in ambush."

"Damned Apaches. I hate them."

"Well, just as the moon came up, we heard this snorting and snuffling sound, then a strange ripping noise, like calico cloth being torn into little pieces."

"What was it?" Wes asked.

"It was Reuben or maybe Rufus being torn into little pieces."

"The big boars have sharp tusks on them. They can rip into a man."

"They ripped into the dead boy all right. Come first light all that was left was a bloody skeleton. But the head was still intact. The hogs hadn't touched it." I stared at Wes. "Why would they do that?"

"I don't know, Little Bit. There ain't no accounting for what a hog will do."

Wes stepped to the brush, then turned and said, "I'm taking this feller well away from camp. Your damned story about them hogs has me boogered."

Chapter Four:
Wes Has Big Plans

We rode into Longview at the noon hour under a sky that had been burned out by the scorching sun. There was no breeze and the air hung heavy as a damp blanket.

Few people were on the street, probably because the sporting crowd was still abed and wouldn't appear until the dark of night.

Casting no shadow, Wes and I rode to the livery stable, the two mustangs in tow.

Longview was a rough railroad town and the smart moneymen reckoned that the arrival of the iron rails would soon bring prosperity on a massive scale to all concerned. Half the buildings that lined the street were saloons. Gunfights were common and most days the town could be depended on to serve a dead man for breakfast.

No doubt about it, the booming town had snap.

The business district, a cluster of hastily

built timber-frame buildings, surrounded the train depot. Wes said there was enough money in the district to bankroll his Wild West show with plenty to spare.

A painted sign hung above the door of the livery.

JAS. GLEE, *prop.*
HORSES FOR SALE AND RENT
Carriage Repairs a Specialty

In person, Jas. Glee, prop. was a tall, loose-geared man somewhere in early middle age. A red beard, shot through with white, hung to his waistband. His eyes were large and expressionless, popping out of a cadaverous face like a pair of black plums.

He wore a threadbare shell jacket of Confederate gray with a corporal's chevrons on the sleeves and thus immediately jumped up several places in our esteem.

"A stall and hay is two-bits per day per hoss," Glee said. "I'll throw in a scoop of oats for two-bits extry."

Wes said that we'd spring for the oats.

Glee gave him a sidelong glance. "You boys staying in town long?"

"I'm visiting kin," Wes said. "Depending on the welcome, it could be one day or ten."

"Don't make it any more than one, John

43

Wesley," Glee said.

Wes was surprised. "How do you know my name?"

"Seen you a few years back when I was visiting with your ma and pa."

Glee turned to me as though he thought there was something I ought to know. "The Rev. James Hardin is a fine man. And his wife Mary Elizabeth is a most singular woman and mighty purty."

"Well, thankee kindly," Wes said, answering for me. "When next I see them, I'll tell them what you said."

"Yes, do that, and add my kind regards," Glee said.

Wes propped the Springfields against the side of a stall. "I'm open to offers for the mustangs and those two rifles."

Glee cast his eyes over the horses, then the rifles. "A hundred is the best I can do. That's giving you thirty dollars apiece for the scrubs when they ain't worth any more'n ten. As for the Springfields, seems that everybody these days wants repeaters, so they'll be a hard sell."

Wes scowled. "Hard sell, hard bargain."

"Hard times," Glee said.

"Done and done," I said. The last thing I wanted was for Wes to fly off the handle and put a bullet into Jas. Glee, prop. Not in the man's own town.

"All right, a hundred it is, payable in gold coin." Then, still smarting a little, Wes said, "Now what's all this about us staying only one day in Longview?"

"The law is after you, John Wesley," Glee said.

Wes grinned. "The Yankee law is always after me."

"Stay here. Let me put up your mounts." Glee led the horses into stalls, forked them hay and then returned, his face grim. "John Wesley, this time it's serious. There's a state police lieutenant in town by the name of E. T. Stakes, known as Ned to them he considers friends. He's been asking about you, talking to your kin and the like."

"Did he mention charges?" I asked.

Glee stared hard into Wes's eyes. "You want to hear this?"

Wes grinned. "Lay it on me, like I give a damn."

"One count of hoss theft and three counts of murder. All four of them charges are hanging offenses in Texas."

"Wes, maybe we should light a shuck," I said.

"Hell, no we won't," Wes said. "I'll find this Stakes feller and talk to him. If he's interested in polite conversation, then fine.

45

If he isn't, well, Texas will be rid of another Yankee lawman."

"Wes, if you kill a state constable, the law will never leave you alone," I said. "They'll come after you until they catch you, or worse."

"The young feller's right, John Wesley," Glee said. "You can bed down here tonight and ride out at first light. I got a nice pot of beef stew on the simmer, if you'd care to make a trial of it, and I can find some whiskey if you're an imbibing man."

Wes seemed to be thinking over that proposition, but he wasn't. "Who's the richest man in town?" he said after a while.

Glee's head jerked back in surprise. "Why, I guess that would be Sam Luck. He owns the bank, a couple saloons, a sawmill outside of town, and maybe a dozen other properties he's foreclosed on in the past twelvemonth."

"Where can I find him?" Wes said.

Glee consulted the nickel railroad watch he took from his pants pocket. "At this time of day, he'll be taking lunch at the Excelsior Hotel."

"Is this Luck feller a carpetbagger?" I asked.

"He's a black man and a close, personal friend of President Grant," Glee said.

"What does that tell you?"

"Yeah, well I can stand it," Wes said. "I don't mind doing business with the devil if I can spend his money."

"Sam Luck is a grinder, a real hard-ass," Glee said. "He ain't likely to give a loan to a ranny he don't know."

"I don't want to borry money," Wes said. "I'm looking for business partners."

I read the question on Glee's face and said, "John Wesley plans to start up a Wild West show."

A second question overlaid the first on Glee's face, but then he articulated his puzzlement. "What the hell is a Wild West show?"

Wes said, "We'll tour the country and bring the frontier to the folks — drovers, Indians, cavalry rough riders, settlers, pretty saloon gals, shootin', scalpin' — you name it. Folks will sit in grandstands and watch."

"And the folks will pay good money for this?" Glee said.

"Sure they will," Wes said. "I'll get rich and so will my partners."

"Hell, boy, all folks have to do is walk into the street to see a Wild West show the likes of what you're talking about. There's one in Longview every damn night of the week."

Wes could look pompous at times.

47

He puffed up and said, "This is why you'll never be great, Mr. Glee. You don't see the big picture. My show will tour the east where folks walk into the street and all they see is high buildings and trolley cars. They'll pay through the nose to see the Wild West right in their hometown of Boston or New York or wherever."

"You're serious about this, ain't you?" Glee said.

"Damn right I am," Wes said.

"Damn right he is," I said.

"Damn stupid if you ask me," Glee said.

"Well, I'm not asking you," Wes said. "Now I'm gonna see that black man and hope he's got a heap more business savvy than you."

Glee shook his head and walked away. Then he stopped and said over his shoulder, "Think about the stew, huh?"

CHAPTER FIVE:
THE MARK OF CAIN

The Excelsior Hotel was a two story building with a generous porch supplied with bamboo and rattan rockers and wooden side tables. Swallows had built their nests in the corners and ollas, beaded with condensation, hung from the rafters to cool the sitters.

"Nice place," I said as we stepped onto the porch. "It looks expensive."

"Where else would a damned carpetbagger lunch?" Wes asked.

We stepped out of the day's intolerable heat into the shaded coolness of the hotel lobby.

A clerk stood behind the front desk talking with a plumed, beautiful officer resplendent in the blue, silver, and gold dress uniform of the U.S. Cavalry. The fussy, bespectacled man shifted his attention from the officer to us, as dusty, shabby and trailworn a pair as ever was. "What can I do for you" — he gave a moment's pause — "gentlemen?"

"I'm here to see Sam Luck." Wes would not put *Mister* in front of a black man's name.

The uppity clerk did. "Mr. Luck is lunching." He had a funny left eye that turned inward toward the bridge of his nose.

"I know." Wes could see that the dining room opened onto the lobby and he stepped toward the door.

"Wait. You can't go in there," the clerk said.

The beautiful officer stroked the blond, dragoon mustache that fell in waves to the corners of his mouth and his nose wrinkled as he regarded us.

Perhaps he believed that we'd spent the night in a pigsty somewhere.

Wes ignored the clerk and strode quickly into the dining room, me limping after him.

The place was full of big-bellied men in broadcloth, their women in silk, and cigar smoke hung in the air like a blue fog. I identified the fragrances of steak, lamb chops, and sizzling bacon and my hollow stomach rumbled.

Wes stood still for a moment, looked around, then yelled, "Sam'l Luck! Show yourself, Sam'l!"

I cringed with embarrassment as every face in the room turned to us. A few seemed mildly amused, but the majority were openly hostile and stared at us with a mix of disapproval and disdain.

"I'm here to see Sam'l Luck," Wes called out again.

After that, things got rapidly out of hand.

The beautiful officer marched into the dining room, a riding crop in his hand. He grabbed Wes by the shoulder and yelled, "Out you go, my buck."

"You tell him, Custer!" a man yelled. And people laughed.

"Who the hell are you?" Wes said, his eyebrows drawing together.

Custer knew he had a captive, adoring audience and made a grandstand play. "General George Armstrong Custer," he grandly announced. "And I'm the equal of an 'undred, nay, a thousand, of you."

As he knew it would, this bold statement drew a round of applause and cheers, and, amid the loud huzzahs, I heard yells of, "Give him hell, General!" and "Remember the Washita!"

Wes hated Yankee soldiers, was widely believed to have shot several, and he took a set against Custer. His hands blurred and an instant later the muzzles of two blue

Colts pushed into the blue belly of Custer's frockcoat. "Back off, soldier boy." His voice was as cold as death.

Looking back, I have to give Custer credit. The man had sand. He wasn't too smart, but he had bark on him and he didn't even blink.

"Pull those triggers and you'll hang like the damned Rebel dog you are," he said.

"Might just be worth it," Wes said, smiling.

Oh sweet Jesu!

John Wesley's knuckles were white on the triggers and America was about to lose a hero.

"General Custer!" A small, frail black man stood up at his corner table. In the sudden hush that followed, he said, "Please allow the gentlemen to draw closer to me without harm or hindrance."

He'd phrased that request so that Custer could extricate himself without losing face.

But I still don't know how things would have ended had a pale young waitress, *in extremis,* not dropped a tray of dirty dishes that clattered and crashed onto the wood floor.

The sudden clamor broke the spell that had plunged the room into silence.

Custer took advantage of it. He lowered

his riding crop and said to Wes, "I'll deal with you later, sir." Then he swung on his heel and stomped away, his spurred boots chiming.

Wes grinned, spun his Colts, and let them thud into their shoulder holsters. "There goes a lucky man."

Custer wasn't the only one who loved to make a grandstand play.

Sam Luck, for indeed that was the identity of the delicate little black man, waved us over to his table.

Wes sashayed across the room like a new rooster in the hen house and basked in the crowd's attention.

He didn't deign to hear, or chose to ignore, the hear-hears after one fat Yankee with broken veins all over his nose and cheeks called out, "We should hang the rascal."

But when Luck ushered us into chairs, the diners settled down and the normal buzz of conversation and the clink of cutlery resumed.

I'd formed a picture in my mind of what Sam Luck would look like, a big-bellied, shiny-faced black man in a loud checkered suit smoking a fat cigar the better to show off the diamond ring on his little finger.

He was none of those things.

Luck was tiny, spare, dusty and worn, like a leather-bound book on a disused library shelf. His skin was coffee-colored, his eyes small and dark as raisins, and his mouth was a thin gash, tight, hard, and mean.

The black broadcloth he wore, once expensive, was much frayed and stained and his linen was yellow with age.

Withal, he was a very unimpressive figure . . . but for the most singular scar that marred his forehead. The letter *R* had been burned into his skin with a hot iron. The brand was fairly small — I could have covered it with a silver dollar — but it was sharp and deep.

I recognized it for what it was, of course.

The *R* marked Luck as a runaway slave who'd once tried to flee his lawful master and was thus never to be trusted again. It was a Mark of Cain that he'd once richly deserved.

Luck made no effort to offer us coffee, but did listen intently to what John Wesley was saying to him about the Wild West show. All the time, the black man's thin fingers crumbled the bread roll on his plate.

When Wes finished speaking, Luck said, "The officer you threatened with death is General George Armstrong Custer. He's leaving for Kansas today to take command of the Seventh Cavalry." Luck's brief smile was the flash of a knife blade. "I rather fancy that the gallant Custer will soon provide enough action against the savages for a dozen Wild West shows."

"My point exactly," Wes said. "I want to bring that kind of frontier excitement to audiences back east and even beyond, to Europe."

When he put his mind to it, Wes could talk like a lawyer, even to a Negro.

Luck brushed bread crumbs off his lap and without looking up said, "No one has come up with an idea like yours before, Mr. Hardin, and it just might work."

"It can't fail," Wes said.

Luck raised his eyes. "Any business can fail. I just lost money on a Mississippi plantation that I was sure I could resell at a profit. Somebody burned down the big house and I was left with six hundred acres of land, half of it swamp."

Wes wouldn't say it, but I did. "Sorry to hear that." My face was empty.

Again Luck's smile was slight and fleeting. "Yes, I'm sure you are."

"Well," John Wesley said, "what do you think of my proposition?"

"It interests me, young man," Luck said.

"I believe your Wild West show idea has potential."

"Good," Wes said, beaming. "How much do you want to invest?"

"Not so fast. First I want to see a business proposal from you."

"What's that?" Wes asked.

Luck steepled his fingers and cocked his small head to one side. "You will draw up a cover letter, executive summary, business and market feasibility analyses and studies, financial data, and supply me with the *curriculum vitae* for all the members of your management team."

"Hell, is that all?" Wes blinked like an owl.

"For the time being, yes," Luck said. "Have it on my desk by the end of next week."

Wes nodded, then turned to me. "You heard the man, Little Bit. Have all that stuff on his desk by the end of next week."

My face said, "Huh?" but I heard the croak of my voice say, "Sure thing, Wes."

"Very well, our business is concluded," Luck said. "Now, if you gentlemen will withdraw and allow me to finish my lunch?"

Wes rose to his feet and I did the same.

"Don't worry, we'll get you all that . . . stuff," Wes said.

Luck nodded. "Good. In the meantime

56

stay clear of Custer. He can be a dangerous enemy."

CHAPTER SIX:
THE WRATH OF CUSTER

"Well, what do you think?" John Wesley asked me.

"Hell, I don't know anything about that business stuff."

"You read books."

"Not about being a tycoon and the like."

Wes thought about that for a spell. "Well, just do what you can."

"I'll need a pencil and paper," I said.

"There's a general store across the way. It'll have what you want."

We stopped in the middle of the street to let a heavily loaded dray drawn by an ox team trundle past.

The wagon kicked up a cloud of yellow dust and when it cleared three men stood staring at us. One of them was Custer and he had his plumed hat set at a fighting angle. He jabbed a finger at Wes. "That's the scoundrel who threatened my life, Constable."

One of the men with the general, a tall, rangy fellow with a magnificent, black cavalry mustache that rivaled Custer's, had a shotgun leveled at Wes's belly, both hammers eared back.

Beside him, a smaller, slighter man, was similarly armed. He had the eyes of a snake and his fingers were crooked on the Greener's triggers. "You are under arrest."

John Wesley tensed, a thing I'd seen before when he was determined to draw down on a man.

But he was bucking a stacked deck and I think he knew it.

It's a hard thing to die in the street when you're but seventeen years old with a great business idea.

"Let it go, Wes," I said. "They'll cut you in half."

"Truer words was never spoke," the rangy man said. "We have reason to believe you are John Wesley Hardin, the man killer. Give us any kind of excuse to gun you right where you stand and we'd sure appreciate it."

A dust devil spun between us and Custer and them, then collapsed. People had gathered in the street and judging by the eager expressions on their faces, they hoped Wes would make a play.

"We're in a hell of a fix, Wes," I whispered. John Wesley knew that as well as I did.

As I said, a man who hopes to have a Wild West show one day doesn't brace a couple hardcases with scatterguns. Not at a range of three or four feet, he doesn't.

Wes tried to brazen it out. "The soldier boy I've already met. Who the hell are you two?"

"I'm not in the habit of giving out my name to low persons," the rangy man said. "But since I'm arresting you and expect to watch you hang, I'm Lieutenant E.T. Stakes of the state police and this here is Constable Jim Smalley."

"What's the charge?" Wes asked.

Stakes' grin was unpleasant. "Don't worry about that, Hardin. You're facing enough murder charges to send you to the gallows."

"My name is Wesley Clements," Wes said. "You got the wrong man."

"Let's go ask Sam Luck about that," Custer said.

I guess that's when Wes knew he was running out of room on the dance floor.

"Go to hell," he said.

"Constable Smalley, the ruffian has two murderous revolvers under his armpits," Custer said. "Do your duty and relieve him of those."

Stakes raised the muzzle of his shotgun. "Be careful, Jim. He can make fancy moves."

Smalley slapped the butt of the Greener. "I got the cure for fancy moves right here, Lieutenant."

Later, John Wesley told me that he'd had a passing fancy to go for his guns and that Custer would get the first ball. But when the muzzles of Smalley's scattergun pressed into his belly and he looked into the man's cold, reptilian eyes, Wes decided it was not the time to make a play.

After Smalley removed the Colts from their holsters, Stakes slapped a pair of massy, iron handcuffs on John Wesley's wrists.

General Custer then stepped forward, his face like thunder. "You damned Texas cur." His lips curled into a snarl as his riding crop slashed across Wes's left cheek, leaving an angry red welt and drawing blood from the corner of Wes's mouth.

Wes took the blow without a sound, then leaned forward and spat a mix of blood and saliva onto the chest of Custer's beautiful coat, right between the parallel rows of gilt buttons.

Enraged and foaming at the mouth, Custer wielded his riding crop and rained cut after cut back and forth across Wes's unprotected face.

I heard Smalley as though he yelled at the far end of a tunnel.

"Hell, General, leave enough of him for us to hang!"

By then I was already moving. I limped as fast as I could to Custer and threw my fist into his face.

Small and stingily built as I was, my punch did little damage, but it made the general back off a step. I followed him, my puny arms windmilling as I tried to land another blow.

Something hard slammed into the back of my head and I saw the ground cartwheel up to meet me.

Then I saw nothing at all.

Chapter Seven:
A Pathetic Creature

I woke facedown in the street, my mouth full of dirt and clots of blood in my nose. How long I'd lain there I had no way of telling.

The business of Longview proceeded around me. People stepped past me on the street and wagons and horses detoured around my prostrate body.

I felt something wet at the back of my head and explored it with my fingers. They came away bloody and stained with manure. At one point, a horse must have crapped on my head as I lay unconscious. No doubt it had occasioned considerable mirth in the passersby.

I attempted to rise but my head spun and I sank slowly back into the dust and dry manure of the street. To add to my misery, a cur dog, as mangy a brute as ever cocked a leg, decided to bark at me and tug at my clothes . . . as though they weren't ragged enough already.

"Git the hell off'n him!" The man's voice came from above me.

I turned my head and beheld Jas. Glee, prop. aim a kick at the dog's ribs. The wily canine dodged expertly and lit a shuck.

"Let's get you on your feet, young feller," Glee said.

"John Wesley has been taken," I said.

"Yeah, I know. There's nothing you can do for him now, boy."

The man helped me to rise and his nose wrinkled. "Lordy, but you smell bad. You got hoss crap in your hair."

"And blood," I said.

"Yeah, that too. I'll take you back to the livery and get you cleaned up."

"They got Wes," I said again.

Glee nodded. "You told me that already."

"They plan to hang him."

Glee nodded. "Seems like. Pick up your hat."

I did as he said and he half-carried, half-dragged me to the stable.

A rain barrel stood at one corner. Glee took off my hat, grabbed me by the scruff of the neck, and plunged my head into the green, scummy water. He dunked me again and again until I thought I must surely drown.

64

Then he raised my head for the last time and, my hair dripping, guided me into the livery where he tossed me a scrap of towel. "Dry yourself good, boy, then let me take a look at your head. I think you've got a bad cut back there."

"Somebody hit me with something, maybe a shotgun butt," I said, rubbing my thin hair with the towel.

"Seems like." Glee shook his head. "You're a pathetic-looking creature for sure."

The cobwebbed clock in Glee's office claimed it was two in the afternoon as I sat eating his stew, my head wrapped in a fat, fairly clean, white and blue striped bandage torn from one of his old shirts. Around a mouthful of beef and onions I said, "I reckon I'll go visit with Wes."

"If they'll let you," Glee said. "Them state lawmen are hard characters."

The wind had picked up and outside sand was blowing. The sky was the color of mustard and the sun a hazy, orange ball. In their stalls, the two mustangs we'd brought in were restless.

Glee walked to the door of the livery and stared down the street. "Custer is leaving, getting into the stage, him and his wife. I reckon she's a right pretty gal, at least from

65

this distance."

"I hope the savages do for him," I said. "Scalp them yellow ringlets from right off'n his head."

Glee turned to me and smiled. "No use in hoping fer something that ain't got a chance of happening, boy. Custer is an Injun-killer from way back. The Sioux, Cheyenne, all them raggedy-assed tribes are terrified of him. One look at the general on his white hoss and they'll cut and run."

"Before the Indians, he was a Reb-killer."

Glee nodded. "Yup, he was real good at it, an' no mistake. That's why they made him a general and him just a lad."

I scraped up the last of my stew, set the bowl aside, and got to my feet. "I'm going to see Wes." I balanced my hat on top of my bandaged head.

"Seems like there's a sandstorm blowing up," Glee said, looking at the sky and not at me. "If'n I was you, I'd step real careful."

Longview seemed a dark, joyless place as I walked along the boardwalk to the town lockup, my steel-caged leg clumping on timber with every step. Maybe it was because of the wind-driven sand that lifted off the street in tattered yellow veils, found every rip and hole in my clothing, and rasped like sandpaper against my skin that the town seemed so bleak.

But more likely it was the melancholy fact that the Yankee law had John Wesley in its talons and would drag him all the way to the gallows.

In those days, the Longview jail was a low, log structure with a single timber door with three massive wrought iron hinges, each hammered into the shape of what the French call a fleur de lis.

Above the door was a rectangular painted sign. *FIAT JUSTITIA RUAT CAELUM*

In keeping with the door, I figured the motto must be written in French, and I had no idea what it meant.

It was only many years later when Wes became a lawyer that he told me it was Latin for Let justice be done though the heavens fall.

Like me, he never forgot that sign.

To the left of the door was the window of the jailer's office. On the other side was a barred window, one of the panes spider-webbed by a stray bullet.

To this day, jailhouses make me uneasy, but I swallowed hard and pushed on the door. It swung open on oiled hinges and I stepped inside.

A tall man rose from the desk opposite from where I stood and his ice blue eyes warned *Stay right where you are and don't make any fancy moves.*

The jailer had a close-cropped square head, like a Prussian soldier's, and a waxed mustache that curled up at the ends in magnificent arcs. But his forehead was disappointing, low and brutish with massive brow ridges that gave him the appearance of the lowest form of Negro.

Nonetheless, his voice was pleasant enough. "What can I do for you?"

He was a good four inches over six feet and I felt intimidated, like a puny David getting his first glimpse of Goliath.

"I'm here," I said, my voice breaking, "to see John Wesley Hardin."

"State the manner of your business," the lawman said.

"No business. John Wesley is my friend and I'm here to visit."

"Comfort him like."

I nodded. "If he needs comforting."

"He does. Any man facing the gallows needs comforting." The jailer ran his eyes over me from the crown of my battered hat to the fat bandage around my head and then to my down-at-heel shoes. His gaze lingered for a moment on the outline of the steel brace that showed through my pants.

"You can see him," he said. "God knows

you've got enough to contend with without me giving you another problem. What's your name, son?"

"Most folks call me Little Bit, but my given name is William, William Bates. Bates by name, Bates by nature, my ma always told me."

"Uh-huh." The jailer lifted the keys from a hook on the wall behind his desk and said, "Ten minutes."

"Thank you kindly," I said.

Perhaps lest I thought him too friendly, the man then said, "Name's Alan Henry Dillard and I'm a hundred different kinds of hell in a fight."

"I imagine you are."

Dillard nodded. "Just so you know . . . you and John Wesley Hardin."

CHAPTER EIGHT:
A DARING PLAN

"Did Dillard search you?" Wes asked.

I shook my head.

"Good, then he trusts you."

"What's your plan, Wes?" ·

There was only one cell, furnished with an iron cot and a straw mattress, a bucket that stank and a framed, embroidered motto on the wall that read HAVE YOU WRITTEN TO MOTHER?

It seemed that the town fathers of Longview were big on instructing the criminal classes.

Wes wrapped his long, fine fingers around the black iron bars of his cell and pushed his face closer to mine. "Little Bit, bring me a pistol. I can break out of here real easy."

I felt like pinching myself to make sure I was awake. "Wes, that's nigh on impossible, This here jail is built like the First National Bank of Texas."

"Listen, and listen good," Wes said. "Dillard said a Negro woman will bring me grub twice a day. Once I have the gun, I'll squeeze out tears, pretend I'm broke up about hanging an all, and set them at ease, figuring I'm just a scared kid. But when the woman brings in the tray I'll" — he made a gun of his thumb and forefinger — "Pow! Pow! — kill her and then Dillard."

"It's way too thin, Wes." In fact, I was horrified. John Wesley's words were emotionless, as though murdering two people meant nothing to him.

"The hell it is thin. Just bring me the Colt and I'll do the rest."

I had to unload the thought churning in my head. "Wes, you're talking about killing a lawman . . . and a woman."

"So what?"

"It ain't right, Wes. It can't be right."

"Would you rather see me hang?" Wes asked.

"No, I —"

"Then it isn't my fault. Dillard and the black woman are just two more damned traitors shoving me toward the gallows. They both need killing."

The jailhouse was a solid building, but I heard the relentless rush of the wind, the hiss of driving sand, and the curses of a muleskinner in the street, his team balking at the storm.

I looked into Wes's eyes, so cold to be almost colorless, like ice in winter.

"Well, Little Bit, will you help me or will you help drag me to the gallows with all the rest?"

My guilty conscience was the joker in the deck, but nonetheless I decided to play the hand Wes dealt me. "I'll bring the pistol."

The ice in John Wesley's eyes melted away in the sun of his smile. "I knew I could depend on you, Little Bit. Come back tomorrow morning and bring the gun." Wes thought for a spell, then said, "And a bag of sour drops."

"Sour drops?"

"Sure. Dillard won't suspect that a kid with a bad leg and a bag of sour drops in his hand is hiding a pistol, now will he?"

The key rattled in the door that led to the cell, and Wes said urgently, "Make sure all six of the Colt's chambers are charged. I'll have some fast shooting to do."

I nodded and turned away from Wes as Dillard said, "Time's up, son."

"I'll see you tomorrow, Wes," I said. "I'll bring you some sour drops."

Dillard didn't even blink. He had no way of knowing that the words I'd just uttered sounded his death sentence.

■ ■ ■

I slept that night at the livery and next morning bought candy at the general store. They had no sour drops so I substituted molasses taffy, long a favorite of mine.

When I returned to the stable, I ate some more of Jas. Glee, prop.'s stew, cold and congealed with fat though it was, then searched through Wes's saddlebags for the old Colt revolvers.

To my considerable distress, only the gun with the loose cylinder was fully charged. The other had three empty chambers.

Wes was adamant that he wanted a fully loaded pistol, and since I had no money for caps, powder and shot, I decided that the defective revolver would have to do.

I had a deal of confidence in John Wesley's shooting skills with any kind of firearm, including a Colt that was falling apart.

As I'd seen Wes do, I shoved the revolver into the waistband behind my back and covered it with my coat.

Glee walked into the livery carrying a fine English sidesaddle and caught me in the act. He placed the saddle on a rack, then stared at me for a long time before he spoke.

"I hope you're not thinking of doing

anything foolish, young feller. If you're planning to brace Al Dillard, forget it." A fly landed on his cheek and he brushed it away with an irritable hand. "Draw down on Dillard and he'll kill you fer sure, like he's done to seven or more afore ye, all of them bigger and meaner men than you."

My belly churned and I racked my brain for the right . . . no, *any* words.

Finally I managed to say, "Wes and me have a lot of enemies. I figured I should go armed."

Glee looked at me, through me, then said, "Can you shoot?"

"Some."

"*Some* don't cut it, young feller. But *real good* does. Can you shoot real good?"

"No, I guess not."

"Then best you leave the pistol here."

"Jas. Glee, prop., that's probably sound advice, but I won't take it."

Glee shook his head. "Then suit yourself, boy. But mind what I said about Dillard. He don't take kindly to sass."

Glee took up the sidesaddle again, studied a small tear in the leather of the cantle, then his eyes shifted to me again. "What I said about Dillard taking no sass, tell that to John Wesley as well."

I nodded. "I surely will."

"Makes no difference, really," Glee said. "He won't listen."

I'd slept late, so by the time I headed for the jailhouse the sun was high in the sky. All traces of yesterday's sandstorm had fled but for grit on the boardwalks and in the corners of windowpanes. A few innocent white clouds drifted in the indigo sky like lilies on a pond and the air smelled fresh with the promise of the new day.

Despite the beckoning morning, I felt ill at ease and the breakfast I'd eaten was a red-hot cannonball in my belly.

I never carried a gun in those days. My wrists were too thin and weak to absorb the recoil, and on those occasions when John Wesley bade me try, I never once managed to hit a mark, be it at ten paces or two.

Thus I was very conscious of the three-pound Colt that dragged down the back of my pants and I was sure that everyone I passed in the street could see it.

In truth, several men gave me slit-eyed looks as they walked by, but that was probably because a ragged little runt who looked like he'd missed too many meals in his childhood, limping along with his left leg in a steel cage, was a sight to see.

When I stepped into the jailer's office,

Alan Dillard glanced up at me from a leather-bound ledger and said, "What you got in your poke?"

My heart jumped in my chest. Had he tumbled to the revolver?

I hesitated, and Dillard prompted, "In your hand, boy."

I was so relieved, I felt like I'd been touched by an angel. "Oh this?" I held up the candy sack. "It's molasses candy. Wes is right partial to it and I thought it might cheer him up."

"Never cared for it myself," Dillard said, making a face. He pointed at the door to the cell with the steel pen he'd been using. "It's unlocked. Ten minutes, mind. No longer."

I nodded my thanks and stepped through the door into the wretched half-light of the cell area.

Wes was lying on his cot. When he saw me he jumped up and a quick stride took him to the bars.

"Did you get it?" He looked like an excited kid asking about a birthday present.

I nodded, moved close to the bars, and turned my back. "Hurry." My anxious eyes were fixed on the door.

It took only a moment. Wes grabbed the revolver and in a trice, fourteen inches of

Colt disappeared into his waistband.

It always surprised me that a man with such a narrow, sharply defined face and thin lips could pout. But Wes did.

Sounding petulant, he said, "You brought me the bust-up Colt."

"I know. It was the one with all the cylinders charged."

"Damn it. I thought I taught you how to load a gun," Wes said, a hint of anger in his voice.

"I didn't have the price of powder and shot. All the money we have is in your pocket." I was a little angry myself, getting little thanks for walking past a named man killer like Alan Dillard with a contraband revolver stuck down my pants.

Wes's smile was a little forced, I thought.

"Well, at least you brought the sour drops," he said, glancing at the paper sack in my hand.

"They didn't have any at the general store, so I bought you molasses taffy."

"I don't like molasses taffy," Wes said, pouting again. "I declare, Little Bit, can't you do anything the hell right?"

I stifled the sharp retort on my tongue as he reached through the bars and pulled me closer to him.

"Listen, earlier the black woman brought

me coffee and said she'd be back around one with my lunch. Dillard came in with her and he opened the cell to let her inside."

This time John Wesley's smile was genuine. "I'll kill them both, then make a run for the livery. Have the horses saddled, ready to go."

He scowled. "Think I can trust you to do that right?"

I didn't answer his question. "Wes, Jas. Glee, prop. says Dillard is a real good gun. I think he'll be hard to kill."

I saw it again, as I'd seen it so often before. Wes puffed up and his handsome young face took on that everybody-look-at-me expression that was so difficult for me to stomach.

"Hard to kill for you, maybe, but not for me. Dillard may be good with a gun, but on his best day he can't shade John Wesley Hardin."

I was Wes's only audience, and not much of a one at that, so all he wanted to hear were his own boasts . . . and he believed every single word of them.

In the event, his plan came to naught.

The door slammed open so violently it banged against the partition wall and two men stepped inside, their spurs ringing.

One of then carried manacles, the other a
rope.

CHAPTER NINE:
YANKEE ASSASSINS

The man with the manacles was E. T. Stakes, the other, holding a rope that I thankfully noted didn't end in a noose, was Constable Jim Smalley. Alan Dillard, the cell key in his hand, stood behind them.

"We're taking a ride, John Wesley," Stakes said, "so gather up what's your'n."

For a moment, Wes's eyes were calculating, figuring his chances against three guns. He obviously decided against making a play. "Where are you taking me, and why?"

"Waco," Stakes said. "Where you'll get a fair trial before you're hung."

Stakes had pouched black eyes and the small, tight, intolerant mouth you sometimes see in elderly nuns. When he smiled, the effect was most unpleasant. "I'll hang bunting on the scaffold myself, John Wesley. Make it look festive for your send-off, like."

"Waco is two hundred miles away," Wes said.

"A hundred and seventy-five to be exact," Stakes said. "But never fear, Mr. Hardin, I'll do everything I can to make your trip an enjoyable one."

"You're a damned liar," Wes said.

Stakes smiled with his lips shut, like a closed steel purse. "Ain't I, though?"

He turned to Alan Dillard. "You took his guns?"

The jailer nodded. "Yeah, they're locked in my desk."

"Who is he?" Jim Smalley looked at me the same way a man does the sole of his boot after he's stepped in dog doo-doo.

"He's nobody." Dillard turned to Stakes. "I'll release the prisoner."

Before the jailer stepped to the cell, I said, "I want to tag along with John Wesley."

It was Stakes' turn to gut me with a withering stare. "What the hell for, boy?"

"Sir, Wes is a friend of mine and I've got nothing else to do." Then I quickly added, "I'm a good trail cook." That was only partially true, but indeed, I could boil coffee and dredge salt pork in flour and fry it with the best of them.

It seemed that I amused Stakes. "You got a hoss, boy?"

I nodded. "Sure do."

He said to Smalley, "What do you say, Jim?"

The man's answer was to step in front of me and pat me down. "What's in the poke?"

"Molasses taffy. I like it, but Wes doesn't."

Smalley turned to Stakes. "He's an idiot."

"I know, but he's an idiot who can cook," Stakes said. "It will take five, maybe six days to reach Waco. Do you want to rustle up the coffee and grub?"

"Hell, no." Smalley thought for a moment, then said, "All right, let the idiot do it."

"What's your name, boy?" Stakes asked.

"Folks call me Little Bit," I said.

"All right, Little Bit, listen up," Stakes said. "I'm a plain man, bacon and pan bread is what I want, and coffee strong enough to float a silver dollar. You got that?"

"Yes, sir."

"Good, then we'll get along." Stakes nodded to Dillard. "Let Hardin out, jailer."

Before the cell door swung open, Wes smiled at me and winked.

I knew what that meant.

He had killing on his mind.

I returned to the livery and saddled my horse, then started in on Wes's mount.

As I looked around for the blanket, Jas. Glee, prop. stopped me.

"Them lawmen already got a hoss fer John Wesley," he said. "They requisitioned one of the mustangs you and him brung in."

"What does that mean?" I said, never having tussled with the word *requisitioned* before.

"It means they took it in the name of the law, boy."

"Wes's saddle is still here."

"No matter," Glee said. "He ain't going fur."

"It's nigh on two hundred miles to Waco," I said.

"He won't get there."

"They mean to kill him?"

"That's my guess."

"But Stakes promised him a fair trial."

"What E.T. Stakes promises and what E.T. Stakes delivers are seldom one and the same thing, boy." Glee put his hand on my shoulder, a fatherly gesture no man had ever done to me before. It felt strange.

"Listen, boy," he said. "The Yankees who currently rule the great state of Texas have had enough of John Wesley and his kind — unreconstructed Johnny Rebs that claim the war didn't end at Appomattox. As far as the government is concerned, a trial would be a waste of time. Better to gun Hardin on the trail and, for the price of a few cents' worth of powder and ball, tie up everything nicely in a big blue bow."

"What can I do?" I felt scared, lost, like a blind man trying to feel his way out of a burning building.

"How badly do you want to keep on living?" Glee said.

I shook my head, bewildered. "What kind of question is that to ask a man?"

"I'll answer it for you, boy. You ain't a man, not yet you aren't. As to the question I asked, if you want to remain above ground, stay here in Longview. If you want to take your chances on getting a bullet in the back, go with John Wesley."

"I'll go. He's my friend."

Glee smiled. "You're learning, boy. That was a man's answer."

CHAPTER TEN:
A MURDEROUS PLOT

I led my horse back to the jail where John Wesley was already mounted on the mustang; his only saddle a ragged blanket, his legs lashed under the pony's belly with a rope.

"Dillard, sell me a saddle or let me get my own from the livery," Wes said. "This hoss has a backbone like the thin end of a timber wedge."

"Sorry," Dillard said. "You'll be less likely to make a dash for it, John Wesley."

"At least give him another damned blanket," I said.

Nobody paid me the least mind.

Stakes gathered up the mustang's lead rope then swung into the saddle.

Jim Smalley followed suit, slid the Henry rifle from under his knee and laid it across the saddle horn. "Let's ride. We're burning daylight and we need to put two hundred miles of git between us and Longview."

I mounted, and then Alan Dillard did something that surprised me.

He stepped off the boardwalk and slipped a jar into my coat pocket. "Pickles. For the trail."

I was dumfounded, but managed to nod and mumble my thanks before I kicked my horse into motion and followed the others.

Since Alan Dillard drops out of my narrative here, let me mention that he didn't live to scratch a gray head. He died of jungle fever on Samoa in 1889 while working as a civilian contractor for the U.S. Navy. It is interesting to note that Dillard passed away in the parlor of the novelist Robert Louis Stevenson, author of *Treasure Island,* who was living in the island nation at that time.

We camped that evening under a disused railroad trestle, the temperature surprisingly cool after the heat of the day. Around us lay a world of broken ground, treeless hills and patches of thorny cactus. The moon rose fat and fair, its pale light banished by the crimson glow of our campfire.

After a hearty supper of strong coffee, salt pork, and sourdough bread, we sat around the fire and I wondered where Wes had hidden the Colt I'd given him.

Only later did I discover that he'd tied it under his arm and then covered the big revolver with his shirt and coat.

Stakes had untied Wes's legs, and it caused considerable merriment in Jim Smalley. "Here now, Hardin," he said, staring at Wes over the rim of his coffee cup. "How far do you think you'd get if you stood up and made a break for it?"

Before Wes could make any kind of answer, Stakes grinned and said, "One step, Jim. I'd gun him for sure."

"Well, E.T., I think I'd let him run for a spell and then go after him. Make it a chase, like."

Stakes nodded. "It would be good sport."

"I won't run," Wes said. "All I ever did was try to obey the law. I'm in great fear that the kin of the men I killed in fair fights will lay for us on the trail and try to do for me."

"Don't worry about that," Smalley said. "We'll protect you, young feller. I mean, we want to watch you hang in Waco, hear that *snap!* when your neck gets broke."

Stakes cackled. "Hell, Jim, it won't be like that." He made a pantomime of a hanging man, his tongue lolling out of his mouth as he made horrible strangling sounds.

Then he smiled. "They don't break necks in Waco. It's too quick and robs the folks of a show."

"I say, Hardin," Smalley said, "when you're standing there on the gallows, piss and crap running down your legs, and the hangman asks if you've got any last words, here's what you say. 'Fancy whores and strong drink led me to this pass, but I had a good mother.' "

Stakes grinned. "You're right, Jim. The women love that."

"I don't want to hang," Wes said, his voice a scared whine. Then, I swear, he squeezed out a single tear that trickled down his cheek like a raindrop. "This will break my poor mother's heart."

"Aw, that's a shame, ain't it, E.T.?" Smalley said. "Even this piece of garbage, the lowest of the low, has a mother."

"Please don't let them hang me," Wes pleaded, his red-eyes fixed on Stakes. "I'm so afraid, Mr. Stakes."

"Sure, sure, kid," the lawman said. "I'll see what I can do."

Smalley almost choked as he suppressed a giggle.

I remember sitting there in the chill of the night, the steel brace cold against the skin of my wasted leg, thinking that even the most naïve circuit preacher would have more sense than the two fools mocking John Wesley Hardin. The preacher would know all too well that it's dangerous to tease the devil.

As most of you will recall, winter came early that year of 1871, and by the time we reached the Sabine River we all shivered with cold.

The lawmen, taking no chances, lashed Wes's feet under his pony again and placed him in the middle of the procession as we prepared to cross the swollen waters.

Wes, playing his role of terrified youngster to the hilt, rambled on about death and life everlasting, and when we were midway across he even launched loudly and tunelessly into a grand old hymn.

"Shall we gather at the river,
Where bright angel feet have trod,
With its crystal tide forever
Flowing by the throne of God?"

"Shut the hell up," Smalley yelled. His horse had stumbled and plunged him underwater and he was soaked to the skin and mad as a rained-on rooster.

"Sorry, Mr. Smalley," Wes said. "As I get nearer to judgment and death, I feel a need for the comfort of religion."

"Wail that damn song again, and you'll be a sight closer to death than you think,"

89

Smalley said.

Wes grinned but said nothing. Taking my cue from him, I also kept my mouth shut.

By the time we reached the far bank of the Sabine we were all frozen and wet, but we rode for two more miles before Stakes called a halt and told us to dismount and prepare a camp.

There was a ramshackle ranch house in the distance, but Stakes said he wouldn't ask for shelter, since the rancher was likely to be kin of his prisoner. "Go ask him if we can borry an axe, and then chop up some kindling," he told me. "Be quick. It's damn cold and we need a fire."

I did as I was told, but when I reached the gate to the property I quickly drew rein.

A sign on the gate, badly printed with a brush and tar, warned:

SHARPS .50 RANGED ON GATE.

And under that, in a neater hand was *There's a hell of a lot of shooting going on around here.*

Stakes' fears were justified. I figured the rancher must be kin of Wes's, right enough.

I opened the gate, made sure to close it, and then rode at a walk toward the ranch house, expecting a bullet at any time.

The wind was cold and bladed through my soggy rags like a razor. The sky was grim, gray as slate, and under that gloomy tyrant the surrounding pines rustled and bowed, as though paying quaking homage.

I was yet ten yards from the house when the door threw open on its rawhide hinges and a one-legged man with a crutch under his armpit and a Sharps in his hands stepped outside.

"Stay right where you are." He was a large, heavy man, his face a brown triangle almost hidden behind a beard and unkempt mane of black hair. His eyes were blue and hostile. "I got a possum in the pot, coffee on the bile, but none o' that's fer you, on account of how I only got enough for my ownself. So ride on. There's no grub here."

Then, to make sure I got the point, he said, "This here rifle gun is both wife and child to me. Just so you know."

I was scared, but I told him that a party of well-armed and determined state police and likely a town constable were camped to the west of his spread and needed to borrow an axe to cut kindling. Then I dropped John Wesley's name, but the rancher seemed unimpressed.

After a moment's thought, he said, "There's an axe in the woodshed over yonder. When you bring it back, leave it at the gate."

He turned, stepped inside, and slammed the door shut on me.

Now, I'm sure the man had lost his leg in the war fighting for the Noble Cause, so I didn't fault him for his lack of hospitality then or now.

But he was a mean old cuss and no mistake. And not a one for sharing.

After I cooked supper, we huddled around the fire and gradually our clothes dried.

Smalley continued to tease Wes, describing the marks on a man's neck after he'd been hung with a hemp rope, and how long it took for the condemned to strangle to death . . . vicious, cruel stuff like that.

For his part, John Wesley stayed silent, although every now and then he forced out a tear and muttered the prayers he'd learned at his mother's knee.

But often I saw him glance sidelong at the lawmen. Then his eyes glittered in the firelight and his teeth gleamed, like a cougar anticipating a killing spree.

And they didn't see it! Idiots!

Those two fools Stakes and Smalley saw only what they wanted to see, and that was a boy demented by terror over the thought of a cruel death on the gallows.

Indeed, the fool does not see the same peril as the wise man, and there's truth.

The next day, we ferried across the muddy, sluggish Trinity then rode north into swamp country that was foreign and forbidding.

Gradually the pines, post oak, and black hickory of our own soil gave way to bald cypress, water tupelo, and shrubs like swamp privet and water elm.

The going across the wet country was exhausting and I felt sick. My face and hands were covered in insect bites. To my surprise Wes made no move, even when we were within a few miles of Waco.

Overtaken by darkness and used up, Stakes halted and we made camp.

He left to obtain fodder for the horses and cornmeal from one of the surrounding farmers, if such could be found in the wilderness. "Keep a close eye on Hardin, Jim," he said from the saddle. "He's scared and he might bolt."

"If he does, he's a dead man," Smalley said. "Depend on it."

Then Stakes said something strange that really upset me. "Hold up on the shooting until I get back. We've got to be in it together, mind."

Smalley smiled and nodded. "He'll keep, E.T."

Stakes' eyes and mine met, tangled, and what I saw in his cold, penetrating gaze chilled me to the bone.

He meant to murder Wes.

Soon.

That very night.

CHAPTER ELEVEN: GUT SHOT

With no moon the sky was dark as printer's ink. Such breeze as there was came chill from the north and carried with it the musty smell of muck and of the swamp pools where lime green frogs jumped.

Jim Smalley sat on the sawn trunk of a tree, his grin malicious. "Not long now, huh, Hardin? I mean the noose a snotty-nosed killer like you so richly deserves."

"Please don't chide me, Mr. Smalley," Wes said, his voice breaking.

I added a few sticks to the fire, then said, "Leave him be. The man is scared enough."

With deliberate slowness, the lawman turned his head to me. "Another word out of you, gimp, and I'll put a bullet in you." His lip twisted. "Who's gonna miss a damned raggedy-assed pauper like you. Me?" He nodded is Wes's direction. "Him? Anybody?"

I said nothing, and Smalley stared at me

for a few moments, and then said, "From now until we reach Waco, keep your ignorant trap shut."

He again directed his attention to Wes. "Hey, Hardin, we haven't even talked about your burying yet." He smiled. "How remiss of me. I mean, a famous shootist like you doesn't want to go under the ground in any old pine box. How about a mahogany casket with a nice glass window so you can see the worms come for you?"

Wes had been squatting by the fire. He rose to his feet and sobbed, "I can't stand this anymore." He stumbled to the mustang and buried his face in the animal's neck, his shoulders heaving as he sobbed.

Smalley's derisive laughter followed him. "Hell, boy, leave the caterwauling for the gallows," he yelled as he slapped his leg, enjoying himself.

John Wesley turned, a gun in his hand and a grin on his face.

And in that awful moment, Constable Jim Smalley knew he was a dead man.

He spiked a terrified, "No!" Then jumped to his feet as his hand dropped to his gun.

He never made it. Didn't even make it halfway.

John Wesley's ball hit the lawman in the belly.

Shock, pain, and the realization that he'd suffered a death wound, slowed Smalley. He took a step back, tried to complete the draw, but suddenly found the Colt was too heavy to drag from the leather.

The revolver tumbled out of his hand and Smalley went to his knees, his eyes on Wes. "Kill me, damn you. I'm gut shot."

Wes grinned. "Hell, I know that, Jim. I aimed for your belly."

Smalley had seen gut shot men before. He knew he had only a few words left in him before the worst waves of pain hit and then all he'd be able to do was scream.

"How did you hide the damn —"

"I've been there before, Jim." Wes smiled. "I'm too old a cat to be played with by a kitten."

"Then get it over, damn you," Smalley said.

"We've got time." Wes's hard mouth stretched in a grin. "I know, I'll sing you a song, help you on your way, like. Hey, Jim boy, do you know this one?"

"As I walked out in the streets of Laredo,
As I walked out in Laredo one day,
I spied a young cowboy wrapped up in
    white linen,

Wrapped in white linen and cold as the
  clay."

Wes took a knee beside Smalley, who was
lying on his back, groaning in pain, his teeth
bared in a grotesque grimace.
"Here's the darlin' part, Jim," Wes said.

"Oh beat the drum slowly and play the fife
  lowly,
Play the Dead March as you carry me
  along.
Take me to the green valley and lay the
  sod o'er me,
For I am a young cowboy and I know I've
  done wrong."

Wes scowled as he rose to his feet, his eyes
savage. "Damn you, Jim. You don't like my
song. I can see it in your face. Well, you
don't know dung from honey, so be damned
to ye for an ungrateful wretch."
He raised his boot and brought it down
fast and hard onto Smalley's bloody belly.
The lawman shrieked, horribly, loudly,
like a damned soul that's just been thrown
into the lowest pit of Hell.
Wes had to raise his voice to make himself
heard. "It ain't my fault, Little Bit. He
would've done the same to me."

I grabbed a burning stick from beside the fire and advanced on John Wesley. "Damn it all, Wes. End his suffering and do it now."

Wes looked at me and smiled. "Oh, all right. On account of how you look right scary holding that there twig. Well, good night, Jimmy boy." And without seeming to even glance at Smalley, Wes casually shot him between the eyes.

The screams stopped. But the racketing echoes of the gunshot seemed to go on and on forever.

"There," Wes said. "Happy now?"

"Yes," I said, my voice flat. "Happy now."

Wes was silent for a while, then he said, "The gun has a bad cylinder. It shoots low. That's why I gut shot him."

"Is that what it was?"

"Yeah, that's what it was. Smalley sassed me all the time, made me feel bad. He was borrowing trouble."

"He surely was. Borrowing trouble, all right." I didn't mention the brutal kick to the dying man's belly and neither did Wes.

But I was sick inside and disappointed, though that's an inadequate word to describe how I felt. *Betrayed.* Yes, that's a better way to put it.

Wes had betrayed my trust in him. I'd always known he was reckless, vengeful sometimes, and too quick to shoot.

But I'd never known him to be purposely cruel.

Until then.

Kicking Smalley had been a wanton, barbarous act and it instilled fear in me. I dreaded that John Wesley might become a monster.

If he wasn't one already.

Wes saddled Smalley's sorrel horse then turned to me. "Should we wait for Stakes to get back?"

"No. Best we get the hell out of here."

Was gave me his petulant look. "He sassed me, Little Bit. Just like Jimmy boy did."

"I know. But Stakes is a state policeman, Wes. Chances are you'll run into him again."

John Wesley brightened at that. "Yeah, you're right. Hell, he might come back here with a bunch of sodbusters."

"Maybe so." To flatter him, I added, "Sodbusters are a real probability. A lot of folks want to shake the hand of John Wesley Hardin."

Wes took the compliment with a smile. "And I ain't near done with my shootist career or started in on my Wild West show yet."

He swung into the saddle, gave Smalley's

body an indifferent glance, then grinned. "Damn it all. I'm gonna charge through life at a gallop and be a great man." His blue eyes glowed in the gloom as I kneed my horse beside his. "Ain't that right, Little Bit?"

And me, weak, craven creature that I was, once again hitched my wagon to my friend's malevolent star. "The greatest."

CHAPTER TWELVE:
A STRANGE ENCOUNTER

A wise man once said that fate is the friend of the good and the enemy of the bad. Looking back, I can only conclude that he was right.

We were destined to make a clean escape, and we did.

Wes was determined to head south through friendly country and visit with his mother and father who were residing in Mount Calm, a tiny hamlet struggling for life at the ragged edge of nowhere.

We rode through the dark of night, constantly checking our back trail for any sign of pursuit. There was none and that pleased Wes enormously.

"Ned Stakes' hoss was tuckered. He won't come after us until first light, if he comes at all." Wes drew rein, then kneed his horse close to mine. "Here's what we'll do. We'll lie low for a spell, eat Ma's good home cooking and grow fat and sassy. Maybe even spark a girl, if there's any to be found in Mount Calm. Once everything blows over, I'll get back to organizing my Wild West show."

Of course, Wes hadn't organized anything so far, but I wasn't about to pop his bubble.

"I can get started on the business proposal for Sam Luck," I said. "Seems to me all we'll have at Mount Calm is time."

Wes was far away, staring through the tree canopy at the black sky with nary a star in sight. He turned his head to me. "What did you say, Little Bit?"

"I said I should draw up the business proposal for Sam Luck."

Wes nodded. "Yeah, you do that. Good idea."

I hesitated before I spoke my mind, but asked finally, "Wes, you sure your folks will make us welcome?"

"Of course they'll make us welcome." He reached into his coat pocket and produced a crumpled scrap of paper. "This is the last letter I got from Ma. Well, a piece of it. I tore off and kept the good part."

He passed the paper to me and I glanced at the small, crabbed handwriting. "It's too dark for me to read it, Wes."

"No matter. I know it off by heart, memorized it, like." He turned his face to the sky again. "Come quickly, Johnny. If you are in Pisgah, come. If you are in Groveton, come. Return home to Ma. I want to tell you so many things and see your sweet face, ere long. Come home, my own John. Come home, Johnny."

Wes dashed away a tear with the back of his hand. "Damn, but that's purty. Ain't it, Little Bit?"

"Sure is. I reckon your ma wants you to settle down."

Wes nodded. "She does, but it's way too early for that. I'll walk a wide path before I'm done."

We let the horses pick their way, and they led us onto a narrow lane between the pines. It was still dark, but ahead of us we saw the glow of lanterns.

I thought it might be a cow outfit rounding up mavericks in the brush and said so to Wes.

"Could be. But it also might be lawmen or the army."

I pulled up my tired horse. "Do we ride around them?"

"We'll dismount and get closer. See what we can see," Wes said.

We swung out of the saddle and walked our horses, always a chore for me on uneven ground. After a couple minutes, I heard a woman's laugh, followed by the bellowing roar of a man.

"Doesn't sound like lawmen or the army, either," I said.

Wes had close-seeing eyes and after he peered into the darkness, he said, "Damn it all. I can't see a thing."

"Let's get closer," I said.

Wes had Smalley's Colt butt forward in his waistband and he adjusted the big revolver for a fast draw. "Little Bit, you see anything that suggests lawmen, holler out I'll cut loose and then we'll ride back the way we came."

I said that sounded just fine with me and we walked on.

The path, no more than a sliver of game trail, led though a pine and brush thicket, then into an open area dominated by the skeleton of a lighting-struck tree that lifted skinny white arms to the dark sky.

After maybe fifty paces, I made out a large wall tent in the distance and next to that a canvas lean-to. The silhouettes of men and a couple women moved back and forth in front of the fire. Beyond the camp, barely visible in the gloom, a parked covered wagon had its tongue raised. Nearby, a tethered mule team stood in a hipshot row.

"Well, what do you see?" Wes sounded on edge.

"Men and women. Travellers more than likely."

"I could use a cup of coffee and some grub," Wes said.

"Then we'll go visiting. It seems safe enough to me."

"We're a pair of drifting farm boys looking for work. Got that?"

"I got it." I led my horse forward and when I was within hailing distance, I yelled, "Hello the camp!"

The answer came immediately. A man yelled, "Good-bye your ownself. Come on out."

"Welcoming folks," I said. "Ain't they?"

Wes said nothing, but I could tell from the stiff, alert set of his head and shoulders that he was wound up tight as a clock spring.

As we drew closer, a man who looked big in the darkness stepped forward and said, "Are ye frontwards or are ye backwards?"

I'd no idea what the man was talking about, but I took a shot in the dark. "We have good mothers."

It took a while for the big man to understand the implications of my answer, but when he did, he said, "Then advance and be recognized, friend." Another pause, then, "If ye'd said ye were frontward there would have been no welcome for you at our fire."

Beside me I heard Wes groan or growl. To this day, I still can't figure the right of it.

The big man walked out to meet us and made a great show of waving us into camp, like St. Peter ushering the righteous through the Pearly Gates.

He was dressed in black broadcloth. Under that he wore a white collarless shirt, mighty yellow and stained. His hat was low-crowned and flat-brimmed, his face wide, fair, and handsome.

The two men with him were clothed in the same fashion and all three were close enough in looks to be brothers.

I guessed that the two women were wives, thin, severe, and modestly attired in black dresses with white at the collars and cuffs.

One of the women smiled at me and said, "Good-bye."

"Indeed," the big man said. "Sleep, put your horses up, and then have coffee."

The other men stepped forward, smiled, and shook hands with us. "Good-bye," they said. "Come again some time."

Wes gave me a sidelong look and I noticed that his thumb was hooked into his waistband, close to the Colt.

"My name is Isaac," the big man said. "And these are my brothers Charley and Milton." He bowed as he introduced the women. "My dear wives Goldie and Estelle."

"Right pleased to meet you, an' no mistake." I figured these folks were tetched in the head.

More so when the man called Isaac said, "After you sleep, we'll teach the word to you about the Contrarians and our faith."

"I could use a cup of coffee," Wes said.

"Yes, yes, of course," Isaac said. "But that comes sooner."

Now, I don't know why I thought I could engage in polite conversation with a man with loco camped out in his eyeballs, but so help me I tried.

"Where are you folks from?" I said.

"Ah, we're headed south for the Oklahoma Territory," Isaac said.

"That's north," Wes said.

Isaac's kin giggled as he said, "Why, of course it is. Very well said, young man. You see, because Oklahoma is north, we're going south." He smiled like a benign favorite uncle. "That is the Contrarian way."

"But you'll never get there," I said.

"But we will," Isaac said. "The good Lord will show us a road."

The woman called Estelle, a pretty young blonde with smoke gray eyes and a small, prim mouth, decided to do some preachifying. "Although it can be very difficult at times — or should that be easy? — we Contrarians live backward."

"Oh, yes, very, very difficult," Isaac said, shaking his head. "And there I state the case dishonestly."

"We sleep during the day and go about our business at night," Estelle said. "We eat dinner as our first meal, and breakfast for our last. But that is just some of the simpler, back-to-front things we do."

"We even tried walking backward," one of the brothers said. "But Charley stepped into a gopher hole and broke his ankle, and Isaac said that such means of locomotion was too dangerous, so now we desist from that."

Wes had been listening with the utmost interest as he studied Estelle's small, high breasts. "Why the hell do you live backward?"

This occasioned another burst of laughter, then Isaac said, "Well, you see, by living backward we won't be a day older tomorrow, we'll be a day younger."

"And eventually," Estelle said, "we'll become children again."

"Why do you want that?" I asked.

109

"To enter the kingdom of heaven, of course," Isaac said.

Estelle warmed to her subject. "In the Gospel of Matthew, chapter eighteen, verse three, Jesus says, 'I tell you the truth, unless you change and become like little children, you will never enter the kingdom of heaven.' "

"And that in a nutshell, boiled down, in brief, is the very basis of our Contrarian faith," Isaac said. "To enter Heaven, we must retrace our steps through life, go backward and become little children again."

The woman named Goldie, who had remained silent, tilted back her head and yelled, "Backward is forward, forward is backward! Hallelujah!"

"Amen, sister, amen!" Isaac said, his arms spread wide.

He turned to me. "Years ago, in my wild youth, I was smitten with a dread disease, given to me by one of the fallen women of the town. One night, after even the mercury cure failed, I prayed that God would cure me, and I heard his voice in my head say, 'Live backward, Isaac. Become a child again.' "

"Hallelujah!" Goldie yelled.

"When I woke up the next morning, I was free of the disease," Isaac said. "And that was when I became the first Contrarian."

"Hallelujah!" Goldie yelled again.

"We don't want you to join us to share in Isaac's miracle," Estelle said.

"That's fine, we won't," Wes said.

"Hallelujah!" Goldie exclaimed. "That means you will."

"No, it means we won't," Wes said.

Now, I don't know how this unreal conversation would have ended, probably with Wes shooting somebody, but the flat report of a rifle shot shattered the shadowed night . . . and we were again in a heap of trouble.

CHAPTER THIRTEEN: A TERRIBLE FRIGHT

A V of dirt spurted between John Wesley's legs, then, over the rack of a Henry rifle, a man's voice said. "Don't make a move, Hardin. I can drop you from here real easy."

Without turning his head, Wes said, "How many, Little Bit?"

I glanced briefly behind me. "Three that I can see. Two shotguns."

"They got the drop on me."

"Seems like."

Feet pounded behind me and a man pushed me aside, so roughly that I stumbled and fell.

Wes cursed and rounded on the man, his hand reaching for his gun.

Too late!

The walnut stock of the Henry swung and crashed into the side of Wes's jaw. He went down in a heap and lay still.

The man who'd pushed me and hit Wes raised his rifle, covering the people around the fire. "You folks kin of his?"

"Yes we are," Isaac said.

"Then I'm arresting you all on the charge of harboring a fugitive from justice," the man said. "There's an eleven hundred dollar reward on this man's head."

From the ground, I said, "They're Contrarians."

The man glanced at me. He had a huge, hooked nose and under it his gray mustache looked like the bow wave of a steamer. "What the hell does that mean?"

"They live backward and say the opposite of what they mean. They're no kin of Wes's."

The man looked confused.

I explained. "We rode into their camp looking for coffee."

"You wouldn't lie to me, boy, would you?" the man said.

I shook my head. "Not about them, I wouldn't. They're all crazy."

Wes groaned and the man leaned over and relieved him of his revolver. "I'm Constable Chance Smith." He nodded to the bearded men with him. "Constables Davis and Jones."

I struggled to my feet.

Smith stared at me, measuring me. "Ned Stakes told me you're harmless, youngster. Looking at you, I'd say he was right." He turned to one of the other lawmen. "Search him. I'd still like to know where Hardin got the gun he shot Jim Smalley with." The constable shook his head as he stepped toward me. "He was mean as a snake in your drink."

After patting me down, the lawman said, "He's clean."

"Good, now you and Davis get Hardin on his feet," Smith said. Then, as though he thought he owed Isaac and his crazy kin an explanation, he said, "We're taking this man to Austin where he'll get a fair trial and then be hung."

Isaac shook his head, and the two women looked distressed.

"No, that is not right," Estelle said. "You're doing that all wrong."

"You got something agin hanging, lady?" Smith asked.

"She means it's not the Contrarian way," Isaac said. "A man should be hung and then tried."

Smith pulled a long-suffering face then nodded. "Whatever you say, mister."

He pushed Wes toward his horse. "Mount up. We're riding." He gave me a hard look. "You too, runt. Hell, I never hung a dwarf with a tin leg afore, but there's a first time for everything, I guess."

As we rode through the darkness, the three lawmen passed a bottle back and forth. They seemed to be in good spirits, maybe because of the eleven hundred dollars reward posted by Hill County for John Wesley's apprehension.

After an hour, more than slightly drunk, Chance Smith declared that he could go no farther and needed some shut-eye. After some coffee, he'd take the first watch, Davis the second, and Jones the third.

Wes was ordered to sit across the fire from Smith with his back against a pine.

"I see you even bat an eyelid, I'll blow a hole in you with this here scattergun," he said. "You understand that, huh?"

Wes, perhaps tired of playing the scared youngster, said nothing. He leaned the back of his head against the tree trunk and pretended to sleep.

Smith motioned with his shotgun and indicated that I should sit next to Wes. "One barrel of buck each if you and your friend suddenly feel ambitious. You catching my drift, runt?"

"I ain't planning to do nothing but sleep," I said.

Smith nodded. "Sleeping your life away, boy. If I was fixin' to get hung, I'd try to stay awake as much as I could." He smiled. "Savor the moment, you might say."

The lawman took another swig from the bottle then lifted his head. "You smell it, boy?"

"Smell what?" I said.

"There's death in the wind."

"I don't smell it."

Smith ignored that because, half drunk, he was talking to himself, not me.

"Smelled it once before, on the night afore the Battle of Champion Hill. Death walked through our camp and then ol' General John C. Pemberton ran around the tents asking everybody he met, 'What's that smell, boys? What's that accursed smell?' "

Smith drank from the bottle and wiped off his mustache with the back of his hand. "The next day Grant and his Army of the Tennessee kicked our asses and piled our Confederate dead in heaps as high as a man." His eyes sought mine in the darkness. "It was a great battle and the field of honor stank like a charnel house. It was the smell I'd smelled the night afore, the smell I smell now. Death just took a stroll through our camp, boy. But whose death?" He smiled. "Not mine, so maybe yours, huh?

116

Or Hardin's."

Beside me, I became aware that Wes's eyes were half open, studying Jones and Davis who, overcome by alcohol, were sound asleep. His eyes slanted under his lids, fixing the location of the lawmen's weapons.

Behind the glow of the crackling fire, Smith laid his shotgun across his knees and sang softly to himself.

"O, I'm a good ol' Rebel,
Now that's just what I am.
For this 'Fair Land of Freedom',
I do not care at all."

Wes watched the lawman with wolf eyes.

"I'm glad I fit against it,
I only wish we'd won,
And I don't want no pardon
For anything I done."

Smith's head dropped on his chest and he jerked awake.

Wes tensed . . . a young man-eater getting ready to spring.

The lawman took another swig and sang again.

"I hates the glorious Union,

'Tis dripping with our blood —"

Smith's voice faded. His head bobbed, lower . . . lower. . . .

"I hates their stripèd banner,
I fit . . . it . . . all . . . I . . . could. . . ."

The lawman's voice ebbed . . . died away . . . grew silent. . . .
He snored softly.
And John Wesley Hardin descended upon him like the wrath of God.

Wes carefully lifted the shotgun from Smith's lap, then stepped to the sleeping constables and grabbed Davis's Colt.
He returned to Smith and let the snoring man have both barrels in the face.
Smith, his head practically blown off his shoulders, died without making a sound.
Davis and Jones woke and sat up. Davis yelled, "What the hell is happening?"
Expertly working the Colt, Wes thumbed two shots into him.
Davis screamed and fell back, sudden blood staining his mouth.
Jones, the youngest of the three, threw off his blankets and scrambled to his feet.
"For pity's sake, don't shoot me," he

called out. "I have a pregnant wife and three young'uns at home."

Wes hesitated, and I thought for a moment he felt inclined to show the young lawman mercy.

How foolish I was. How unspeakably stupid.

The concept of mercy was as alien to John Wesley as sin is to a cloistered monk. He smiled, then shot the crying, sobbing Jones between the eyes. Standing in the red glow of the firelight, gun smoke drifting around him, Wes looked like the devil incarnate.

At the time I said nothing. Nothing at all.

He turned to me then, his face like stone, his eyes lost in pools of darkness . . . and he pointed his *murderous revolver* at my head.

Sweet Christ save me! I stood transfixed, terrified to move.

John Wesley smiled. "Did you think I'd shoot you, Little Bit?"

"I don't know."

"I don't know either. Maybe I would. Maybe if you did me wrong I'd gut shoot you."

"I would never wrong you. I'm your friend."

Wes waved the Colt around the clearing. "Was this my fault?"

Fearing for my life I didn't hesitate. "No,

Wes, not your fault. Smith said he smelled death. He said death walked through our camp."

"He was right."

"Wes, quit smiling like that and put the gun away," I said. "You're scaring the hell out of me."

He did neither.

"I smelled it too, Little Bit. Death walked close to me and it looked like a column of black mist and stank like a rotting thing. I've seen it before, you know. Sometimes it watches me and says nothing. It just stares and stares with its cold eyes."

Now I was really boogered. I stood there and pissed myself. Warm urine streamed down my legs and trickled onto the toes of my shoes.

"It wasn't my fault. They should never have arrested me." Then, like a man suddenly waking from a trance, Wes grinned and let the Colt drop to his side.

"Little Bit, how come you just pissed all over yourself?"

CHAPTER FOURTEEN:
A GRIEVING FATHER

John Wesley armed himself with a brace of revolvers he took from the dead men, but he decided to leave their horses behind, as they'd attract too much attention to us.

We stuck to our original plan to stay with his folks in Mount Calm where we'd be safe and welcome and took to the trail at first light.

I must admit that I rode with a heavy heart, the deaths of the three constables, especially Jones, weighing on me. And consider this — the death of Smith put paid to the lie that Wes would not pull the trigger on a man who'd worn the gray. He knew Smith had been at Champion Hill, heard him say so, yet he blew off his head with a shotgun.

Need I say more?

And one more thing . . . I'm often asked how many men Wes had killed after he dispatched the three constables. I've heard it suggested that he'd killed one man for every year of his life; like that Billy Bonney kid did later, up New Mexico way.

Wes was seventeen when he gunned Smith, Davis and Jones, and by then I reckoned he was creepin' up on Bonney's twenty-one.

Some folks will tell you different.

But, hell, I know better because I was there.

Mount Calm lay in the middle of the east Texas hill country. A store, a school, and a handful of whitewashed houses were splattered across flat, sandy ground like spilled milk.

Wes said there was talk of the railroad laying a spur to the place, but nobody, including his pa, put any stock in that.

James Gibson Hardin was a tall, slender man, a Methodist minister by profession, who bore, I fancied, a resemblance to the great Jefferson Davis of blessed memory. The Reverend Hardin didn't exactly welcome his prodigal son with open arms, but neither did he send him away.

In contrast, Wes's mother, Mary Elizabeth, an attractive, stiff-backed woman, showered kisses on her son and called him, "My golden boy," and "My dearest Johnny."

After remarking how thin Wes had become, she hurried into the kitchen and left her husband with Wes and me in the parlor.

"Three state constables, you say, John?" Rev. Hardin's face was pale as death, his high, intelligent forehead wrinkled with emotion.

"It wasn't my fault, Pa," Wes said.

"It never is, John."

"They were damned Yankees and they arrested me only because I was a Texas boy. Said they were going to torture me and then see me hang." Wes looked at me, his eyes pleading. "Ain't that right, Little Bit? Weren't they taking me to the gallows?"

I remembered Smith, who'd fought for the Cause, and I didn't answer right away.

The Rev. Hardin noted my hesitation and said, "Don't bring Little Bit into your lies, John. The Bible says, 'Thou shalt not kill.' If I am to believe what I hear, you've already broken that dictate a score of times."

"I was defending myself, Pa. The Yankees hate me and want to see me dead. It's not my fault."

"Son, you're a liar and a killer," the elder Hardin said. "I fear that there is no place for you in God's heart." He paused for just a moment. "Or in mine."

Mary Elizabeth opened the door and

stuck her head into the parlor. "Johnny dear, roast beef and taters on the table, and plenty of it."

She glanced at me and I saw that she was trying to be cheerful, even charming, I guess, but the strain in her blue eyes and the deepening lines on her face betrayed her true feelings. "You too, Little Bit. You need some weight on those skinny bones."

Mary Elizabeth had been listening at the door. That much was obvious, and she'd been wounded by what she'd heard.

The meal was awkward to say the least — silent, like a wake for dead kin. But I ate heartily, by no means sure where my next grub might come from.

Mary Elizabeth tried, God bless her. She and the reverend had ten children together, though two had died young, and she chatted about the family and what they were doing.

But her husband's silence and John Wesley's slow-simmering anger was not conducive to polite conversation. Even when Wes mentioned his plan for a Wild West show, though his mother clapped loudly and declared, "How wonderful!" it was greeted by a stony silence from his father.

When the tense meal was over, the Rev. Hardin lit a cigar. "John, I've been thinking things over and have asked the Good Lord for guidance. I want you to go to Old Mexico and remain there for —"

"How long?" Wes interrupted, astonished.

"I don't know. Years maybe."

"The Yankees never forget, Pa, They're mighty long on hatreds and short on forgiveness."

"As we Texans are ourselves," the reverend said.

"What the hell will I do in Mexico?" Wes asked.

"No profanity, John, please," the reverend said, speaking behind a cloud of curling blue smoke. "Find honest work, I suppose."

"As a laborer?" Wes said.

"If that's all you can do, then yes, that's the kind of work you must find."

Wes sprang to his feet, his eyes blazing. "I'd die before I'd blister my hands on a damned shovel."

"The boy is right, James," Mary Elizabeth said. "Johnny's delicate constitution is not suited to the laborer's trade."

"Then what is he suited for, my dear?" the reverend asked carefully.

It was a loaded question, mildly asked, and I awaited Mrs. Hardin's answer with some unease.

She rose to the challenge, exclaiming,

"The stage! You heard Johnny say that he wants to put on a show. He has the looks, the poise, and the erudition to become a fine actor. Why, he might even perform in Shakespeare like the noble Booth brothers."

She dragged me into the talk. "Is that not so, Little Bit?"

I hedged. "It's a Wild West show, ma'am."

"Yes, and a most singular idea it is," Mrs. Hardin said. She raised her pretty eyes to her son. "You'll be very good at it, Johnny, and, I declare, become rich and famous quicker than . . . well, quicker 'n scat!"

Before Wes could speak, his father rubbed his forehead and said, "I grow weary, Mary Elizabeth. I will retire to my study, re-acquaint myself with Holy Scripture then seek my bed early."

He rose to his feet. "John, Little Bit, there's a zinc bathtub out back. I strongly suggest you both use it."

"And I have a fresh bar of Pears soap all the way from England," Mrs. Hardin said. "I know how delicate your skin is, Johnny, dear."

CHAPTER FIFTEEN: UNWELCOME NEWS

The next morning at breakfast, the Reverend Hardin said that John Wesley and I could stay with him for a couple days before leaving for Mexico. Wes said nothing, but I saw by the expression on his face that he was unhappy with this arrangement.

Everything changed early the next day when a man named Crow Duplin knocked at the door and was admitted by the Hardin maidservant, then ushered into the parlor where we all were.

I figured that Duplin got his name from the black crow feathers he wore in the band of his gray kepi. He had a long, sad face and eyes so saggy his bottom eyelids showed red rims.

The Rev. Hardin said, "Well, Crow, what errand brings you to my home so early in the morning?" Belatedly, he introduced us. "My son John you know, and this is his friend Little Bit."

"Pleased to make your acquaintance, I'm sure," Crow said.

I'd thought him a Texan, but he spoke with a strong English accent. He grinned, revealing few teeth and those black, and pumped my hand with the greatest show of affection.

"In answer to your question, Reverend," Crow said, "I'm on a mission of the greatest moment, and it concerns young Master Hardin, here present, and those who would do him great bodily harm."

Crow grabbed my hand again and pumped that already punished extremity even harder. "Howdy do?" He grinned wider than before. "This is indeed a plumbed and squared pleasure."

"Likewise, I'm sure," I said, withdrawing my crumpled fingers.

"Before we hear what you have to say, can I offer you coffee, Mr. Duplin?" Mary Elizabeth said.

Crow bowed with all the flair of an Elizabethan courtier. "Now, as to that question, dear lady, if I say no, you may think me an ungrateful wretch. But if I answer yes, then I fear I may put you to the greatest inconvenience."

"It's no trouble at all," Mary Elizabeth said. "I'll bring you a cup directly." Her gray morning dress rustled as she turned and headed for the kitchen.

"Let's hear your news, Crow." Wes seemed quite unconcerned, nibbling on a corner of toast left over from breakfast.

"And there it is in a nutshell," Crow said. "A forthright question from a forthright youth. And I will answer it honestly and in full. Duplin by name, Duplin by nature, I always say."

"Proceed, Crow," the Rev. Hardin said, a tinge of impatience in his voice.

"And proceed I will, with the greatest dispatch." Crow bowed low, then accepted a cup from Mary Elizabeth "I was a-sitting in my cabin with the missus, discussin' our hard times like, and me sayin' that I was much afeerd of more coming down —"

As though she felt the need to explain Crow's straitened circumstances, Mrs. Hardin interrupted. "Mr. Duplin has twelve children, Little Bit, and, unfortunately, most of them are simple."

"All of them, dear lady, except for little Nancy," Crow said after a sip of coffee. "She's as smart as a whip, that young 'un."

Wes and his father exchanged irritated glances, and the reverend said, "So, Crow, you were sitting in your cabin, and . . ."

"And Mrs. Duplin, bless 'er heart, hap-

129

pened to glance out the window, and what does she see?" Crow waited expectantly.

Wes snapped, "Tell us."

"Sojers! Blue coat sojers!"

The Rev. Hardin was much taken aback by this intelligence and displayed the utmost agitation as he exclaimed, "Soldiers? Here in Mount Calm?"

"Yankee sojers as ever was." Crow bowed as Mrs. Hardin took his cup. "A score of black cavalry and a white officer."

In her sudden anguish, Mary Elizabeth dropped the cup and it smashed on the wood floor. She ran to Wes and threw her arms around his neck. "My poor Johnny, the God's cursed Yankees are after you."

"Indeed they are, ma'am," Crow said. "Upon my inquiring as to their presence in our little town, the officer said, 'We're hunting a damned scoundrel, traitor, and murderer by the name of John Wesley Hardin. Have you seen him?'" Crow wrung his hands in agitation. "When I said that I hadn't, the officer said, 'Then we'll tear apart every house in Mount Calm until we find the rogue.'"

The Rev. Hardin immediately grasped the seriousness of the situation and cried out, "John, into the root cellar without delay. You too, Little Bit." He quickly reached into

130

his pocket and pressed some money into Crow's hand. "You have done my family a great service."

I thought so too, but Wes seemed to have a different opinion. Despite the considerable amount of money in his pocket, he brushed past Crow without a thank-you.

Not for the first time, I realized that gratitude and generousness were not two of Wes's virtues.

For his part, Crow reached out to take my hand again. But I placed that tormented appendage behind my back, smiled, and tipped him a little bow.

Much pleased by this, Crow himself bowed. "It's been a real treat meeting you, Mr. Little Bit."

"And for me too," I said.

"Quickly now," Rev. Hardin said, grabbing my arm. "There's no time to be lost."

From outside, I heard the thud of hooves and the jingle of cavalry bits. The Yankees were at the door!

Chapter Sixteen:
Across the Rio Grande

To my dying day, I will never understand why the soldiers ransacked the Hardin home, but didn't search the root cellar. Perhaps it was because the underground cellar was small and had not been used in some time, thus its single door was partially overgrown with brush and was difficult to see. Whatever the reason, our hiding place went undiscovered, and Wes and I remained there until dark.

Coyotes yipped in the hills when we heard footfalls approach the cellar.

Wes had retrieved his pistols before we fled from the house and he pointed them at the timber door. He grinned and whispered in my ear, "If a Yankee opens that damned door you're going to see a hell of a fight."

"John Wesley, it's me. Don't shoot." It was the Rev. Hardin's voice. He knew better than to walk up on Wes without being announced.

"Are the Yankees gone?" Wes asked.

"Yes, about an hour ago," his father said. "They did some damage in the house and your mother got a black eye trying to stop them."

"Open the damned door," Wes said. "I'm going after the one that did it."

"Too late for that, son," Mr. Hardin said. "The Yankees are long gone, and the soldier that struck your mother told his officer that it was an accident."

After the door creaked open on rusty hinges, Wes clambered outside. "Describe him, Pa." His voice was shaking with fury.

"He was a Negro, John, and they all look alike," the reverend said. "How can I describe him, that he was a man with a black skin?"

"Then I'll kill them all," Wes said. "That way I'll be sure of getting the right one."

"Revenge is a dish best served cold, John. It will wait. Your mother wasn't badly hurt and I have other plans for you." The reverend wore a wide-brimmed hat and an oilskin. He carried a new Henry rifle, an odd thing for a man of the cloth.

Drizzling rain slanted in a shivering wind and everywhere around us the lost, lonely land was hidden in darkness.

"Your horses are saddled and I'll escort

you as far as the Rio Grande," Mr. Hardin said.

"We don't need an escort," Wes said, his face stiff as a board.

"I know you don't, son. But I want to make sure you do as I told you." The reverend turned his attention to me. "Little Bit, I know you're much attached to novels of the more sensational kind, so I brought you this." He handed me a cloth-bound volume with gilt lettering on the cover.

"It is the historical work, *Quentin Durward,* by the late Sir Walter Scott. I hope you'll find time to enjoy it."

Indeed, I had read the story of dashing young Quentin before.

You will recall that Sir Walter's tale is about a young Scots cavalier in search of honorable adventure. By his senses, firmness, and gallantry, he becomes the fortunate possessor of wealth and rank and then gains the hand of a beautiful lady whose family tree is as noble as his own.

I'd read the work years before (and, oh, how I wanted to be Quentin!) and was eager to reacquaint myself with its entrancing prose. I thanked the Rev. Hardin profusely and put the book under my coat out of the rain, where Quentin Durward's pure heart could beat against mine.

A few minutes later we took the trail to Mexico. Wes was silent and sullen, but his father sat tall and alert in the saddle, his eyes constantly reaching out into the darkness around him.

He needn't have worried.

The rain grew heavier, the wind colder, and no hostile traveller would venture forth on such a night.

We reached the north bank of the Rio Grande at daybreak, under a sky that stretched formless gray as far as the eye could see. The rain had lessened, but the drizzle fell steadily. Having no oilskin, I was thoroughly soaked.

The Reverend Hardin shook my hand and then his son's. "You will be safe in Mexico, John. Lay your guns aside and find good, honest work. Son, take the word of God in Psalms to heart, 'He shall be like a tree planted by the rivers of water that bringeth forth his fruit in his season; its leaf shall not wither; and whatever he doeth shall prosper.' "

The reverend pointed to the Rio Grande where stately wading birds hunted frogs and minnows in the shallows. "There is your river of water, John. All you have to do is cross it and whatever you do will prosper."

Wes took this advice with ill grace. Without another word, he swung his horse away and rode into the river.

The Rev. Hardin said to me, "Little Bit, when you get settled, see that John writes his mother. She does worry about him so."

I nodded. "I will make sure he writes at least once a week."

We shook hands and parted. The Reverend Hardin rode away and did not look back at his son.

My soul was weighed down by a burden I couldn't fathom. Maybe it was the leaden sky, or maybe it was because of the mysteries and dangers of Mexico, then an unknown land to me.

Or maybe, in my heart of hearts, I knew that James Hardin's dreams for his son would never come true.

He was a fine man, the Reverend Hardin, but born to parlous times.

CHAPTER SEVENTEEN:
KILLINGS AND
THE JOY OF MESCAL

The ride south of the border took close to three weeks. We rode hard during the day and camped at night, arriving in October.

The Mexican village lay about three miles south of the river and it wasn't much — modest adobe buildings clustered around a central plaza. A fountain stood in the middle of the square, but it was dry as dust and didn't look like it had run water since the time of the old Spaniards.

But there was a cantina with a blue coyote painted on the outside wall. The smoke that rose from its chimney smelled of mesquite and the tang of fried beef.

Until then, John Wesley had been silent since we crossed the border. "I could sure use some breakfast."

"I'm feeling sharp set my ownself," I said. "Then let's eat."

Four other horses already stood at the cantina's hitching post when we dismounted. That surprised me because their saddles were double-rigged Mother Hubbards, popular in Texas at that time. Only white men sat such a rig.

Hungry and cold as I was, I didn't give the presence of white Texans another thought, but I should have, the way things turned out.

The owner of the place was a small, plump man, with a round, pleasant face that bore a worried, almost fearful expression.

The reason was not hard to find.

Four white men sat at a table, sharing a bottle of what I later learned was mescal, the strong, smoky and potent liquor of Old Mexico. They were a wolfish, uncurried bunch, who looked like they'd just come in off the trail. All of them wore dusters, good boots, and fancy spurs, and each carried a brace of revolvers in tooled holsters.

Such men bring trouble with them, and I sensed it, but Wes seemed totally indifferent.

After the worried little Mexican sat us at a table and took our order for tortillas, beef and frijoles, Wes got up from his chair and stood with his back to the blazing log fire.

He looked over at the four men and smiled. "Ahh, it does a man good to warm his butt at the fire after a long ride."

138

It was at this point that the proprietor put a bottle of mescal and two earthenware cups on the pine table in front of me. I draw this detail to your attention only because I have always believed that bottle of mescal was the first step on my long road to the hopeless drunk I later became.

As I said, Wes stood in front of the fire and made a remark that the four men seemed to take with considerable good humor. But appearances can be deceptive when it comes to hard cases of that kind. Even rabid wolves can smile.

One of the four, a redhead big in the chest and shoulders, sporting a magnificent, sweeping handlebar mustache I'd have given my eye teeth to own, grinned. "You quit blocking the fire, sonny, or I'll warm your ass for you over my knee."

The others laughed and Wes laughed with them.

"Hey, that's funny. A real thigh-slapper." Then the laughter drained from Wes's face, his eyes a bright, piercing blue. "Now come here and let me see you put me over your knee." Suddenly he was on the prod.

Wes was touchy, and I knew he felt that being called *sonny* was an insult to his manhood.

The four men at the table wanted trouble

and they were not shy about bringing it. The big redhead looked around at the others and grinned. Then he slowly rose to his feet, with a considerable, easy elegance I must add.

"You gonna lower your britches, youngster, or am I going to do it for you?"

"Studying on it," Wes said, "I reckon I'll leave that up to you."

Lacking gun leather, John Wesley's Colts were shoved into each side of his waistband, butt-forward, in what some now call the cavalry draw position. They were hidden by his coat.

This mode of carry was much favored by another famous shootist, but more of him later. First things first, as I always say.

The big man, his spurs ringing, stepped across the cantina floor. Then he stopped, his eyes locked on Wes's face.

The Mexican proprietor, steaming plates in hand, stepped between them and said to Wes, his voice tremoring, "Senor, your food is served."

In recent years I've heard men say that the redhead's name was Archie Keller or Kenner and by the time he clashed with Wes, he'd killed seven men. They say he was mean enough to pour water over a widow woman's kindling, and so profane, he used the Holy Bible for cigarette papers.

Maybe these things are true enough, but what isn't true is that he saw his own death in Wes's eyes and backed down real quick. Hell, he wasn't scared of Wes any more than he was scared of me. I'm convinced he knew that killing what he thought to be an unarmed, beardless boy would do little to enhance his gun reputation.

As it was, let's call him Archie Keller. He just grinned, willing to let it go. "Yeah, you go eat your breakfast like a good boy."

And there it might have ended.

But it sure didn't.

One of the others at the table, a young towhead with the eyes of a carrion eater, said, "Aw hell. I'll take down the pup's britches an' whup him good, Arch."

The towhead got up in a hurry and advanced on Wes. But I had my good foot resting in a chair and I pushed it into him.

The man got all tangle-footed with the chair and fell.

Keller turned his head to see what had happened.

And that was all the break John Wesley needed. In an instant, his guns were in his hands.

The big Colts bucked as he slammed two shots into Keller and then another hit the towhead in the throat as he struggled to free himself from the chair and get to his feet.

Keller, hit twice in the chest, lay dying on the floor as Wes covered the other two men at the table with his revolvers.

"You brought it," he said. "You want I should finish it?"

But the two survivors wanted no part of Wes on that day, and by the horrified look on their faces, on any other.

"We're leavin'," the older of the two said, so fast there was no space between his words.

"Then leave," Wes said.

Death rattled in Keller's throat and all the life that was in him left.

The towhead lay gagging on his own blood for a spell, then, after making a horrible, gurgling sound, he too gave up the ghost.

Wes glanced at the two bodies. He stood slender and significant like some kind of avenging angel. "Take these two and bury them across the border. I will not have Texans lie in foreign soil."

The older man got up to do as he was told, but the younger man, hard-faced and defiant, his eyes reckless, said to Wes, "I'll remember you. There will be another place and another time."

That was not a wise thing to say to John Wesley Hardin when his blood was up and his eyes were cold as a killing frost.

Wes raised his Colt and shot the man just where his hat met his forehead. His suspenders cut, the youngster hit the floor with a thud and lay still.

"For God's sake, Wes!" I yelled. "For God's sake!"

"This was not my fault." Wes's eyes flicked from me to the older man, who was ashen and looked like he might puke at any second. "He threatened me and I will not leave a sworn enemy on my back trail." He glared at the fellow Texan. "Now you have three men to bury."

The man had bark on. He dug deep and rediscovered his courage. "I hope I'm around when they bury you."

Wes smiled. "You figure on living another fifty years, huh?"

"You won't live that long," the man said. "One day you'll run into a man who's just as hard as you, and he'll kill you. You'll get it in the back and die on a saloon floor with your face in a spittoon."

Wes shook with anger, or maybe a goose flew over his grave. "All right, I'll turn my back on you right now. Then shuck the iron, old man, and we'll see who bites the ground."

"Kid, you go to hell." The man turned away, his talking done.

Then, with the help of the Mexican, he dragged the dead men out of the saloon and into the dusky gloom of the dank, drizzling day.

Our food lay cold on the table, but I'd lost my appetite anyway. I picked up the dark blue bottle. "What the hell is this stuff?"

"Mescal. It's made from some kind of cactus." Wes absently studied the three blood trails that smeared across the floor like the tracks of snails. His eyes held nothing. No regret. No interest.

"Is it good?" I asked.

"How should I know?" Wes said. "Try it."

The mescal poured into my cup like a glittering river of gold and smelled like the smoke from a campfire in Paradise. Saliva jetted from the back of my tongue as I put the cup to my lips and drank.

Oh, heavenly elixir! My lover! My new companion!

Thus was born my love affair with alcohol that burns just as passionately today as it did then. Although I no longer drink (The Sisters of Charity frown on alcohol) I remain in constant mourning for the loss of my dearest, but most treacherous friend.

I drank and drank again.

Wes said, "Go easy on the busthead, Little Bit. We got riding to do." He looked at me with a puzzled expression. "I never known you to indulge in liquor before."

"I never knew how good liquor was before," I said.

Indeed, the booze was working its magic quickly on my tiny body. My leg no longer hurt and I felt that I was drifting on a pink cloud three feet above the floor. For the first time in my life, I realized that the world was a wonderful, shining place and that I'd at last found my niche in it.

I'd let the genie out of the bottle and I vowed never to cork him up again.

CHAPTER EIGHTEEN:
A TERRIBLE WOUND

"Give me that!" John Wesley snapped. He grabbed the bottle from the table and threw it into a corner where it smashed into pieces, the golden liquid spilling like angel's blood over the floor. "Now, listen up. We're heading back across the border and heading for Gonzales County. I got huggin' kin there, the Clements brothers. Fine, upstanding folk."

My brain was fuzzy and I'm sure I had a silly grin on my face. "But your pa —"

"I know what's best for John Wesley, not my pa," Wes said.

"But, Wes, you promised —"

"Damn you, I promised nothing." He stared hard at me, then waved a hand around the cantina. "I crossed the border to get away from trouble, but all it did was follow me, like, like some kind of plague. Lookee, three men dead through no fault of my own. Hell, we've only been in Mexico an hour and we've already worn out our welcome."

Before I could say anything, Wes waved the Mexican over. He'd been jabbering away to a couple peons who'd just walked in. All three regarded us with fearful eyes.

"Hey you, get over here," Wes yelled.

The little man shuffled over to our table.

Wes said, "You want to invest in my Wild West show?"

The Mexican was confused. "I-I don't understand, senor."

"Hear that," Wes said, directing his attention to me. "How are we going to raise money for my show in greaser towns?" He turned to the Mexican. "Get lost."

The little man scurried away, no doubt thanking his lucky stars that he was still alive.

"On your feet, Little Bit. We're heading back to civilization."

I rose and staggered a little.

With that casual cruelty that came so easily to him, Wes said, "Hell, just what I need, a drunken cripple."

"I'll be all right," I said.

"Sure you will, once the bug juice wears off. You'd better be. The Clements boys don't suffer fools gladly."

"I'm not a fool, Wes," I said with all the

dignity I could muster.

I saw the flipside of the John Wesley Hardin coin.

"Of course you're not, Little Bit." He smiled, his hand on my shoulder. "I was just joshing you. Hell, you're going to be my business manager one day, aren't you?"

"Sure thing, Wes." The alcohol had made me mellow.

We recrossed the Rio Grande and camped that night in a stand of post oak and bois d'arc, a stone's throw from a willow-lined stream where blue and silver fish jumped.

It was way down in the fall. The rain, though intermittent, seemed widespread. Every now and then a shower rattled through the trees. Urged on by a north wind, it soaked everything.

For the first time in my life, alcohol, my beautiful new mistress, showed what hell she could cause. The mescal hangover she inflicted on me was the ninth circle of Dante's Hell.

Wes, of course, was highly amused, and teased me constantly. He made a masterful show of bolting down the cold tortillas and beef he'd brought from the cantina and expressed the wish that he had a bottle of mescal to wash it down.

In addition to a churning belly and my other miseries, my bad leg ached. Once when I moved it closer to the fire, I cried out from the sudden pain.

"What the hell was that?" Wes said.

"My leg hurts real bad," I said.

"Which one?"

"Which one do you think?"

"Let me have a look at it."

"I got to take off my pants," I said.

"Lord a mercy, can I bear the shock?" Wes grinned.

Raindrops ticked from the oak branches and I heard the rumble of distant thunder as I pulled down my pants. The leather and steel contraption around my wasted limb gleamed in the firelight.

"That leg is thin, by God," Wes said. "Like a stick."

"Don't you think I already know that?"

"How the hell does it hold you upright?"

"It doesn't. The steel does."

"Where does it hurt?" Wes asked.

"Up here, right at the top of my thigh."

Wes's strong, nimble fingers undid the buckles that strapped the cage to my leg, then he set it aside. He looked at my leg again and his eyes flew wide open. "Damn. Take a look at that."

I looked down and saw what Wes saw. A

149

huge sore — raw, red, deep, and streaked with yellow pus — had formed under the leather strap, caused by its constant rubbing against my skin. The ulcer was about twice the size of a silver dollar and it smelled bad, like rotten fish.

"How long have you had this?" Wes looked queasy.

"It started just after we left Longview. And it's been getting worse since."

Wes said nothing.

I said, "What can we do about it?"

"I don't know. I'm not a doctor." Wes picked up the steel brace, rusty in spots. "You can't wear this. The leather will rub on the sore again and make it worse."

"I can't walk without it." I felt sweat bead on my forehead.

"Then I'll carry you to your horse. The Clements brothers have womenfolk up in Gonzales County and they're known to be good at patching up wounds."

"This isn't a bullet hole."

"I know, Little Bit. It's a sight worse."

But the worst was still to come. That night the fever struck.

CHAPTER NINETEEN:
TALK OF THE CHISHOLM TRAIL

I was burning up, out of my mind with fever as we made our way to the cousins. Time meant nothing to me, but I learned later it took almost two weeks. Wes wasn't happy about it, but he never left me by the side of the trail. The concerned triangle of John Wesley's face drifted in and out of my consciousness.

He held wet leaves to my forehead, and from the far end of a scarlet tunnel I heard him say over and over, "You'll be fine, Little Bit, just fine."

I remember (or did I imagine?) grabbing him by the front of his coat, babbling to him about the pale men who stood in the shadows, watching us.

And Mage was there. But, unlike the rest, his face was black as mortal sin and his eyes glowed with a sable fire.

They were all there . . . all the men Wes had killed. They stood still as graven statues.

Watching.

Silent as the grave.

"Look! Look, Wes!" I yelled.

A white mule stepped among the trees, a gambler's ghost. On him sat a man who held a walking cane across the saddle horn. The man smiled and made a gun of his fingers and thumb and he fired at the back of Wes's head.

I heard the bang of the pistol as the man's thumb fell, and blood, bone, and brain haloed around Wes's shattered skull.

I cried out in my terrible fear. "Oh merciful Jesu!"

"It's thunder, Little Bit," Wes said. His face ran scarlet with thin streams of blood and rain. "It's only thunder."

I clutched at Wes again. "Don't leave me. Wes, I'm sore afeerd."

"It's the fever. The fever makes a man see things." He held a cup to my mouth. "It's water. It will help cool you down."

I drank greedily and noisily. "Did you see Mage? Over there by the post oak. He's come back from hell, Wes."

Wes smiled. "Hell, you can't see a black man in the dark."

"And I saw a white mule."

"A gambler's ghost . . . just passing through."

I grabbed for him again. "Beware of the man with the cane, Wes."

"I surely will, Little Bit."

I lifted my face to the cool rain and opened my mouth to catch the drops. Then I lapsed into a troubled sleep again, my dreams filled with dead gamblers and pretty, laughing saloon girls in rainbow-colored dresses and the man with the cane who pushed me aside with a terrible curse.

Him I feared most of all.

"You cut it close, Little Bit," the man's voice said. "For a spell there, I figured you were gonna cash in fer sure."

The face of a young man I didn't know swam into focus.

"Where am I?" My voice was thin as a wafer.

The young man answered. "At my brothers' ranch in Gonzales County. We're south of a town called Smiley if'n you feel inclined to go on a tear with the whiskey and gals."

"Not hardly," I said.

"Figured that." The man smiled. "The name is Gip Clements. My brothers James, Mannen, and Joe own this ranch, including the bed you're lying in."

"How long?"

"A week since Wes brought you here more

153

dead than alive."

"For sure it's winter then. Where is Wes?"

"Talking with my brothers. He plans to help them drive a herd up Kansas way."

I felt a spike of panic and tried to sit up in the bed. "My leg —"

"Is doing just fine," Gip said. "Brother Joe's lady says you'll be up and about in no time. Another month, maybe so."

I pushed down the sheet, terrified of what I might see, and pulled up the borrowed nightshirt. The sore on my leg had shrunk in size and was no longer red and angry. When I touched the puckered skin around the wound there was only a little pain.

"You got Mae Ellen to thank fer that," Gip said. "She says looking after you was like caring for a little, hurt dickie bird."

"Thank her from me. Thank her most kindly."

"You can thank her your ownself. She'll bring you some rabbit and onion soup right soon."

"When does the herd leave?" I asked. My heart thumped in my chest. If Wes was going, I didn't want to be left behind.

"The gather isn't finished, but I reckon Wes and my brothers will head 'em north by the middle of next week."

"I've got to be on the drive. Tell Wes I

need to talk to him. Better still, bring me my leg brace and I'll go tell him my own-self."

Gip smiled at me. "Hell, Little Bit, your leg ain't fully healed yet. Strap on all that damned steel and it will open right up again." He gave me a sympathetic look, or tried to. "Besides, a scrawny little feller that keeps as poorly as you ain't gonna be much help on a two month cattle drive up the Chisholm. That's rough country, to say nothing of fire, flood, an' wild Indians."

Well, that was a boot in the teeth. But I managed to keep a brave face.

"I'm a good cook," I said.

"We got plenty of them, good and bad. And assistant cooks."

"Then I could be the assistant cook to an assistant cook," I said.

"You'd better talk with John Wesley. He's the one doing the firing and hiring." Gip shook his head. "Don't get your hopes up."

The door opened and he said, "Ah, here's Mae Ellen with the grub. Put meat on them scrawny bones o' your'n."

Gip left and Mae Ellen said, "How are you feeling, Little Bit?"

"Good enough to go on the trail drive," I said.

Mae Ellen, a pretty, worn girl who probably looked older than her years, smiled. "Not this time, Little Bit. You've got to rest up and get your strength back."

As she put the tray on my lap, I said, "I want to thank you for taking care of me."

"You were no trouble. Just like a little sick animal." She straightened up and worked a kink out of her slim back.

I tried the soup, but it was still too hot. I didn't want Mae Ellen to leave, so I said a stupid thing. "You saw me naked, huh?"

She smiled. "I've seen worse." She stepped to the door. "I'll be back to look at your leg. Old Ma Atsa is a Navajo witch woman and she gave me a new salve to try."

"Will it work fast?" I asked.

Mae Ellen laughed. "We'll see."

Then she was gone and all that remained was a lingering scent of lavender and a lonely, empty space where once a woman stood.

CHAPTER TWENTY:
I JOIN THE CATTLE DRIVE

"Damn it all, Little Bit, I had to kill another man. After I shot him, he lingered for a couple days and I just heard he died an hour before sunup this morning." John Wesley sat on the edge of the bed. "And you can't pin this one on me. It wasn't my fault."

"What happened?" I said, not really wanting to know.

I mean, Wes was Wes. When a man did or said something he didn't like, Wes killed him.

Simple as that.

"Well, me and a couple Clements boys fell in with some vaqueros, as Joe Clements called them, and one of them suggested a card game."

"Poker?"

"Nah. Some greaser game called Spanish Monte," Wes said. "I'd never heard of it before."

"I saw it played years ago by a couple

Rangers," I said. "Now that I study on it, one of those boys said he was quarter Mexican, something like that."

Wes looked irritated. "Hell, Little Bit, is this your story or mine?"

"Yours, Wes. Proceed."

"Well, we played a couple hands and I started to get the hang of it." Wes held up his left hand and showed the silver ring on his little finger. "I don't wear this ring for nothing, you know."

But he did.

Wes had no claim to the professional gambler's ring, since he didn't play cards for a living. The few times he tried, he invariably lost and for a while would become sullen and dangerous.

"So we played another hand. All the while them Mexicans are jabbering away in that heathen language of theirs that nobody understands but them —"

"We never had any dealings with Mexicans before," I said.

"That's because they're all flannel-mouths," Wes said. "I don't like them."

"So you played another hand . . ." I prompted.

"Yeah, and I had a queen. I tapped my card and said, 'Pay the queen.' "

"The queen loses in Spanish Monte, as I recall."

"Damn it, Little Bit. That's the position the Mex dealer took," Wes said.

I cut to the chase. "So you shot him." The rabbit and onion soup lay sour in my belly.

"Hell no, not the dealer. Two other fellers," Wes said. "Him, I just chunked over the head with my gun and cleaned his plow real good."

I opened my mouth to speak, but Wes held up a silencing hand.

"The two fellers with him rose up and started in to shuck iron. Well, I shot one of them in the gun arm, near took the damned thing off, and t'other through the lungs."

"And what happened after that?"

"I told you. The Mex I shot through the lungs died this morning. They cut the arm off the other one, but he ain't expected to live either. Lost too much blood, like."

"What about the law?"

"Hell, there ain't no law in this part of Gonzalez County, except for what a man makes for himself. But the white folks around had a good laugh with me afterward and told me I did a fine thing shooting them two. They got no liking for Mexicans, especially the kind that cheat at cards." Wes rose to his feet and stretched. "Wasn't my fault, Little Bit," he said through a yawn. "They should have paid the queen."

I changed the subject. "Wes, I want to go on the cattle drive."

He stared at me, the imp of amusement in his eyes. "Little Bit, how the hell would you make Abilene? If things go bad, it could take three mighty hard months to get there."

"I'll take my chances." It was boastful talk coming from a skinny pipsqueak with a bad leg and eyes too big for his little pale face.

And John Wesley knew it. "You figure to ride herd, Little Bit? Maybe bring up the drag on a half-broke pony with the where-withal of a cougar that would like nothing better than to break your damned fool neck?"

Desperate, I lied in my teeth. "Gip said I could be the assistant cook's assistant."

"Gip said that?"

"Sure did," I said, blinking.

"You'd carry water and firewood on a gimpy leg?"

"I'd surely like to give it a try." Then I told another lie. "I'm stronger than I look."

Wes considered that for a while, then said, "Little Bit, we can't nurse a man who doesn't pull his weight, not when we're driving sixteen hundred head of wild steers up the Chisholm. If you fall behind, we'll leave you."

"I won't fall behind."

"Apaches, bears, thirst, hunger . . . that's what you'll face if you can't keep up with the herd," Wes said. "Best you stay here and make plans for the Wild West show and draw up them business documents that Sam Luck needs."

"Wes, you're my friend, and you're ramrodding the drive. I want to go with the herd. Don't let me down."

Wes sighed. "All right, Little Bit, you can help the cook. But don't expect any special favors from me. You drop out, you'll be on your own."

"Thank you, Wes. I won't let you down."

John Wesley crossed the floor, picked up my leg brace and tossed it on the bed. "Then get the hell up," he said, unsmiling. "You've laid there too long."

CHAPTER TWENTY-ONE:
MURDER ON THE CANADIAN

We didn't own the cows we were to drive north. John Wesley and the Clements boys made the gather for three fellers by the names of Jake Johnson, Columbus Carroll, and Crawford "Doc" Burnett. They weren't cattlemen either, but were contracted by ranchers to supply the drovers needed to drive their herds to Kansas and the railheads.

Back in those days, none of the Texas cattlemen could afford to hire their own cowboys, so they left it to the contactors to sign up out of work punchers, men on the scout looking to get away from the law, and any dancehall lounger, porch percher, or footpad willing to fork a bronc for eighty cents a day.

Being a lowly assistant of the cook's assistant, I got twenty-five cents, but was allowed to ride in the Studebaker chuck wagon that was invented by good ol' Charlie Goodnight.

The cook was an irritable, abrasive man, as they all were, but since a ten-pound cannonball had run away with his right leg at Gettysburg he took a liking to me, probably because we were both gimps.

His assistant was a stove-up cowboy named Lou. He was a few years past middle age, had a long, sad face and an alarming habit of, at the drop of a hat, shedding sudden tears for the woman he'd loved and lost years before. Her name was Sarah, but he imparted no further information, though I often pumped him for more.

John Wesley took a dislike to him, declaring that shedding tears for a woman wasn't manly. It was unbecoming of a Texan.

As for me, Lou never asked me to do too much by way of hauling water and firewood, so I liked him just fine.

At the end of February 1871, Columbus Carroll and Jake Johnson pushed north for Abilene with sixteen hundred beeves. Wes was in charge of a second herd of the same size that left a week later.

Wes and Jim Clements were paid handsomely, each receiving a hundred and fifty a month, but getting the herd to Abilene intact was a heavy responsibility. Just keeping order among a dozen hands, most of them hardcases, was no easy task.

That's why, for the first time in his life, John Wesley drew gun wages. It indicated how his reputation as a named shootist was growing.

Needless to say I was immensely proud of him as we left Texas at Red River Bluff and crossed into the Oklahoma Territory. We pushed north without incident and followed the Chisholm into the Nations.

Fifteen herds crossed the Red on the same day and the trail became a great winding river of Texas beef headed for the railheads and Yankee bellies.

Then John Wesley killed an Indian on the south bank of the Canadian that even now, many years later as I enter my dotage, I can only call cold-blooded murder.

One early evening as the herd rested, Wes took me on the back of his horse to show me the river we'd have to cross the next morning. The Canadian was a slow moving waterway at that time, bounded by red mud flats and treacherous quicksand and was swollen by the recent rains.

"Once we cross, we're halfway there, Little Bit." Wes drew rein on a brushy rise overlooking the river. "Ain't it a sight to see?"

And indeed it was. The setting sun tinged the sky scarlet and jade and the Canadian looked like a river of molten brass. The night birds squawked at the sentinel stars and far off coyotes talked.

"Want to ride closer, Little Bit?" Wes said. "If your leg will stand it."

My steel cage stuck straight out from the side of the horse, but the sore had healed pretty well and I had little pain. "Sure. I'd like to be the first of the outfit to drink water from the Canadian."

Wes turned his head and grinned at me. "I'll join you and we'll both boast of it in our old age."

As we rode down from the rise toward the river past a stand of salt bush, the horse shied. Wes grabbed for the horn and yelled, "What the hell?"

Mind you, I heard that from the ground where I'd landed in a heap, scared to move, worried that I'd discover a brand new misery. A moment later, as I rubbed dirt out of my eyes, I heard a shot.

Then a terrible scream.

I was in time to see a young Indian boy topple forward into the brush, a scarlet rose blossoming on his chest.

Wes swung out of the saddle, and then stepped warily toward the body, Colt in hand.

The young Indian, a Kiowa as we later

165

learned, was dead, his black eyes dully staring into nothingness.

"He had a bow and arrow," Wes said. "I saw it plain."

I rose slowly to my feet and stepped to the body. Half-hidden in the brush lay three dead cottontails and the boy, for that's what he was, still clutched a small bow.

"He was rabbit hunting," I said.

"The hell he was. He was trying to bushwhack us."

"Wes, he's only a boy. No more than twelve or thirteen years old, I reckon."

"Older than that," Wes said. "Look at him. He's a warrior."

"He was just a boy hunting rabbits," I said.

But John Wesley wasn't listening. A hint of a triumphant smile tugged at the corners of his mouth. "Since I started this drive, the only talk I've heard is Indians, Indians, Indians, and that they'd recently killed two white men in the Nations. Everybody is scared of them — except me."

He prodded the slim, brown body with his toe. "Hell, I'm no more afraid of a damned Redskin savage than I am a raccoon in a tree. I was anxious to meet one of them on the warpath and now I did." His smile grew wider. "And I done for him."

Wes reached into his pocket, produced his

Barlow, and opened the blade. "I think I should scalp him. That's what you do with an Indian you've killed, isn't it? Or should I cut off his ball sack for a tobacco pouch?"

"Wes, leave him be," I said. "Damn it, you killed him. Isn't that enough?" My face was blazing.

Wes looked at me. He smiled and closed the knife. "Well, I don't know how to scalp a man anyway. Mount up, Little Bit, and we'll go down to the river and have a drink like we planned."

I shook my head. "It's getting late. We should head back to the herd."

"Suit yourself," Wes said.

But suddenly he wasn't smiling any longer. "I sure never took you for a damned Indian-lover, Little Bit."

The next morning, Wes took Jim Clements and some of the drovers to see the dead Indian and they all agreed that he'd been a fearsome warrior. A puncher named Gray scalped the boy and gave the scalp to Wes who kept it for a couple days before he threw it away. He said it was a filthy thing.

Chapter Twenty-Two: Strong Drink and Wild Women

The Osage Nation was the last Indian reservation we had to cross before entering Kansas and the tribal elders demanded a tax of ten cents a head to let us through.

John Wesley told them to go to hell and pushed the herd north.

That led to another killing and a second dead Indian.

The morning after Wes's meeting with the Osage, he and most of the hands were out scouting the trail ahead of us.

I helped the cook prepare breakfast — cornbread and fried salt pork. The meal is stuck in my memory because of what happened later that day.

Wes had not yet returned when half a dozen Osage rode into camp, demanded their tribute, and started to cut out cattle.

The cook and me, with only two good legs between us, could only stand and watch. He hurled cusses at the Osage now and again that the savages pretended to not understand.

One of the two hands left in camp, a young fellow by the name of Tin Cup Sam, looked at me, his eyes scared. "Are they gonna massacree us?"

"I sure hope not," I said. "I'm not up for a massacree this morning."

"Well," Tin Cup said, "I'm going to fetch my pistol."

The cook agreed. "Me too. I will not be murdered by thieving savages."

How this would have ended I don't know. The cook was only halfway to the wagon when Wes and the rest of the hands rode into camp.

He drew rein and said to me, "What the hell's happening, Little Bit?"

"The Indians are taking some of our cattle," I said.

"The hell they are." Wes swung his horse around and rode to the chuck wagon where an Osage with a bright red scalp lock had dismounted. He demanded food from the cook, all the while brandishing a *bloodthirsty tomahawk* of the largest size.

As I watched Wes swing out of the saddle and approach the savage with a determined stride, I very much feared for my friend's safety. But he ignored the Indian and

169

stopped beside the warrior's horse, which bore an ornate silver bridle cunningly inlaid with a beautiful blue stone the Navajo call lapis lazuli.

After examining the bridle closely, Wes advanced on the savage, his hand on his pistol. "That bridle was stolen from our camp. I'm taking it back."

A huge, brindle steer that had wandered into camp was grazing close to the smoky fire built to keep the flies away. The Osage walked his horse to the steer, pulled a pistol from his belt and pushed the muzzle into the animal's forehead. "If I cannot keep the bridle, I will kill this cow."

"Harm that animal and I'll kill you," Wes said.

To my surprise, *shock* I should say, the stupid savage pulled the trigger!

The brindle steer bellowed in pain and then it staggered a few steps before its legs buckled and it fell.

Wes raised his Colt and slammed a shot into the Osage's head. The Indian's dead body joined the steer on the bloody ground.

Turning to the hands, Wes grinned. "Well, he killed the beef and I killed him. I guess now we're all even."

This drew a cheer from the punchers as the remaining warriors fled.

The cook, with the single mindedness of the truly dedicated, glanced at the Indian, then at the dead steer. "Looks like we're having beefsteaks for dinner tonight, boys."

The cook had made a good joke, and we all laughed.

A couple days later, we crossed into Kansas and drove the herd toward Cowskin Creek, about twenty miles south of Wichita.

At this juncture I would like to ask all ladies of gentle breeding to forbear reading from here to the end of this chapter of my narrative, for I will talk of whiskey and loose women and wish to spare your maidenly blushes.

I was up on the wagon seat with the cook and his assistant, when a delegation of well-dressed gentlemen met us on the trail and hailed John Wesley in a most friendly manner. After what seemed like a congenial conversation, the men left after a deal of smiles, handshakes, and back slaps.

Wes then explained to the assembled hands that the businessmen had extended everyone an invitation to visit their new town, Park City by name, and be prepared to whoop it up.

Privately Wes told me that he'd mentioned to one of the men, a Mr. Millard, that Park

171

City, soon to rival Wichita as a cattle town, might be the ideal spot to debut his Wild West show. "I told him I'd act out how I killed the Kiowa warrior to save a fair maiden from a fate worse than death and how, though badly wounded, I bested the murderous Osage. And he was very interested." Wes slapped me on the back. "Park City could make us rich, Little Bit."

And so it was that Wes veered the herd a few miles west of the Chisholm and followed a wagon road into the town, a raw, rough settlement that smelled of newly sawn lumber and boasted three saloons, a hotel and bath house, a dancehall, and cattle pens large enough to accommodate up to five thousand cattle.

There was no church and no school, but the place was booming.

The saloon whiskey passed muster and, to punchers fresh off the trail, all the girls were pretty and wild as cougars.

Wes and I raised a few pints to celebrate his eighteenth birthday a couple weeks away and his obvious success as a shootist. Half drunk and loving it, we staggered from saloon to saloon, bottle to bottle, woman to woman.

Despite my unprepossessing looks — for was I not a pale, twisted, little goblin? —

the girls took a liking to me and treated me like a sick puppy, cooing as they stroked me and kissed the top of my head.

As you no doubt have already guessed, I lost my virginity that very day . . . and have never regretted it.

Suffering from massive hangovers we headed back to the Chisholm the next morning. All agreed wholeheartedly with John Wesley when he said, "Boys, I reckon a good time was had by all."

Wes never again mentioned Park City and his Wild West show in the same breath. That was just as well. After the railroad bypassed the town, it died a quick death.

Finally its dust was blown away by the prairie winds and today there is no sign that Park City ever existed.

CHAPTER TWENTY-THREE: DEAD MAN'S TRAIL

After fording the Little Arkansas River, Wes pushed the herd into Newton Prairie where the Chisholm widened from a mile to nearly three. There was plenty of good graze, and room for following herds to pass us if they needed to.

One Mexican trail boss didn't cotton to swinging wide around our herd. He wanted to push us aside and go straight on through.

Well, when that idea didn't set too well with John Wesley, I knew bad things were bound to happen.

The stage was set for a killing.

Things went from bad to worse when the point of the boss vaquero's herd collided with our drag and cowboy cusses were exchanged in English and Mexican.

The cook, his assistant, and I went back to see the fun in time to hear Wes yell to the Mex trail boss, "Go the hell around!"

The air was thick with yellow dust as our

hands started to turn the Mexican herd. Fistfights broke out all over the place, but since the scrapping was done from horseback, no great damage was done to either side.

But the boss vaquero was on the prod and mad enough to bite the head off a hammer. He swung back to the rear of his herd, grabbed a Henry from a wagon, and galloped back to the point again, a chaotic scene of tussling, cussing punchers and vaqueros, bawling steers, and dust so thick I could hardly see a hand in front of my face.

Beside me, the cook shook his head. "Son, this ain't gonna end well, mark my words."

The old-timer was right. The herds were all tangled up and the whole sorry affair was turning into a regular donnybrook. Above the din, I heard Wes yelling orders, but nobody seemed to be paying him any heed.

A paint pony bucked out of the melee, the puncher's chaps flapping as he white-knuckled the horn. He nearly cannoned into the boss vaquero who swung out of the saddle and stepped into the cartwheeling dust, his rifle up and ready.

I didn't see what happened next because of the lack of visibility, but one of the hands later told me how it all shook out.

The Mexican trail boss, his name was Jose, or so I was told, spotted Wes through the murk and took a pot at him. He missed then stepped forward and fired again.

Another miss.

His Henry jammed, probably from grit and dust, and he shifted the rifle to his left hand and drew a Colt with his right. He advanced, shooting every few steps, but did no execution.

For some reason John Wesley was carrying a revolver so old and abused it had shot loose and the cylinder wobbled.

It happened time after time to those old cap and ball Army Colts. I blame roosters who loaded so much powder into the chambers they had to shave the balls to allow the cylinder to turn.

I don't think Wes figured he'd get into a gunfight that day, and he paid for his lack of oversight.

Still mounted, he fired several times at the advancing Mexican, and only God knows where the balls went.

"Git off the damned hoss, Wes, and hold the cylinder!" Jim Clements yelled. He was unarmed and could not join in the shooting scrape.

The hand I spoke to afterward told me, "Well, ol' Wes jumps off'n the pony, holds

176

onto the iron with both hands, an' cuts loose. His ball burns the Mex across the thigh and then his piece locks up solid and he can't shoot no more."

It seems the vaquero then charged Wes and the two fell into the dust and began to grapple, bite, and eye-gouge.

When guns were drawn on both sides and it looked like the shooting was about to become general, Jim Clements stepped into the fray and separated the warring parties, including the principal combatants who were rolling around on the ground.

"Here," Clements yelled, "this won't do! All hostilities must end. We were all drunk and didn't know what we were doing."

It wasn't much by way of a peace talk, but Wes, always canny, agreed to a truce, knowing he couldn't open the ball again with a useless gun. But back at camp, nursing a shiny, black bruise under his right eye and a chawed ear, he was a powder keg, vowing revenge on the Mexican who had so roughly handled him.

The fuse was lit when a hand rode in and said, "Boss, the Mexicans are pushing their herd up again, comin' on fast."

Enraged, Wes threw away the beefsteak that he'd been holding to his black eye and armed himself with his own Colts, stuck into shoulder holsters. He and Jim Clements then rode out of camp, two men well skilled in the use of arms and on fire with a blazing rage and the urge to kill.

Once again my narrative must resort to hearsay, but since Jim Clements himself relayed the details of the gunfight that followed, you can depend on my accuracy.

"When the Mexicans saw us coming, six vaqueros, including the one they called Jose, circled around toward us, their weapons drawn," Clements said. "After a merry quip, Wes put the reins in his teeth, drew both Colts and charged. Never, since the late war ended, had a Southern cavalier advanced on a superior enemy so gallantly.

"Firing at the gallop, Wes shot Jose through the heart and the wretch tumbled off his horse with a terrible cry and died. Then a vaquero, cursing in the vilest fashion, rode directly at John Wesley, his gun blazing. Cool as ever, Wes would not be stampeded. He turned in the saddle and, working his Colts with great rapidity, shot the Mexican cur in the head. The man was dead when he hit the ground, and good riddance."

Clements said that he and Wes then captured four of the Mexicans.

"Two of the vaqueros, both very young, said they'd had nothing to do with the affray, and, out of the goodness of his heart, Wes let them go. But the other two, after agreeing to surrender, were filled with typical Mexican deceit and treachery. They pulled their murderous pistols and fired point-blank at John Wesley."

Clements said that both vaqueros missed, but Wes didn't.

As Wes told it to me later, "The first I shot through the heart and he dropped dead in a moment. The second I shot through the lungs and Jim shot him, too. The man begged me not to shoot him again, and put up my guns. Hell, I knew the greaser was a goner anyway."

The shooting of the traitorous Mexican assassins made John Wesley a hero, and I, as his best friend, bathed in his reflected glory.

Cowboys from other herds dropped into camp just to catch sight of the famous kid shootist. Cowmen — I'm talking of great cattle barons, not one-loop nesters — shook his hand and told him what a fine fellow he was.

Wes took the opportunity to speak to these powerful and wealthy men about his Wild West show and introduced me as his, "part-

179

ner and business manager." My narrow little chest swelled with pride.

A few expressed interest, but again, due to circumstances, in the end it all came to nothing.

CHAPTER TWENTY-FOUR:
ABILENE, QUEEN OF THE WEST

Our herd reached the bedding grounds of the Chisholm in late May 1871 and joined another hundred thousand Texas cows waiting to be sold and shipped. Just thirty miles south of Abilene, the resting cattle spread out along the North Fork of the Cottonwood River.

On June 1, Columbus Carroll sent word that John Wesley and his drovers should join him in town to be paid off. Of course, I went along with them. My jaw dropped when I first beheld Abilene. Its teeming populace and majestic buildings overwhelmed my reeling senses.

Why, the Drovers Cottage hotel where we went to draw our wages had a hundred rooms! And the Alamo Saloon, a shining palace dedicated to gambling and the god Bacchus, had a forty-foot frontage on Cedar Street, two engraved glass doors, and a full orchestra that performed morning, noon, and night!

Abilene was a booming, bustling, bespangled city to rival ancient Athens, Rome, and Babylon and even the modern capitals of London, Paris, and Berlin.

I'd never seen the like before.

As Wes and I rode along Texas Street I turned in the saddle and said, "I never knew there was this many folks in the whole country."

"In the whole world." Wes was trying his best to avoid looking like a rube, but his eyes were big as silver dollars, as were mine, and his head was on a swivel as it turned this way and that.

The street was a sea of people in town for the summer season, speculators, commission men, cowboys, gamblers, outlaws on the scout from mysterious places, and careful-eyed gunmen who looked at nothing but saw everything.

Solid, red-faced businessmen in broadcloth planted themselves in the middle of the street and made deals with cattle buyers wearing uncomfortable celluloid collars and cattlemen in high-heeled boots and wide-brimmed hats. The crowd broke around them like a sea around rocks.

Here and there ladies, many of them pretty, passed by.

Staid matrons, in collar-and-cuffed brown cotton, rubbed shoulders with saloon girls whose scarlet mouths, bold eyes, and candy cane dresses marked their calling.

I even saw a parson who walked among the throng, brandished a Bible like the sword of Gideon and railed against the evils of strong drink, fallen women, gambling, and mortal sin in general. Nobody listened to him of course, but the old boy had sand. His stovepipe hat was punctured with holes where inebriated punchers had taken pots at it.

It was mighty dangerous to wear a top hat in Abilene in those days.

Wes and I looped our horses to the hitching rail then stepped onto the broad veranda in front of the Drovers Cottage. An old-timer sat in a rocker smoking a pipe. He smiled and nodded as we walked to the door. Wes's jingle-bob spurs rang with every step.

"You boys just get in?" the old man said.

"Seems like," Wes said.

"Well, don't fergit Wild Bill's bath at four sharp. It's a sight to see. I tell that to all the young fellers come up the trail."

I would've questioned the old-timer further, but Wes said, "Yeah, we'll be sure to do that, pops," and opened the door.

Away from the burning heat of the day, the hotel lobby was a cool, dark oasis of polished wood, red velvet, and shining brass. Dirty and trail worn, the smell of horses on us, we stood for a moment, a bit awed and uncertain of what to do next.

The desk clerk solved that problem. "What can I do for you gentlemen?" Better dressed than anyone I knew in Texas at that time, he didn't raise an eyebrow at our dusty, sweat-stained trail clothes and three-months-without-a-bath odor.

Too many rich cowmen, who I bet sometimes looked and smelled worse than we did, walked through the door of the Drovers Cottage.

"Mr. Hardin to see Mr. Columbus Carroll," Wes said with stiff formality.

"Ah yes, gentlemen, he's expecting you," the clerk beamed, as though we were the most honorable of honorable guests. "Mr. Carroll is in the salon, first door to your left."

Note that he said *salon,* not *saloon.* The Drovers Cottage was a classy place and catered only to the best.

The *salon* was a large room shaded by leafy potted plants and beautifully appointed with heavy leather chairs, mahogany side tables, and Persian rugs on the floor. A discreet bar with three barkeeps stood against the far wall and a massive stone fireplace promised plentiful heat when the winter blizzards struck. A three-piece orchestra played "Oh Wed Me Not to Grandpa" as we walked inside.

The room was crowded with cigar-smoking men and a few sleek women, but Carroll spotted us through the blue fog as soon as we entered. "John Wesley! Over here!"

Every head turned in Wes's direction and I realized that his fame had already spread far and wide, even to the hallowed halls of Abilene. And he was only eighteen years old.

He wore his Colts and basked in the admiration of the awed crowd as he walked tall and vital to Carroll's table . . . the deadly young shootist come to collect his gun wages.

And I, like a moth following a flame, stepped after him, doing my best to reflect just a gleam of his vibrant light.

Columbus Carroll sat alone at a table that bore a decanter of whiskey and crystal glasses on a silver tray, a cedar humidor of cigars, and a large tin box.

With every eye on John Wesley, the conversation died away to a murmur as Carroll complimented him on bringing the herd in on time with minimal losses. He then announced, louder than was necessary, I thought, that he was paying Wes a hundred dollar bonus for a job well done.

Such largess was greeted with gasps from the assembled patrons and not a few shouts of, "Hear, hear!" and "Stout fellow!"

Wes had the good grace to blush, and this endeared him even more to the crowd, especially the ladies. I felt a thrill that I was friend to such a great and famous man.

CHAPTER TWENTY-FIVE: WILD BILL'S BATH

My wages amounted to twenty-three dollars, but Columbus Carroll deducted a dollar for four cups I'd broken on the drive. Still, twenty-two dollars was more money than I'd ever had in my life.

John Wesley bought a bottle of Old Crow and shared it as we sat in tubs in a Chinese bathhouse on Texas Street. A couple young Oriental girls with soap and washcloths helped us bathe after pointing to a sign on the wall that read LOOKEE NO FEELEE.

Wes thought this a good joke. Helped along by the bourbon, we were in high spirits when the owner, a small, slender man wearing some kind of heathen robes, approached us and gave a low bow.

"Gentlemens, you leave pretty damn soon. Wild Bill come for bath four o'clock, very prompt. He like bathhouse to himself."

It was only a little after noon, so Wes said, "Hell, we got plenty of time."

The Chinaman bowed again. "Maybe so, but Wild Bill always on time and get angry if anyone else in tub." He shook his head. "Bill a bad man when angry. Go bang! Bang!"

"How come he likes to bathe alone?" I asked.

The two girls giggled behind cupped hands and the owner said something sharp in the Chinese tongue that hushed them instantly.

Then to us, he said, "Bill bathe every day. Very strange thing. That why many peoples come to watch."

There may have been some twisted, Oriental logic there, but I failed to grasp it.

"But you told us he likes to bathe alone," I said, accepting the bottle from Wes's soapy hand.

Again the girls giggled and the owner, I later heard that his name was Willie Chang, silenced them with a glance.

"Peoples arrive after Bill in tub. Peoples leave before Bill get out of tub. This always the way."

"So he's shy," Wes said, grinning.

"No shy," Chang said. "Bill never shy."

"Then what is he?" Wes asked.

Chang looked over his shoulder then leaned closer to us and his voice dropped to a conspiratorial whisper. "Wild Bill have *xiao niao.*"

"What the hell does that mean?" I said.

The girls giggled again, but Chang, his wrinkled face solemn, didn't stop them.

"In Chinese, *xiao niao* has very bad meaning. It mean, *little birdie.*"

Wes looked at me, then exploded into raucous laughter. "You mean Wild Bill Hickok has a tiny dick?" he yelled.

Chang was alarmed. He waved his hands at us and made a hushing sound. "No! No say! Wild Bill kill you for sure, by God!"

Wes laughed so hard he slipped backward into the tub and bubbles rose to the surface from his open mouth. He surfaced, choking from soapy water and laughter. It was a good two or three minutes, the girls slapping his naked back, before he could talk again.

Finally he could. "Well, don't that beat all. Wild Bill keeps a little birdie in his pants." Thinking about Wild Bill's shortcomings sent Wes into convulsions again, to the wretched Willie Chang's babbling distress.

He flapped around us like a beheaded chicken and yelled, "You go now. Now nice and clean mens. Two-bits each. Go, go, go!"

Well, I reckon Wes had gotten his money's

worth because he made no objection and was still laughing as we left the bathhouse and crossed the street. He headed directly for a store with a sign in the window that proclaimed

SOLOMON LEVY, MEN'S CLOTHIER
BESPOKE TAILORING A SPECIALTY
All Boots and Shoes Sold At Cost

Wes bought a dark suit off the rack and a new shirt and hat. He tried the celluloid collar that came with the shirt but tossed it aside, telling Levy that it could choke a man.

At first I couldn't understand why he removed his guns and spurs and didn't put his flashy silver hatband on the new John B. Then it dawned on me that he didn't want to look like a lowly, working cowboy but a businessman of some standing.

You've all seen the tintype likeness he had made after we left the tailor's store. I'm sure you'll agree with me that, standing tall, Texan and handsome, he succeeded very well . . . but for those cold, Hardin eyes that not even a new hat and fancy suit could soften.

As for me, I tried a broad-brimmed Stetson myself, but Solomon Levy, a man of some perception, told me I looked like a "damned toadstool." I finally settled on a brown bowler, and Levy, much impressed, said folks would take me for a visiting English duke, or at least a lord.

I didn't believe him.

The hat was dusty, as though it had lain on a shelf for a long time, there being no great demand for bowlers in Abilene until I came along.

In the West at that time, people who took regular baths were as rare as tears at a Boot Hill burying, but a man who partook of the tub every single day, rain or shine, was agreed by all to be one of the frontier's most extraordinary sights.

Wes and I, tanked up on Old Crow and feeling no pain, got in line outside the bathhouse with two dozen other people of both sexes (Bill's long hair and fine mustachios made feminine hearts flutter) and waited with growing impatience for the witching hour of four when the doors opened.

"Wes, when we get inside, if you value our friendship, to say nothing of our lives, don't mention" — I glanced around me then dropped my voice to a whisper — "you-know-what."

"Not a word," Wes grinned.

"Wes, listen to me. Wild Bill is quick to

191

take offense and mighty sudden on the draw and shoot."

"So am I."

"Well, just don't slight his manhood, is all."

"You know all about that, huh, Little Bit?"

I don't think he was going out of his way to be cruel, but surely he knew it hurt me. "Yeah. I know all about that."

"The door is opening," Wes said, smiling in anticipation.

Wild Bill Hickok was already relaxing in the tub when we spectators filed in to share a moment with the great man. Like his friend Custer, he was indeed a beautiful sight. His golden hair spilled over broad shoulders and his eyes were a clear, gun smoke gray.

A result of his nocturnal lifestyle, his skin was pale and pink as a woman's. Bill's cheekbones were high and downy, and he had a habit of looking down at them under his long lashes, as though inspecting a speck of dust. The mannerism made him appear shy.

Beside me a woman sighed and bobbed a little as her knees turned to jelly.

Behind him, on either side of the tub, stood two hard-eyed women of the lowest sort, each cradling a shotgun across their breasts.

When he spoke, Bill's voice was pleasant to hear, somewhere between a tenor and a baritone, well modulated, with just a trace of the nasal Yankee accent I despised so much.

"Good evening to all of you and welcome," Bill said, steam rising from his tub. "Some of you already know the ladies behind me. On my right is High Timber, currently a hostess at the Bull's Head Saloon, and on my right, the one and only Little Nell, proprietor of the Naughty Kitty cathouse."

That last drew a cheer from the men and frowns from the ladies, especially when Nell dropped a little curtsy and batted her eyelashes.

To my wondering gaze, the women were a sight to see. High Timber stood at least six-foot tall and was as skinny as a bed slat. On the other hand, I reckoned Little Nell would probably dress out at around three hundred pounds. Both had eyes that were as warm and friendly as tenpenny nail heads.

Wild Bill shrugged apologetically. "If any ranny draws a gun in my presence this evening, High Timber and Nell will immediately fill him full of buckshot. They've both killed their man in the past, so be warned." He smiled. "Now, enough unpleasantness. After my ablutions are complete, a hat will be passed among you. Please give generously."

High Timber cradled her scattergun under one arm, then leaned over and passed Bill a brown bottle with a white label.

"One more word, ladies and gentlemen," Wild Bill said. "As my bath progresses, you will see me partake of liberal doses from this here bottle. It's . . . what the hell is it?"

Bill turned the label to him. "Ah yes, Dr. Simms Trophy-Winning Tonic for Genteel Folk. It's guaranteed to cure the rheumatisms, ague, toothache, cancer, consumption, running sores, and female miseries. It will also fill you with new pep and energy, improve sight and appetite, and soothe fussy babies."

Bill held the bottle high, revealing a muscular, if soapy arm. "Dr. Simms tonic can be purchased at Will Gardener's general store for the cost of just one dollar a bottle. But if you say, 'William sent me,' you will receive a ten cent discount."

Before he returned the bottle to High Timber, he added, "Buy Dr. Simms Tonic for Genteel Folk today. Accept no substitute."

The two young Chinese girls approached Bill's tub with all the reverence of Vestal Virgins and poured liquids from pink, blue, and white bottles into the water. Immediately the scent of wildflowers filled the room with an underpinning of sandalwood, pine, and exotic Oriental spices.

As Wild Bill sniffed, then nodded approval to his acolytes, Wes whispered in my ear, "I can't see his dick. Can you see it?"

I shook my head, terrified that Bill, who was reputed to have the ears of a bat, might hear.

"Damn it all," Wes whispered. "He's got so much parfume in there, the water turned blue." He was silent for a moment, then added, "He did that on purpose."

I said nothing, enthralled as the rest of the crowd, as the bathing ritual continued.

One of the Chinese girls held up a bar of amber soap. Pears, I noticed, the kind John Wesley's ma used.

"I," Wild Bill said, "use a fresh soap for every bath. What's left, I donate to the poor."

This drew a ripple of applause, but Wes said, "The hell with the soap. I want to see his damned manhood."

The girls used sponges the size of soup dishes to wash Bill all over, and even plunged their hands into the water to get at his private parts . . . much to the wide-eyed interest of Wes.

Bill then began to regale us with tales of his derring-do on the wild frontier.

I vividly recall him telling us how he galloped through the entire Comanche nation, killing two score of savages en route, ere he reached a cavalry fort to warn of an impending Indian attack.

In later years, when I became a writer of dime novels, I used a fictionalized account of this true adventure in my book *Wild Bill Saves the Day or The Warlike Wrath of William.* I should add here that this volume is still available for purchase wherever fine books are sold.

Alas, we must come to an end. After the girls poured a couple buckets of water over Bill's golden head and then produced huge towels of snowy whiteness, his shotgun guards announced that the proceedings were concluded.

After Bill shook himself off and lit a cigar, his announcement that the hat would be passed around precipitated a stampede for the exits, and Wes and I found ourselves back out in the street.

"I would have put a dollar in the hat if I'd seen his pecker," Wes said.

"Disappointing," I said.

"Damn right it was. And I plan to tell him so."

CHAPTER TWENTY-SIX:
JOHN WESLEY BACKS DOWN

Early that evening, Columbus Carroll offered John Wesley a hundred and forty dollars a month to look after his herd until the buyers shipped them out. "But first tell me how are you with Wild Bill. I want no trouble on that score."

"I stand square with Bill," Wes said. "We have no problems."

"Then the job is yours," Carroll said.

Wes readily agreed to stay on since two of his gambler friends, Ben Thompson and Phil Coe, were in town. Both men were good with a gun, but neither had the status, nor the shooting skills, of Wes and Wild Bill.

That brings me to the undercurrent of gossip that had swept Abilene since Wes arrived — if there was a showdown between Hardin and Hickok who would prevail?

To my certain knowledge, bets were already being placed. Even Wes's erstwhile friends, Coe and Thompson, had a wager going.

Ben bet a thousand dollars on Wes and Coe put the same amount on Bill. Both confidently expected to be the winner.

That evening as Wes and I left the Alamo, matters almost came to a head. As was my rapidly growing habit, I was half drunk, Wes less so, when Wild Bill met us on the boardwalk.

He carried two ivory-handled Navy Colts at his waist, butt forward in black leather holsters and was dressed in his gambler's finery, a massive silver ring on the little finger of his left hand. He smelled like . . . well, you know when a man opens the door of a bawdyhouse and gets his first whiff of that wonderful odor of perfume, soap, bonded bourbon, and just a hint of sweat? That's what Bill smelled like.

No wonder I thought him a truly magnificent specimen. I'd always longed to be Wes, now Wild Bill was also a source of my adoration.

Ha! Pale, puny, prattling pygmy that I was, I still dreamed big in those days.

As we approached Wild Bill, Wes smiled and touched his hat.

Maybe there was something in that smile that Bill didn't like. A touch of, "I know-what-you-ain't-got" perhaps.

Bill's shaggy eyebrows drew together and he growled at Wes, "Here, why are you wearing those guns in town? Take them off and give them to me or face arrest and a seventy-five dollar fine."

A huge moon hung over Abilene that night and its light turned Wes and Bill into silvered statues. Neither man moved a muscle, for just the twitch of an eye could open the ball.

"My friend and I are just enjoying a promenade before bed, Marshal," Wes said. "We're taking in the sights, like."

"I don't give a damn what you're taking in, get those guns off." Bill didn't seem to be in much of a mood for compromise. However, he did seem to be in the mood for a killing.

Wes smiled. "I always comply with the law."

Whiskey made me speak out of turn. "Man is the noblest of all animals, but separated from law and justice, he is the worst." I smiled at Bill. "Aristotle said that."

Without looking at me, Wild Bill said, "Did he though? Tell me where he is and I'll put a bullet in him. He's lying." Then to Wes, "Give me those guns, boy. I won't tell you again."

200

You all remember what came next. God knows, it's been repeated a thousand times in print.

Wes drew his guns and offered them to Bill butt-forward, then spun them in his hands so the muzzles were pointed at the marshal's head.

In my novels, I christened this, "the road agent's spin," and the name seems to have stuck.

The story goes that Bill looked at the Colts, hammer-back and ready, and said, "John Wesley, you're the gamest and quickest boy I ever saw. Let us go and have a drink and I'll be your friend."

Except it didn't happen like that.

Wes did the trick with his revolvers all right and then said, "Still want to take my guns, Marshal?"

"I reckon," Bill said. "Try to use them Colts, boy, and I'll gut you like a hog."

Only then did I see moonlight gleam on the blade of the wicked knife in Wild Bill's hand, the point sticking into Wes's belly. Where it came from I'll never know.

Bill was that fast.

Wes was a revolver fighter. Knives were an anathema to him, a barbaric weapon used only by Mexicans and red savages. The pig sticker pricking the skin of his belly gave him pause. He swallowed hard. "I was josh-ing, Marshal."

"I wasn't," Bill said.

Man, he was pushing on that blade pretty good.

Wes had sand, but he wasn't up for a cut-ting. He let go of the Colts and let them hang from his trigger fingers.

Bill turned to me. "You with the plug hat, come take his guns. And do it slow."

I did as I was told, then Bill stepped back and the blade disappeared again. "You can pick up your guns when you leave town."

Wes knew Wild Bill had put the crawl on him, but he put a brave face on things.

"Would you really have used that blade on me?" He smiled, or at least tried to. "Answer me that."

"Would your guts be all over the board-walk if you hadn't surrendered your guns? Answer me that." Bill didn't smile. He grabbed the Colts from my hands and said to Wes, "Next time I see you carrying guns in Abilene, I'll kill you."

"There won't be a next time, Marshal," I said. "This was all just a misunderstand-ing."

"I don't like misunderstandings. Bad things happen when I misunderstand people." Bill turned away and his boots clumped along the boardwalk until he melted into the darkness.

Wes stood where he was for a long time, then he said, "Next time, I'll make sure there's six feet of ground between us."

"Wes, let's go back to the herd and then blow this town."

John Wesley didn't answer right away. Then he said, "What do you think? Can I beat him, Little Bit?"

"I think it would be a draw. And that means two men dead on the ground."

"Unless I shoot him in the back."

"They'd hang you for sure."

Wes nodded. "All right, let's go get a drink, and we'll talk about plans for my Wild West show." He spat. "Hickok isn't going to be in it."

Chapter Twenty-Seven: Death of a Carpetbagger

Looking back, I consider that Saturday evening when John Wesley and Wild Bill almost got into a shooting scrape as the night that never ended. We drank some more . . . well, a lot more . . . at the Alamo bar and then repaired to the dining room to get a bite to eat.

Wes was quiet, almost sullen. Every time I mentioned his show, he cut me off with a curt, "Not now. We'll talk about it later."

He brightened up a little when Eddie Pain, the one-armed Mississippi gambler, joined us at our table and ordered the waiter to burn him a steak.

As Wes and Pain ate, they discussed the gambling scene on the riverboats and in Denver, and how pretty the ladies were in New Orleans. Wes talked about his Wild West show. Pain declared it a capital idea then sang a few verses of "Goodbye, Eliza Jane," a popular song that was sweeping the nation, and told Wes that he should put it in his show.

Pain showed Wes a beautiful Alsop .36 caliber revolver that he kept in a shoulder holster, away from the prying eyes of Wild Bill.

"A fine weapon indeed," Wes said, turning the Alsop over in his hands.

Thus the final hours before the clocks tolled midnight might have passed pleasantly enough due to Pain's convivial company, had not the Yankees spoiled it as they do everything.

Two big-bellied bullies, with the look of carpetbaggers about them, barged into the room and loudly demanded the best table, the prettiest waitress, and the oldest bourbon in the house. Both wore broadcloth, and the watch chains across their bellies, cunningly wrought from gold coins, must have weighed two pounds apiece.

Florid, forceful and, in the event, foolish, the older and bigger of the two pounded his fist on the table and yelled, "If there are any damned Texans in here, I advise them to leave now." He drew a Colt and placed it on the table in front of him. "I'll shoot any Texas scum who doesn't leave because I can't abide their rebel stink. The Texan hasn't been born yet that can corral me."

The two carpetbaggers thought this a good joke and laughed so uproariously they didn't notice Wes slowly rise from his chair.

But the other diners did.

A dead silence fell over the room as Wes said, "Eddie, let me have your pistol."

The gambler slipped the Alsop into Wes's hands.

Talking softly across a quiet drawn as tight as a bowstring, John Wesley said, "I'm a Texan."

Standing there in his new suit, I thought Wes a brave sight. He was not as flamboyantly picaresque as Wild Bill, but he still cut a dashing figure.

How could I have been so stupid as to think there would be no gunplay? Why did I believe that both parties would call it all a misunderstanding and settle their differences over a drink?

I should have known better.

The big man, used to lesser mortals stepping out of his way, picked up his Colt. "Why, you insolent young pup. I'll teach you some civilized manners."

The fool, for that's what he was, adopted the traditional duelist's stance. The right side of his body turned to Wes, the arch of his left foot behind his right heel, revolver straight out in front of him at eye level.

He and Wes fired.

And missed.

The carpetbagger's ball hit Pain's good arm, shattering bone.

The big man, sobering quickly, decided he wanted out before Wild Bill heard the shots and got there. He ran for the door to the street and Wes fired again.

The .36 ball hit the fool just as he cleared the doorway. Struck behind the left ear, the ball exited the carpetbagger's mouth and scattered teeth, bone, and brain matter all over the street.

Wes spared a quick glance at Pain, who groaned pitifully in his chair, and ran for the door.

I went after him and saw him jump over the dead Yankee then crash into a man toting a deputy's star. He pushed the deputy away and then slugged him over the head with his revolver.

Before the lawman dropped, Wes vaulted onto the unconscious man's horse and headed at a gallop for the bedding grounds on the Cottonwood.

Abandoned, all I could do was step back inside and check on Eddie Pain.

"Murder! Murder!" The Yankee's companion ran through the dining room, hands fluttering in the air, his eyes wild.

"Get the marshal!" somebody yelled.

"Get me a damned doctor." Pain groaned. "Damn, getting shot in my only good arm is hard to take."

The carpetbagger, his large nose covered in warts, stopped and pointed an accusing finger at Pain. "He and the assassin were in cahoots," he yelled. His stabbing finger jabbed for my heart. "And so was he!"

"You go to hell," I said.

"Damn you. Now I'll do for you!" The Yankee reached into his coat, but ere he could draw, Wild Bill strode into the room and quickly disarmed him.

"Do we have a dead 'un?" Bill looked around.

The warty man cursed and attempted to wrench his revolver from Wild Bill's hand.

In one swift, elegant movement, Bill skinned one of his Navy Colts and slammed the barrel over the carpetbagger's head.

The man groaned horribly, dropped to his knees then stretched his length on the floor.

Bill was as drunk as a hoedown fiddler and all the more dangerous for that.

"Over there, Marshal," a respectable-looking citizen said. "By the side door."

Bill crossed the floor in a couple long strides and got down on one knee beside the dead man.

After a while he rose to his feet, staggered a little, then told everyone what we already knew. "He's as dead as mutton." Wild Bill burped then politely excused himself. "The ball entered the back of his head and came out his mouth. Took most of his teeth with it." His eyebrows knitted together and asked if anyone knew the dead man.

"He came into the dining room with the gentleman who's currently unconscious on the floor," the respectable gent said.

"Who done for him?" Bill asked.

"It was that young Hardin boy," a pretty woman said. She wore green eye shadow and had pink rouge on her cheeks.

"Damn," Bill said. "That boy is causing me no end of trouble. And he buffaloed Mike Williams, my deputy."

"Bill," Pain said, "I'm bleeding to death here."

"I see you, Eddie. You'll keep. You've been shot before."

Pain grimaced. "The dead man, whoever he is, shot first. Wes was defending himself."

"Defending himself? Even when the victim was making a run for it?"

"He could have come back, Marshal," I said.

"Maybe so." Bill looked at me for a moment, then said, "You know where Hardin is?"

I shook my head.

"No matter. By now, he's probably with Columbus Carroll's herd down on the Cottonwood and it's out of my jurisdiction."

Bill's deputy staggered into the room. He held his hat in one hand and rubbed a bump on his head with the other.

"How are you, Mike?" Bill asked.

"I got a headache."

Bill kicked the unconscious man who was drooling from the mouth and didn't look good at all. "Take this down to the jail and lock him up, Mike."

"What's the charge?" the deputy asked.

"Carrying a firearm contrary to the town ordinance. If he pays his seventy-five dollar fine, I'll let him go later."

"Bill, for God's sake, he put a bullet in me," Pain said.

Wild Bill nodded. "I know, Eddie, but you can't charge a man for shooting somebody by mistake. I've studied on the law books and there's nothing that says it's a crime."

Since Bill later killed Mike Williams, his deputy, by mistake, maybe it's just as well that the law took a lenient attitude toward the odd, accidental shooting in those days.

As Williams hauled the eye-rolling, weak-kneed Yankee to his feet, Bill said, "Somebody go get the undertaker."

"Bill," Pain cried, "for God's sake!"

"Oh yeah, and bring Doc Henderson. We have a wounded man here." Bill laid a hand on Pain's shoulder. "Eddie, a man with only one wing should stay away from the likes of John Wesley Hardin. You lose t'other one, hoss, you might as well blow your brains out." He smiled. "Though how you'd hold the gun, I do not know."

Through clenched teeth as his wound throbbed, Pain said, "Bill, you're all heart."

Wild Bill smiled. "That's what folks say about me." He turned his attention to me, his gray eyes searching into mine. "Come here, little mouse," he said, curling his finger.

When I stood in front of him, my eyes were level with the middle button of his frockcoat.

The crowd in the dining room grew noisy again as they talked about the killing, but Wild Bill leaned over and whispered into my ear. "Tell your friend to stay out of Abilene. I'm writing off this killing as self-defense, but if John Wesley kills another man in my town, I'll gun him." He straightened. "Tell him that."

"I sure will. I reckon once the buyers pick up the herd, we'll head for Texas."

Bill nodded. "Live longer that way."

Chapter Twenty-Eight: The Vengeance Posse

John Wesley had booked us accommodations at the Alamo, but since he'd skedaddled, I couldn't afford two rooms, or even one, so I bedded down in the livery stable.

That night, aided by a lantern and moonlight, I remade the acquaintances of Quentin Durward in the novel the Reverend Hardin had given me and a pint of cheap bourbon. By the time I rolled into my blankets, I'd started one and finished the other.

Come the cold dawn, I woke with a splitting headache. It was a miserable chore to saddle my horse and ride out under a sky ominous with thunderheads.

I didn't linger in Abilene, but rode directly to the Cottonwood, arriving in a pouring rain and soaked to the skin. Wes immediately pumped me for information.

I told him what had transpired after he

ran out of the Alamo dining room. "Wild Bill gave me a message for you, Wes. He told me to tell you to stay out of Abilene."

Wes smiled. "Well, that ain't going to happen, is it? I'll buckle on my guns and head for the Alamo any time I want. I don't back off from any man, except my pa."

"Bill's taken a set against you, Wes. He's made that clear."

"Like I give a damn."

Wrapped up in my own cold, wet misery I said nothing.

We sheltered under a canvas tarp rigged from the chuck wagon and a small, smoky fire burned between us and gave no warmth.

I sat hunched over, a damp blanket across my shoulders. My leg was playing hob and the ulcerous sore had opened again. In pain, dog-tired from the ride from Abilene, I was in need of hot coffee and dry clothes.

I had neither.

Wes, wrapped up in his ownself as usual, didn't notice or care.

He finally drifted away to join the other punchers who kept boredom at bay by drinking, gambling, and arguing about everything and anything. He and four other cowboys gathered under a larger tarp, held in place by tree limbs. Their fire was bigger and a blackened coffeepot smoked on the coals.

Between me and the others lay fifty yards of open, muddy ground — a vast distance for a sick, weak, and shivering gimp like myself.

Driven by a north wind as cold as a stepmother's breath, rain peppered the mud and birds rose out of the trees against a sky that looked like broken coal. I watched a coyote approach the horse line, think better of it and slink away, raindrops silvering his shaggy coat.

I fancied I could smell the coffee, distant though it was, and determined to make the effort. Rising to my feet, I stood for a few moments to let my reeling head settle, then stepped from under the tarp.

Unfortunately, as I bent my head, the brim of my bowler hat hit the edge of the canvas and about a gallon of water poured down my neck, so icy I thought my heart would stop. Thus it was that by the time I reached Wes's tarp, I was wetter and even more miserable than before.

No one greeted me — the assistant to the assistant cook didn't stand very high in the cowboy hierarchy, well below the drag rider in fact — but I heard no objections as I poured myself a cup of coffee and found an out of the way corner to seat myself.

Then John Wesley, that unpredictable chameleon, stepped to my side with a bottle in his hand. He smiled, poured a stiff shot of Old Crow into my cup, and said, "This will warm you up, Little Bit."

What to make of such a man?

One minute disinterested and uncaring, the next kind and concerned. Was John Wesley a knight in shining armor or an unmitigated knave?

I never did find the answer to that question. With Wes gone and me in my old age, I guess I never will.

Later that day, a rider on a blown horse galloped into camp with news of a killing. His slicker dripping water, he swung out of the saddle and stepped directly to Wes. "Billy Cohron is dead. Shot in the back."

Wes knew and liked Cohron and the news staggered him. "Who did it?"

That was typical of Wes. His first thought was of revenge.

"Greaser by the name of Bideno," the cowboy said. "Him and Billy quarreled about something and then a couple minutes later Bideno snuck up behind him and triggered a shot into him." The drover's voice broke as he added, "Billy lingered long and he suffered something terrible the whole time."

Billy Cohron was a likeable fellow and a steady hand who'd come up the trail as boss herder for Colonel O. W. Wheeler. As I recall, he'd been married just a six-month before his death.

The Wheeler herd was bedded down close to our own.

"Where is Bideno?" Wes asked.

"He rode south on a stolen hoss," the cowboy said. "I guess he's headed for the Nations."

"When did this happen?" Wes let his breath out in a rush, then his mouth tightened into a hard line.

"Day afore yesstidy," the drover said.

"Hell, and you're only telling me now?"

The drover, his name was McKenzie, thought about that a moment then said, "Wes, like I told you, poor Billy lingered. Nobody knew right then if he'd live or die, so we loaded him into a wagon and took him to Abilene. That's where he breathed his last, and then everything was confused."

"Nothing confusing about who shot him though, is there?" Wes asked.

"No, I guess not." McKenzie reached inside his slicker and brought out a folded paper. "Brung you a letter from Colonel

Wheeler. It says it all, or so he told me."

Wes read the letter silently, then read it aloud for the benefit of the hands who crowded around him.

"To John Wesley Hardin, Esq.

"By now you have heard the news of William Cohron's death at the hands of a foul and treacherous murderer, whose name is not fit to mention here. Given your skill at arms, it is my request, seconded by fellow cattlemen, that you pursue this vile killer and bring him to justice.

"I have sent out riders on swift horses to square you with the herds now coming up the trail, in the matters of fresh horses and provisions. If you are willing to undertake this task, which will be to your credit if you do, please inform this courier.

"May God ride with you and may you seek out and destroy the fiend who robbed us of a fine man, loving husband, and Southern patriot.

"Yours Respectfully.

"Colonel Oliver Walcott Wheeler.

"There it is, boys. This letter touches my heart and stirs my blood," Wes turned to the courier. "Please inform the colonel that I accept this commission and, as God is my witness, I'll bring this vile assassin to justice."

It was a pretty speech, and, pursuant to what we were talking about earlier, perhaps indicated how John Wesley saw himself . . . as an avenging knight of the plains.

Not a black knight, mind, but a Sir Galahad in shining armor, pure of body and spirit, and always ready to take up a noble cause . . . so long as there was killing involved.

For breakfast the next morning I drank coffee laced with whiskey. It was not in me to stand aside and not play Sancho Panza to my delusional Don Quixote. Sick, tired, and used up as I was, I saddled my pony under a vast, scarlet and jade sky alongside Wes and a surly puncher named Jim Rogers then joined the others as they rode out of camp.

"We must catch that murderer before he reaches the Nations," Wes told us. He looked at me. "Little Bit, we got some long-riding across hard country ahead of us. Can you stand the pace?"

Made brave by the whiskey, I said, "Wes, my horse's nose will be up your sorrel's behind the whole way."

Brave talk from a cripple, and a sickly or at that, but we were all young in those da and more than slightly crazy.

The rain had passed and by the time

reached the village of Newton the hot sun had dried my clothes and I felt better.

Johnny Cohron, Billy's brother, was waiting for us outside the Wells Fargo office with another cowboy named Hugh Anderson. The two men joined our avenging posse and we reached Wichita, seventy-five miles south of Abilene, that evening.

I got drunk that night and felt like death when we headed south again at first light.

Colonel Wheeler had arranged horse changes with the herds coming up the Chisholm and we switched mounts every few miles.

Riding those half-broke mustangs was an ordeal for me, but I gritted my teeth and kept at it. I would have no man accuse me of being a quitter.

Wes was jumpy as a frog in a frying pan, worried that we'd lose Bideno. He was still somewhere ahead of us.

But when we rode into the cow town of Sumner City, our luck changed.

Wes asked a passerby if a vaquero wearing a big sombrero, riding a good horse, had blown into town recently.

The man said, "He sure did. Right now he's over to the Silver Spur saloon." Because westerners are a naturally curious breed, he asked, "He a friend of your'n?"

"No," Wes said. "No, he sure ain't."

Our little posse rode up to the Silver Spur and dismounted. Wes sent Cohron and Rogers around the back of the saloon to cut off that avenue of escape. Wes and Anderson stepped into the saloon.

Me, I was left to my own devices since I didn't carry a gun. I followed Wes.

The saloon wasn't busy at that time of day and when Wes and Anderson entered with guns drawn, the bartender quickly realized that something was afoot. He stared at John Wesley, a question on his face.

Wes said quietly, "Mexican. Big hat."

The bartender nodded and used the glass he was polishing to point to the door that led into the restaurant.

Wes stepped through the door and recognized his man.

Now, in Wes's memoirs, he claims he said to Bideno, "I am after you to surrender. I do not wish to hurt you, and you will not be hurt while you are in my hands."

Well, I was there and what he really said was, "Get up, Bideno. Take it in the belly like a man."

The Mexican had a cup off coffee halfway to his lips, but he dropped the cup, cursed, and clawed for his holstered Colt.

Wes fired. Shot Bideno smack in the

middle of the forehead.

I heard a *Ping!* as Wes's ball hit a potbellied stove against the far wall after crashing clean through the Mexican's head.

Johnny Cohron took Bideno's bloody sombrero for a souvenir.

And that's all there was to it. Just another routine kill for John Wesley.

Bang! You're dead.

CHAPTER TWENTY-NINE: WES STRIKES IT RICH

Shortly after we rode back to the Cotton-wood, a deputation from Abilene arrived in camp with a purse made up by some wealthy cattlemen. It contained a thousand dollars and a flowery letter that thanked Wes for killing Bideno.

Now, let me tell you something about that. It was the worst thing that could have happened to John Wesley.

Years later, in the harsh Wyoming winter of 1903, I interviewed Tom Horn for a dime novel before he was wrongly hung for murdering a boy by the name of Willie Nickell. I recall Tom saying to me, "The worst lesson I ever learned in life was that wealthy citizens would pay me for killing people they considered undesirables. It was a hard lesson and it led to my downfall and death."

Well, Wes had learned that same lesson . . . and it would kill him just as surely as it killed poor Tom.

By my count, John Wesley had killed around thirty-one men and he could justify every single one of them. To his mind, all of them were men who needed killing.

I never heard Wes say that his conscience troubled him or that dead men haunted his dreams at night. He believed that thirty human beings lay in dank graves because they were bad, wicked, criminal, or just plain wrong.

It was entirely their fault, not John Wesley Hardin's.

In his own eyes, Wes was not a killer but a lawful executioner dispensing his own brand of justice to evildoers of every stripe.

I pen this now as an old man, but at the time I didn't think on all this so deeply. All I knew was that Wes would lead and I would follow.

That was the nature of things in those days.

"Little Bit," Wes said to me a couple days after our return. "Do you not agree that I'm a man of substance, respected by rich and poor alike?"

"I'd say that."

Since he'd not given any of the posse members, myself included, a red cent out of

224

his reward, he still had a thousand dollars in his pocket, plus most of his trail wages. To me, that was wealth beyond imagining.

"Then there's no reason why I shouldn't visit Abilene is there?" Wes asked.

I smiled. "Just one."

"You mean Wild Bill?"

"As ever was."

"I have nothing to fear from him. Since I killed Bideno, I'm bull of the woods in Abilene."

"Reason enough for Wild Bill to gun you, Wes."

"I'm a respectable businessman in the cattle industry and I'll soon own a Wild West show. Hickok is drunken trash. He wouldn't dare draw down on me." Wes used a stick from the fire to light his cigar. "If I kill him, who would blame me? Any future trouble between us will be his doing, not mine."

I drank from the pint of whiskey I'd bought in Sumner City and set aside for when my leg got to aching real bad and listened to the night. We were so close to the river I heard fish jump. A cool breeze carried the odor of longhorns and trampled mud, the only reminder of the great cattle herd that had been there for a little while.

"Tomorrow," Wes said, his cigar glowing red in the dark, "we'll ride into town, get noisy, get a woman, get drunk, and be somebody."

I laughed out loud. "Sounds good to me, Wes, so long as Bill doesn't spoil the party."

"He won't. He knows better than that."

I leaned my head to the side. "Think you can take him?"

Wes nodded once. "Damn right I can. Any day of the week."

My leg brace lay beside me and I picked it up. I slept with it on in those days. With Wes around, there was no telling when we might have to light a shuck in a hurry.

"How is the sore?" Wes asked.

"It's all right."

"You're lying to me, Little Bit. You look like you got one foot in the pine box."

"What foot? The good one or the bad one?" I smiled, feeling the drink.

"Hell, maybe both." Wes lit the lantern close by and held it high. "Let me take a look at that damned thing."

Orange light splashed over me like wet paint as I dropped my pants and revealed the open, weeping wound at the top of my thigh. It was as big as a man's palm.

Wes stared at the sore for a long while, then said, "That settles it. We're riding into Abilene tomorrow and you're seeing a doctor."

John Wesley was rich and famous, and oh how I basked in his attention.

He shook his head. "Little Bit, I've asked you this before. Even with the steel brace, how do you stand on that leg? It's as skinny as a carpetbagging Negro's walking cane."

"It isn't easy. Pains me some." I reached for the brace, but Wes pushed it out of reach.

"Leave that off until you see the doc." He saw the doubt on my face and added, "I'll help you into the saddle." He laid the lantern aside and poured coffee. "Want some?"

I shook my head. "Still got whiskey in the bottle."

"Well drink it down. We'll pull out of here at first light." He studied me for a spell, then said, "Damn it, Little Bit, how do you live?"

"Well enough, I guess."

"No, I mean how do you *survive*? You look like, I don't know, one of them little white-faced goblins in the fairy stories my ma used to read to me when I was a younker."

"Goblins survive, Wes, and so do trolls and imps and dwarves and gnomes," I said. "Somehow or other, they manage to live. For me, all survival takes is will and the ability to delude myself."

Wes grinned. "You want to be six foot tall,

don't you?"

"No, just as tall as you."

"It ain't going to happen."

"I know that."

"When I have my Wild West show I'll put you in a tent and show you off as a freak. I could charge folks two-bits to see you and shake your hand."

"Like Wild Bill taking his bath," I said.

"No, not like Wild Bill. He's six feet if he's an inch. You're just a nubbin'."

I corked the whiskey bottle. "Whatever you think is best, Wes."

"Ah hell, I was only joshing. I won't put you in a tent."

"Then where will you put me?"

"Why, behind a desk where you belong. Even a crippled goblin can count our profits, huh?"

"That sounds better," I said.

"Damn right it does," Wes said.

Before I drifted into an alcohol-troubled sleep, I remember thinking that come tomorrow, maybe the doctor could fix my leg . . . but some of the wounds Wes so casually and thoughtlessly inflicted on me would never heal.

Chapter Thirty:
Doctor's Orders

We rode into Abilene through a blue dawn and the town was sound asleep. All the dust and drama of the night before had been laid to rest with the rising of the sun. Like Mr. Stoker's vampires, Wild Bill and the rest of the sporting crowd were abed behind shades and would not rise again until the sun began its scarlet descent to the horizon.

When we reached the doctor's house, Wes lifted me from the saddle and carried me inside without effort, as though his arms cradled a child.

Doctor John Henderson, a young man with black hair and earnest brown eyes, directed Wes to sit me on the edge of the examination table.

Wes handed the physician my leg brace. "This is his. It gave him a sore" — he pointed to the top of his thigh — "right there."

Doc Henderson's nurse was middle-aged

and not pretty. She had one of those tight, prim mouths you see on women who exist on a diet of prune juice and scripture. Her eyes were small, blue, and intolerant. She snatched the brace out of Wes's hand. "Please be seated in the waiting room."

Then it was lecture time. "The carrying of firearms is not permitted in Abilene."

"So I've been told," Wes said. "Doc, holler when you need me."

After Wes stepped out of the room, the doctor examined me. "How long have you had this?"

I nodded at the brace. "Off and on, as long as I've been wearing that."

"For the time being, we'll keep the wound wet and make sure it doesn't get infected," Henderson said. "Don't wear the brace until I get this healed." He smiled at me. "Can you do that? Will your friends find you a place to stay and help you get around?"

"Oh sure, Doc." Of course, that was a boldfaced lie.

Without the brace, I'd have to lie in bed. Where? And who would look after me? Wes might push me around in a wheelchair for a while, but then he'd get bored, ride out of town, and leave me to my own devices.

Abilene was not a place for an impoverished, helpless cripple. Without the brace, all I'd be able to do was die of neglect and starvation.

"Just do what you can, Doc," I said.

Doctor Henderson put various salves on the wound, one of them that smelled suspiciously of honey, and then he bandaged the wound.

Wes was called back to the surgery and the doc said, "Your friend will need plenty of bed rest and help getting around."

"What about his brace?" Wes asked.

"He can't wear it until his wound heals," Henderson said.

"Can he ride?"

"No. I'm afraid not."

"Just as far as Texas," Wes said.

The doctor smiled. "Not as far as the edge of town."

To say that Wes looked unhappy is an understatement. It was obvious that taking care of an invalid didn't enter into his thinking.

"He's not even kin," he said.

That comment raked across my heart like a knife blade. It hurt a sight worse than my leg.

"I'm sure you will help," the doctor said.

"It's Christian charity after all," the nurse said.

"Then you take care of him, lady," Wes said.

"Wes, I'll be no trouble," I said. "I promise." God help me, I even winked at him, trying to allay his fears.

It didn't work.

"How long will it take his leg to heal, Doc?" Wes asked.

Henderson shrugged. "It's too early to tell. Weeks, maybe a couple months."

Wes looked at me with an odd mix of pity and irritation.

"The patient is not strong. He's suffering from malnutrition and, I suspect, alcohol abuse. The prognosis is far from good."

"But with God's grace and abstinence, he can recover," the nurse said.

"Yes. Yes indeed," the doc said. "But he'll need first rate care."

That was not what John Wesley wanted to hear. "Hell, we could be snowed in here come winter."

Henderson smiled. "Come fall, you mean." He glanced at the door. "Well, I have other patients waiting." To me he said, "Keep the dressing clean and come back and see me at the end of the week. Nurse Meadows will let you out."

"Your bill for today will be two dollars." The woman gave me a hard look that said

And don't even think of telling me you can't pay it.

Desperate, Wes clutched at a straw. "Doc, can he stay here with you? That way you can treat him real good. He's quiet and doesn't eat much." Then, as an afterthought, "And he has some money."

Henderson shook his head. "I'm afraid that's impossible. I don't run a hospital here." He smiled. "Now, if you'll excuse me?"

It was obvious from Wes's hangdog expression that he knew he'd run out of space on the dance floor. He picked me up and stepped to the door.

Nurse Meadows let us out and handed Wes my brace. "Two dollars, please," she said when the door of the surgery closed behind us.

"Pay the lady, Little Bit."

Outside, Wes lifted me into the saddle, then led my horse and his in the direction of the Alamo. The day had brightened and a few women in morning dresses were out and about, shopping baskets over their arms, faces set and determined as they hunted only the best bargains.

A brewer's dray trundled past, the barrels creaking against their retaining ropes. The

233

team of four magnificent Percherons in the traces had hooves as big as soup plates, and I fancied one of those would be the ideal knightly mount for Quentin Durward.

Wes had been fuming silently since we left the doctor's office, but as we passed an alley on our left, I intruded into his quiet. "Wes, lead my horse into the alley there."

"Hell, piss at the Alamo," Wes said.

"I want to put my brace back on."

"The doc told you not to do that."

"Yeah, well I'm doing it. The doctor told me not to drink, and I'm doing that, too."

"Your funeral," Wes said, frowning.

Secretly, I think he was relieved.

Once in the alley I sat down, dropped my pants, and buckled on the steel cage. The doc had wrapped a fat bandage around the top of my thigh and when I stood I discovered that it padded the wound pretty good.

"How does it feel?" Wes asked.

"All right."

He stared at me and wrinkled his nose. "You sat in dog crap."

CHAPTER THIRTY-ONE:
THE SNORING MAN

John Wesley decided against the Alamo where we'd be likely to run into Wild Bill and instead we headed for the American Hotel, less grand but safer.

Not that Wes was afraid of Bill, but he knew he'd get used up in a gunfight, even if he proved the victor. Wild Bill was no bargain. He had sand. He'd take his hits and put lead into a man as long as he'd strength to pull the trigger.

As Wes told me, "Let sleeping dogs lie."

Gip Clements was in town and he joined us at the bar of the hotel saloon where we proceeded to get pretty drunk.

Wes had taken the wise precaution of keeping our horses close and under saddle. I believe his carefulness saved his life later that night.

A friend of Gip's, a man named Charlie Cougar, joined us at the bar. I didn't know the fellow, but he seemed a good sort and stood his round. So I have nothing bad to say about him . . .

Except that he snored with a racket like a freight train in a tunnel.

Now, people often ask me, "Is it true that John Wesley Hardin killed a man for snoring?"

And my answer is, "Well, he did, but it was an accident."

As Wes said later, "Hell, it was all Cougar's fault. How was I to know he'd sit up in bed the very moment I fired a warning shot across his bow?"

Some of you may have a different opinion on that killing, but in my heart of hearts, I can't blame Wes. By one in the morning all four of us were roaring drunk, talking nonsense and seeing double.

Wes said, "I don't want to meet Wild Bill in this state so we should go to bed and sleep off the whiskey."

Gip and Charlie agreed that it sounded like an excellent plan and so did I, though nobody much cared about my opinion.

Wes booked a room for all of us, but Charlie insisted on sleeping alone, so he got the one adjoining.

Staggering, Wes and Gip threw off their clothes and, wearing only their long johns, threw themselves on the bed and were asleep within seconds.

Me, I found myself a corner and tried to make myself as comfortable as I could. My hurting leg was numbed by whiskey, but the rough pine floor was hard and I couldn't drop off.

Ten, fifteen minutes passed . . . and then the snoring erupted.

Remember, the partition walls in frontier hotels were paper-thin and the noise of Cougar's snoring was horrific, a racketing ripsaw roar that reverberated around the room and rattled the portrait of Robert E. Lee on the wall.

Gip shot up in bed like a man waking from a nightmare. "What the hell is that?"

"Charlie Cougar is snoring," I said. "Seems like."

"Hey, Charlie!" Gip yelled. "Turn over for God's sake. You're waking up the whole damned town."

Cougar's bed creaked, the snoring stopped and Gip's head, that seemed to be as heavy as an anvil, hit the pillow again.

A slow count to ten . . . and the stentorian serenade of the ear-shattering slumberer started again.

Wes sat up and groped for the Colt on his bedside table. "I'll scare them snores the hell out of him." He thumbed three fast shots through the partition wall . . . and the snoring abruptly stopped, followed by the sound of a body hitting the wood floor.

For a few moments, Wes listened into the cold, echoing silence, then he whispered, "Hell, Gip, I think I shot too low."

Gip nodded. "I think you did. I reckon you done for ol' Charlie an' no mistake."

This verdict was confirmed when voices were raised in the hallway and on the stairwell.

"Get the marshal!" a man yelled.

I heard the door to Cougar's room open and then a woman shrieked, "Murder! Murder!"

Gip Clements jumped out of bed, put on his hat, and pulled on his boots. "Wes, I'm heading back to Texas. Wild Bill will gun us fer sure."

"I'm with you," Wes said.

I crossed to the window and looked out, just as a hack pulled up and disgorged four deputies. "The law!" I yelled.

Gip ran to the window, saw that the lawmen were already inside the hotel, and jumped.

Like Gip, wearing only his underwear, boots, gun belt, and hat, Wes was ready to follow when I yelled, "What about me?"

Without a word, he picked me up and

threw me through the open window. I fell two floors and hit the sandy ground with a thump.

A moment later, Wes landed feet first beside me. "Let's go!" he hollered.

I thanked my lucky stars that I fell on my butt. If I'd landed on the steel brace it would have split me open like a ripe watermelon.

Wes hauled me to my feet and we made a dash for the horses, still saddled in the hotel corral. Well, I didn't dash, but Gip and Wes did.

The moon was up and Texas Street was bathed in a soft, mother-of-pearl light that was soon streaked by gunfire. Balls thudded around me as Wes and Gip rode out of the corral, Gip leading my horse.

Fear helped me climb into the saddle and we rode out of Abilene at a gallop, followed by searching gunfire and a cloud of yellow dust.

Wes pulled his horse beside mine, laughing, and yelled, "Damn, Little Bit, I never shot a man for snoring before." He shook his head. "I guess there's a first time for everything."

That reminds me to hammer home the point I made before. I'm sick and tired of some rooster coming up to me and asking,

"Is it true that Hardin shot three men for snoring?"

Sometimes it's three men, sometimes four, and even five.

Let me put the record straight yet again. Wes shot only one man for snoring and it was an accidental killing. Nobody can pin a murder charge on him. Hell, if you want to blame somebody, blame Charlie Cougar for sitting up in bed at the wrong time.

CHAPTER THIRTY-TWO: THE DARK STAR

We rode into Texas in August.

To my surprise, Wes talked about hanging up his guns and going straight. "It's time to get the Wild West show organized, Little Bit. I reckon we could be up and running in a year, maybe less."

"Gip, you reckon the Clements boys will help us?" I asked.

"Sure they will. And Wes has kinfolk all over Texas who'll pitch in money. You can lay to that."

I was pleased that John Wesley was finally considering a settled, peaceful way of life. "We have cowboys aplenty, Wes. Now all we need is some tame Indians."

"A lot of them around," he said.

"Where?"

"Oh, up Montana way and places. Blanket Indians they call them, since they got whipped by the army and depend on government beef. They're a raggedy-assed bunch, but with some paint and feathers, they'll work just fine."

I smiled. "Wes, you know, I think we can do it."

"Damn right we can. And we can round up buffalo by the hundreds. The Plains are covered with them." He drew rein then stood in the stirrups, a young man, eyes alight dreaming his dream. "Think of it, boys" — he made a sweeping, circular motion with his hand, building a stadium in the air — "an Injun buffalo hunt right there in the arena . . . the buffalo stampeding around and around, the savages whooping and hollering and shooting arrows, the dust, the noise . . . the crowd cheering."

"Hell, Wes, folks will pay big money to see that," Gip said, catching Wes's enthusiasm.

"Damn right they will."

"But don't you go shooting them Redskins," Gip said. "You'll need them alive."

"Nah, I'm done with all that. From now on, John Wesley Hardin is a respectable businessman, an entre . . . ontre . . ."

"Entrepreneur," I supplied.

"Yeah, that's what I am," Wes said.

You'd be right in saying that Wes was really happy . . . and so was I.

As usual, I should have known better.

John Wesley was born under a dark star.

Its light was black . . . black as midnight. Sometimes a man can't get out from under that somber glow, no matter how hard he tries.

I didn't know it then, but I know it now. Wes was doomed from the moment he was born . . . and, God help me, I hastened his inevitable end.

A month later, we rode up on the Clements homestead in Gonzales County. It was more fortress than home, a frame cabin with a shingle roof, the windows backed by heavy oak shutters. The walls were covered with gun ports and pockmarked by bullets.

At that time the saying was, "If you're a fugitive from Yankee justice and on the scout, there's a welcome waiting for you at the Clements' house." Wes and I relaxed for a time, enjoying the peace and quiet. Indeed, his guns hung on a nail in the wall the whole time we were there.

He had once been sweet on a girl whose pa owned a general store in Nopal, a small town up in DeWitt County close to the Gonzales County line. Along about October, he decided to ride up there and get reacquainted.

Of course, I decided to go with him.

"To keep me out of trouble, Little Bit?"

243

he asked.

"To keep that Bowen girl out of trouble."

Wes laughed.

Neill Bowen welcomed us to his store with a smile, and then told us to help ourselves to cheese and crackers while he dealt with another customer.

Nopal was a dusty, ramshackle little burg, scorched by sun and scourged by wind. It didn't have a single redeeming feature, no place to go where you shouldn't be, not even a saloon. I think a hundred people existed there, maybe less.

John Wesley would soon put that miserable, humble little hamlet on the map.

The trouble began a few minutes after we arrived when a black state policeman, wearing brown canvas pants and a faded blue shirt stepped into the store. He was a tall, lean, muscular man who wore a Colt cavalry style on his right hip. His name was Green Paramore and he'd killed his man in the past, but I didn't learn that until later.

The Negro and Wes saw each other at the same time, but Wes was trying to live up to his peaceful ways. "There's crackers and cheese, but eat them outside."

The lawman wasn't much of a one for conversation. He skinned his Colt and said,

"Hardin, throw up your hands or I'll drop you right where you stand. You're under arrest for murder."

Wes, always a consummate actor, pretended to be nervous. "Look out, old fellow. That iron is likely to go off, and I don't want to be shot by accident."

"Then unlimber those pistols and hand them over," Paramore said. "I see a fancy move and I'll kill you."

"Very well then. You've got the drop on me fair and square." Wes slowly and carefully drew his Colts from the holsters and extended them to the lawman, butts forward.

I knew what was about to happen next and the breath bunched in my throat.

Suddenly those pistols cartwheeled and flamed lead.

Paramore, his eyes bugging out in his black face like boiled eggs, took two balls in the forehead and dropped as though his legs had been swept from under him, dead before he hit the floor.

"John Wesley," Neill Bowen yelled. "Outside!"

Wes stepped over the body of the dead man and hurried to the door.

John Lackey, a mulatto policeman from Tennessee, sat astride a fractious mule, but

245

he snapped off a shot at Wes and missed.

Wes fired and the man toppled out of the saddle. Squealing like a strangled piglet, he quickly climbed on board again and lit a shuck, flapping his chaps.

Wes thought this so comical he didn't fire again, contenting himself to double up with laughter.

I didn't laugh. I knew that after this shooting, hard times would come down fast.

And they did.

CHAPTER THIRTY-THREE: THE RELUCTANT HUSBAND

Just a week after the Paramore killing, a posse of Negro policemen came down from Austin, vowing to collect John Wesley's scalp and tack it onto the door of the nearest outhouse.

Wes was told by kinfolk that the lawmen were camped near the DeWitt County farm of a man called Monroe and that they were constantly drunk and had abused the fellow's wife and teenaged daughter.

This last enraged Wes and he strapped on his guns determined to uphold the honor of white, Southern womanhood.

My knight rode forth, but I was again sick in bed at the Clements home and couldn't follow him.

Since I wasn't there, I'll pass over what followed quickly.

As I heard it from Wes, he rode into the drunken Negro camp and cut loose with his *avenging six-guns*. He killed three of the vile riffraff and put the rest to flight.

Needless to say, he returned to a hero's welcome.

"Wes, surely that makes two score," Gip Clements said as the whiskey ran freely.

It seemed that the whole of Gonzalez County had turned out to honor Wes.

Despite being ill, my pride in him swelled. I recall that a hush fell over the house as the merrymakers strained to hear the answer to Gip's question.

And Wes, as usual, rose to the occasion. He struck an orator's pose. "I do not count blacks, Mexicans, or Indians in my score. So the number of white miscreants, carpetbaggers, low persons, traitors, and troublemakers I have put in the grave must stand at twenty-two."

This brought a chorus of delighted huzzahs and the fiddler struck up "Home with the Girls in the Morning." I cheered louder than anyone else.

Again I must beg my reader's indulgence, as I pass lightly over Wes's marriage that took place around that time . . . for no other reason than he took it so lightly himself.

His bride was a dark-haired lass named Jane Bowen who was fourteen at the time, Wes four years older.

"I'm not a family man, Little Bit, preferring the company of rough men," he told me after the wedding. "Jane's duty is to have children and I will support them the best I can."

I've heard some people say that they were a devoted couple.

They were not.

Wes was a negligent husband. He and Jane seldom slept together under the same roof, even after she gave birth to their first child when she was fifteen.

Oh, how I wish, for the sake of the ladies, that I could pen a romance worthy of Miss Charlotte Bronte or Miss Jane Austen and cast John Wesley and his bride aglow in the light of love as they embarked on their path to marital bliss.

Alas, I cannot.

Thus, we must leave poor Mrs. Hardin — of the unkempt hair and the *Oh my God, what have I done?* look in her eyes — alone and lonely in her small home above her father's general store, and go on to more manly pursuits.

On June 8, 1872, Wes told me that he was driving a herd of grade horses to Louisiana for sale to the army.

Though still thin and wasted, I had recovered from my illness and asked if I could follow along.

As always, Wes was reluctant. "Little Bit, I'm riding with Jess and John Harper, rough men who are quick on the trigger and take no sass."

"I can keep my mouth shut and pull my weight," I said.

That made Wes smile. "How much weight, Little Bit? I swear you don't go seventy pounds."

"I can cook. You know that."

"Yeah, you're pretty good at rustling up grub."

"Well?" I said.

I guess I caught Wes in a good mood because after three months of marriage he was eager to take to the trail again.

"All right, you can ride with us, but don't ask me for wages, or the Harper brothers either. After the drive, if I think you've been worth it, I'll pay you something."

"Sets fine with me," I said.

"How's the leg?"

"It will hold up."

"How's the leg?"

I hesitated a moment, then said, "It's been better . . . and worse."

"Same thing applies as I told you the last time. You fall behind and we're leaving you."

"I'll stick."

"You'd better." Wes smiled. "Them Apache bucks would love to get ahold of you, Little Bit."

CHAPTER THIRTY-FOUR: DOWNED BY BUCKSHOT

We never did reach Louisiana.

Wes got bored with the drive and gave up when we reached the Sabine River. He sold the herd to the Harper brothers for what they would pay, then we headed back for Texas.

Oh, I almost forgot, at a burg called Hemphill in Sabine County, Wes put a hole in a lawman's shoulder for giving him back-talk. It wasn't a fatal wound, so it's hardly worth mentioning here. But that officer surely scampered after Wes plugged him.

My leg was troubling me, so Wes decided we should stop off at Trinity Station and rest up for a spell. The town was a shabby, dusty little settlement without snap or character, but it was close to the Trinity River and was a stop on the Houston and Great Northern Railroad. For the life of me I couldn't figure out why.

Most of the houses and stores clustered

around the station, but the pride of the metropolis was the John Gates Saloon at the corner of Caroline and Parke streets. A banner slung across the building's false front proclaimed 5¢ BEER & 10-PIN BOWL-ING

"Hell, that's the place for us, huh, Little Bit?" Wes said. "I like to bowl."

As I climbed off my horse at the hitching rail, the breath caught in my throat and I was filled with a sense of foreboding . . . dread you might say. I wanted to tell Wes how I felt, but I knew he'd laugh at me and call me an old woman, so I bit my tongue.

Hell, the panels on the saloon's timber door were shaped like a cross. I took that as a bad omen.

And it was.

That day, poor, timorous, craven creature that I was, I almost caused the death of John Wesley Hardin, the greatest man of his era.

The John Gates was a saloon like any other, its raw whiskey and warm beer like any other. The only thing that set it apart was a space at the rear set aside for bowling.

I prevailed on Wes to leave his pistols behind the bar, since the risk of running into the law in Trinity Station was remote.

He readily agreed and handed his Colts to

the bartender. With a whiskey at his elbow, he looked around the saloon . . . and saw someone he knew. "You see that fellow over at the table with the shotgun at his side?"

I looked at the man in the French mirror behind the bar. "I see him."

"His name is Phil Sublett and he killed a carpetbagging black man by the name of George Stubblefield with that there scatter-gun."

"Then he's a patriot," I said.

"Damn right he is. And a farmer."

Sublett glanced over at us and Wes raised his glass. "Howdy, Phil."

Sublett, a tall, thin man with a goatee and roughly cut brown hair, joined us at the bar. He had hard, blue eyes that never looked at you directly, as though he constantly found items of interest in the corners of the room. "Howdy, Wes. It's been a while."

"Seems like." Wes introduced me. "This here is Little Bit."

Sublett gave me a quick, disinterested glance, and dismissed me. "Been hearing things about you, Wes."

"People talk."

"They say you put the crawl on Wild Bill Hickok."

Wes puffed up a little. "He tried to corral me, but now me and William are on the square."

"Glad to hear it," Sublett said.

"You're farming, I heard."

"Not for much longer. I'm tired of pushing a plow, staring at a mule's butt all the damned day."

"You should go into the cattle business, Phil," Wes said. "A man on a hoss can see forever if his eyes are good."

"Something to keep in mind. Let me buy you a drink and maybe we'll bowl later, huh?"

"Sounds good to me," Wes said, fingering his gambler's ring. "What are the stakes?"

"Two-bits a game too much for you?"

"Hell, that's for maiden aunts playing Old Maid," Wes said. "Lets make it fifty cents."

"I'm your daisy." Sublett's unsmiling face was stiff.

I realized then that this man was no friend of Wes. I thought maybe he was jealous of Wes's reputation and fame and was glad my friend's guns were behind the bar.

After Wes and Sublett left for the bowling pins, I took a bottle to the table, stretched out my bad leg and concentrated on the whiskey.

As Wes and Sublett yelled and argued the rules, I got slowly drunk . . . then faster drunk . . . then I-don't-give-a-damn drunk.

I even lowered my pants and poured whiskey over the open wound on my thigh . . . and passed out from the sudden shriek of pain.

I don't know how long I was unconscious, but when I raised my head I heard John Wesley yell, "Damn you for a cheat, Sublett! Keep it up and I'm gonna put a bullet in your damn belly!"

They had switched from bowling to cards.

Wes was a bad gambler and a sore loser. I'd feared something like that could happen. I didn't know that he'd stashed away a sneaky gun or I'd have felt a sight worse.

"And damn you for a scoundrel, Hardin!" Sublett roared. "Come outside and give me six feet of ground."

Wes held a small revolver of the bulldog type with its muzzle jammed into Sublett's belly.

I figured that a killing was only seconds away, but during the time I was out, other men had come into the saloon. I heard shouts of, "No, that won't do!" and, "Put away your weapon!"

Well, to my surprise, Wes calmed down and shoved the bulldog into his pocket, saying that his temper had gotten the better of him.

Urged by the crowd to shake hands, he

and Sublett did just that and everyone repaired to the bar where some rooster ordered rum punches all round.

But Phil Sublett didn't stay. Shotgun in hand, he walked out of the saloon and into the darkening street, his face thunderous with anger.

Wes had lived by the gun for so long that he had the instincts of a hunted wolf.

I watched bleary-eyed from my table as he got his guns from the bartender and shoved them into the shoulder holsters.

As lamps were lit in the saloon against the crowding darkness, Wes drank little, his gaze fixed on the door.

Then came the moment of hell that I dreaded.

Sublett's voice echoed from outside, harsh and challenging. "Hardin, get out here and meet me like a man!" he yelled. "You'll eat supper in hell tonight, by God."

A silence fell on the saloon . . . except for my drunken sobs, the consequence of my fevered thoughts. *Phil Sublett, the failed farmer who envied John Wesley enough to kill him, was outside with a murderous shotgun . . . he planned to slaughter a man of virtue . . . a man much finer than himself . . . my Quentin Durward . . . my knight without compare . . . my hero . . . my friend . . .*

Wes stepped to the door.

I stumbled to my feet. "No, wait," I said, slurring my words. "I'm coming . . . I'm going . . . I mean, I . . ."

Wes threw me a look, ignored me, and stepped outside.

A moment later, I heard the blast of a shotgun and the sharper bark of Wes's Colts.

"Wes!" I screamed, foolish drunkard that I was. "I'm coming!" I staggered to the door, fell, and scrambled to my feet again.

"You, get back here!" a man yelled.

But I ignored him and lurched outside.

Wes stood in the shadows to the right of the saloon door. A lantern at the corner of the building cast a shifting circle of light onto the street and entrance to an adjoining alley.

I stumbled to Wes, tears in my eyes, and grabbed him by the lapels of his coat. "John Wesley," I yelled, "I'm with you! Together we can whip this whole damn town!"

Wes cursed and pushed me away. I stumbled back and pulled him with me . . . into the lantern light.

Sublett's shotgun roared and Wes staggered, hit hard.

The damned, yellow-bellied assassin then turned tail and ran. Wes, leaving behind a trail of blood, went after him.

Rapidly sobering, I stumped after him.

How well I remember that night.

There was no wind. It was as though the town held its breath, waiting for what was to happen. A yellow dog with amber eyes snarled at me as I thudded past and its gleaming fangs were white as ivory. Ahead of me, I saw Sublett turn into an unfinished timber building.

Wes, bent over and reeling, went after him.

Then a shot.

Followed by silence.

Wes staggered out of the building and stood with a supporting hand on the doorjamb. He saw me and said, "I put a hole in him, but he's gone."

"Are you hit, Wes?" I asked, knowing full well he was.

"I'm done for. He got me in the belly." He dropped to a sitting position, scarlet blood leaking through the fingers of the hand that clutched his stomach.

A crowd gathered around him. I kneeled beside him, but Wes threw my arm off his shoulder and yelled, "Get the hell away from me. You've killed me."

As you might guess, that was a wound, but then Wes was hurting and thought he was at death's door, so I forgave him.

He looked around at the concerned faces

of the people. "My time is short."

"No!" a woman screamed.

"You good people are witnesses to my last will and testament," Wes said.

"I'll get Dr. Carrington," the screaming woman said.

"No, not yet. Listen to me, all of you."

The crowd of maybe two-dozen quieted down.

Wes said, "My money belt holds two thousand dollars in gold and there's another five hundred in silver in my saddlebags. Give the money to my wife in Gonzales County, along with whatever my horse, saddle, and guns will bring." He grimaced as a wave of pain hit him. His voice got weaker. "Tell my dear Jane that I honestly tried to avoid this trouble. But my foeman done for me with a scattergun. Such is the way of cowards."

Then, before unconsciousness took him, he said, "Bury me in Gonzales County. Don't let my body lie in foreign soil."

Willing hands carried Wes to the doctor's office, bloody, like a gallant matador gored in the arena. I followed, heavy of heart.

Dr. Carrington, an intelligent man of middle age, said that the big silver buckle Wes wore on his money belt had taken most of the shotgun blast and saved his life.

However, two buckshot had succeeded in doing their deadly work. They had ripped into his belly and were lodged between his backbone and ribs.

"They have to come out," the doctor said. "I can give you something to dull the pain."

John Wesley, that fearless stalwart, said, "I'll have no truck with opiates. Cut away, Doc, and be damned to ye for a butcher."

Well, that's not really what Wes said, on account of how he fainted when he heard the diagnosis. But had he been conscious, he would have said something of that ilk, I'm sure.

Thus I may be accused of putting words in my hero's mouth that he did not utter. But then, how else am I to express his noble, gallant and generous nature?

Chapter Thirty-Five: Thirty-Six Dead Men

The town of Trinity Station harbored a nest of traitors.

John Wesley was still recovering from his terrible wounds when a grand jury convened and indicted him for the attempted murder of that vile hound Phil Sublett!

There was no appeal against this grave injustice and Wes, wounded though he was, had to flee the town by dark of night, like a common criminal.

He became a hunted animal, relentlessly pursued by posses. I'm proud to say that, weak and sick as I was, I rode with him through those trying times. On the scout, we slipped from one hideout to another, and finally found refuge in Angelina County at the home of Dave Harrel, a Hardin family friend.

But the state police would not leave us alone. Three or four times packs of hunters rode close to the house.

Sitting in the Harrel parlor, Wes said to me, "Little Bit, the wound in my belly is festering and I need medical help. I think I've no option but to surrender."

I was not in good shape myself. The wound on my thigh had grown to twice its size and it smelled. We'd had little to eat since leaving Trinity Station and I'd lost weight. The calf muscle of my bad leg was about as big around as a walnut.

"A jury will clear you of all charges, Wes," I said. "Sublett shot at you first."

"Damn right he did." After some thought, Wes said, "Yeah . . . maybe I should take my chances with the law."

"You're a respectable businessman, Wes. And you'll soon have your own Wild West show. There isn't a jury in Texas that will convict you."

But Wes suddenly seemed a little hesitant. "Dave Harrel's wife is making up a salve for my wound. She says her ma used it on her pa after he came back from the war all shot up and it worked wonders." He began to reassemble the Colt he'd been cleaning. "Now I study on it, I guess I'll wait a spell, see how the salve works."

All at once, I was exasperated. "Wes, you must see a doctor. A gut shot man needs more than hog fat and aloe."

"That means surrendering," Wes said.

"Yes, that's what it means."

"Well, I —"

A fist pounded on the front door of the house and a man's voice yelled, "Open up in the name of the law!"

A few moments later Dave Harrel stepped into the parlor, his face pale. He held a shotgun in his hand. "State police," he said, dropping his voice to a whisper. "At first I thought it was road agents."

"How many?" Wes asked.

"Two. That I can see anyway."

Wes rose, wincing, from his chair, the unhealed belly wound punishing him. "Dave, keep them talking. And give me the scattergun."

"I don't want no trouble." Harrel's thin, brown hair was plastered to his head in damp strands.

A fist pounded on the door again. Louder.

"That's up to them, isn't it?" Wes grabbed the shotgun from Harrel's unresisting hand and slipped through the back door.

"Let's go talk to them, Dave," I said.

Two men stood outside, one with a revolver in his fist.

"What can I do for you worthy gentlemen?" Harrel said, his face beaming with pretended good humor.

So far, so good, I thought.

"We have reason to believe that a murderer by the name of John Wesley Hardin is hiding in this residence," the lawman with the Colt said.

Unfortunately, Harrel froze. His throat bobbed, but no words came out.

"He's not here," I said.

The lawman was a big fellow with hair as a black as a Sioux Indian's and a dragoon mustache of the some shade. He was huge, like a force of nature is huge, as though he could lower his head and butt his way through the house from front to back. "We were told Hardin is riding with a lame little runt. Is that you?"

"It sure is," I said. "And it's a great honor."

Well, that was honest enough.

The roar of a shotgun immediately followed my declaration and the big lawman took a barrelful of double-aught buck right in the face.

No matter how big he is, how tough and mean he is, a man can't suffer a blow like that and live.

As he fell, the officer's face reminded me of a smashed raspberry pie I once saw on a baker's floor. It was a sight I'll never forget.

Yet as he went down, the lawman's dead

finger twitched convulsively on the trigger and his ball slammed into Wes's thigh.

The other policeman, much younger, wide-eyed and nervous, glanced down at his brother officer and promptly bent over and threw up so violently I could tell what he'd had for his last three meals.

After the man straightened, saliva trailing from his mouth, Wes pushed the muzzle of the shotgun into his belly. "I can make it two real easy. You want to go for a deuce?"

The youngster tried to speak, but couldn't. He retched a couple of times, then said, "I've never seen anything like that before. His . . . his face . . ."

"Lead in the face can make a mess of a man," Wes said. "Now state your intentions and be quick."

The lawman shook his head. He had brown eyes as pretty as a woman's. "I'm out of it."

"Only if I say you're out of it," Wes said.

The youngster made no answer. I doubt if he could.

"All right, you're out of it. I'm in a good mood today." Wes nodded in the direction of the dead man. "Load what's left of that onto his horse and get the hell away from here."

Harrel, leaning against the wall of his

house, looked sick to his stomach, as though a yellow, porcelain mask covered his blunt features, but he helped get the dead lawman across his saddle. He stepped back and stared at his hands, holding them up in front of him, a horrified light in his eyes. His hands and forearms were streaked with scarlet runnels of blood, mixed with gray fragments of bone and brain. "Ahhhh . . . ahhhh . . ." he hollered, somewhere between a groan and a shriek.

"Damn you, wash them off!" Wes yelled. "Wash your damned hands!" Harrel's wails had unnerved him and he turned on the young lawman. "Get him the hell out of here!" he roared. "Now!"

The officer mounted, gathered the reins of the other horse and led it away, the pulped head of the dead man swaying with every motion.

Harrel, stripped to the waist, frantically worked the handle of the pump. The water cascaded over his hands and turned red.

Mrs. Harrel, a handsome woman with heavy breasts and hips, rushed outside with a bar of yellow lye soap and a towel, and helped her husband wash.

"Martha, did you see?" Saliva gathered at the corners of Harrel's mouth. "Did you see his head?"

"I saw it." She turned to Wes. "Go away. Leave us alone and never come back."

"Bang, Martha," Harrel said, wonder in his voice. "Bang, and he'd no face left."

"I know, Dave. I know how it was."

Wes stepped beside me, the shotgun still in his hand. Blood oozed from his wounded thigh. "Little Bit, I've killed 37, but now they're starting to get lead into me. I think my luck is changing for the worse and hard times are coming down fast."

"Wes, we should head back to Gonzalez County where you have kin," I said. "They'll find a doctor to take care of you."

"The Yankee law will hunt me down no matter where I go," Wes said. "They'll never forgive me for taking a stand against tyranny."

Harrel was drying his hands on his towel. He'd calmed some, but looked at Wes as though he was some kind of dangerous, uncaged beast.

"Where is the nearest law?" Wes said to him.

"That would be Richard Reagan, the sheriff of Cherokee County," Harrel said.

"Where's he live?" Wes asked.

"He has a farm a couple of miles south of here," Harrel said.

"Bring him. Tell him I want to surrender."

"Canada, Wes," I said. "We could go to Canada."

John Wesley looked at me as though I'd just crawled out from under a rock. He looked back at Harrel. "Bring him, Dave. Tell him I'm shot through and through and damned tired of running."

CHAPTER THIRTY-SIX:
HELL ON EARTH

Sheriff Richard Reagan was a tall, slender man with a kindly face. He was a careless dresser, but everything he wore was much washed and clean. Men of such appearance have dutiful wives and that is to their credit. He carried a holstered Colt that looked ill at ease on him, as though he considered it more badge of office than weapon.

Reagan arrived with four, hard-eyed deputies, but they remained outside while he and Wes repaired to the Harrel parlor.

Since nobody objected, or even seemed to notice me, I joined them.

Reagan got right to the point. "Dave Harrel led me to believe that you wish to surrender."

"He led you along the right path," Wes said. Covered by a cloth, his holstered guns were on the parlor table, as was the bulldog revolver.

In his memoirs, Wes says Reagan agreed

to all kinds of conditions before he surrendered. He said the sheriff treated him like a superior kind of person, a God-fearing patriot who'd been persecuted by greedy carpetbaggers and vindictive Yankee lawmen.

The first part of that is not true, of course.

Wes made only one condition. Seriously wounded and fearing that he was dying, he begged Reagan to take him to a doctor who could save his life. "I don't want to leave my wife a grieving widow at so tender an age."

Reagan took Wes at face value. The face in question looked as contrite as a sinner's at a tent revival and was strained from pain.

"I will see what I can do," Reagan said. "But first you must surrender your firearms."

"Willingly. They have caused me nothing but trouble." Wes stepped to the table, pulled aside the cloth and picked up his guns.

Then tragedy struck.

An overzealous deputy who stood near the window saw what Wes was doing and opened fire. The ball hit Wes in the knee and he cried out in pain and dropped to the ground.

"Murder!" I yelled, angry that my friend

now had four bullet holes in his body, two of them inflicted by so-called peace officers.

Reagan crossed the floor to the window and severely reprimanded the sullen deputy who made no attempt to apologize. He then kneeled beside Wes. "I'm sorry, old fellow. That was an honest mistake."

A mistake, yes, but not an honest one. The law had it in for John Wesley and seemed determined to kill him one way or the other.

I know they preferred a rope, but a bullet would do.

Wes was taken to the nearby town of Rusk to be held in a hotel owned by Sheriff Reagan where his wounds were treated and he was allowed to greet the many admirers who called on him.

I saw an immediate improvement in his attitude.

Wes liked people and they in turn liked him. He treated each visitor as though he or she was the most important, interesting person in the world. In those days, before prison ground him to dust, Wes was outgoing and charming. His love of life and inner glow cast a flattering light on all who came in contact with him.

But these were just a few of the attributes that made him a great man. Had the vengeful law left him alone, Wes would have found fame and fortune and a statue of him would stand in every town square in Texas.

On September 22, 1872, John Wesley was taken to Austin to stand trial. I did not join him right away because I felt too sick to travel.

Wes didn't appear to be troubled by my desertion, saying only that I should take care, say my prayers, and stay away from strong drink and fancy women.

I was sleeping rough and took a job as a saloon swamper to pay for my whiskey and the doctor who treated my leg.

The doc managed to help the recurring wound on my thigh, but warned that my bad leg should be amputated as soon as possible since it was withering away, possibly cancerous, and undermining my health.

I told him I never had any health to undermine, and he agreed that seemed to be the case.

"But," the doc said, "that doesn't alter the fact that the leg must be amputated, sooner rather than later."

The swamper job soon proved to be too much for me, but I felt well enough to take the trail to Austin, then a boomtown thanks to the arrival of the Houston and Central

Texas Railroad.

The saloon owner, who'd either taken a liking to me or pitied me, gave me an old army greatcoat, cut to fit a much bigger man than me, and a paper sack with salt pork, a chunk of smelly cheese with blue stuff in it, and half a loaf of sourdough bread.

I was grateful for the coat. The early morning I reached the city it was pouring rain and a cold fall wind blew from the north.

After making some enquiries from a prim matron in the street, I discovered that Wes had been incarcerated in a broken down jail on the Colorado River.

The place was a hell on earth, the woman told me, and she warned that I should stay well clear because the jailors would think I looked like a desperate character, inclined to all sorts of mischief.

I didn't need further instruction on how to find the jail. Its stench could be detected from a mile away. The hellhole was jammed with such a reeking, heaving, mass of humanity that in the summer the prisoners stripped naked to survive the intolerable, humid heat.

I was allowed to speak to Wes through a grill in an iron-studded door that wafted a stink like bad morning breath.

After an exchange of pleasantries, Wes whispered, "Little Bit, bring me a hacksaw blade. I'm going to cut my way out of here."

I felt a jolt of alarm. "Wes, if you're caught, they'll gun you for sure."

Wes's teeth flashed white in the gloom of that place. "The guards are all kin, or friends of kin. They'll turn the other way."

"Are you sure about that?"

"Hell, this is Gonzales County, my home range. Of course I'm sure." He crooked his finger and I put my face closer to the grill. "Manny Clements is in town. Tell him to have a horse ready for me on the south side of the jail."

I never liked Manny Clements much, a big, overbearing bully of a man, but I had to bite the bullet, as they say. "When?"

"Bring the saw later today and I'll be ready by midnight tomorrow."

"I'll be with Clements when you break out."

"Yeah, you do that, Little Bit. Now go get me the saw blade."

I had no money to buy the hacksaw blade and when I stepped into a dry goods store with the intention of stealing one, the suspicious owner kept his eyes on me the whole time I was there. Finally I was forced to leave empty handed.

My only option was to find Manny Clements.

Since Clements usually hung with a town's sporting crowd, I doubted he'd be up and about much before noon, and it was still not yet ten.

My horse stood hipshot in the rattling rain outside the dry goods store. He needed a place to shelter and so did I. The Houston and Central Texas train station lay close by, so I gathered up the reins and walked my mount up the slanted loading ramp to the platform. We found shelter under the wooden awning. I sat on a bench then pulled the paper food sack from under my coat. I ate the piece of cheese and crust of bread that was left. It didn't satisfy my hunger, but it was better than nothing.

About two inches of whiskey were left in my bottle, so I drank that and began to feel a little better, though I was still cold, damp, and shivering. I coughed incessantly.

The sky was gray to the horizon, but black thunderheads piled one on top of the other to the north and promised more rain, more misery, and the perplexing problem as to where I'd sleep that night.

It seemed that I'd have to depend on the

generosity of Manny Clements, a man not noted for his giving nature.

I was so lost in a tangle of thoughts, none of them pleasant, I didn't notice the ticket agent step onto the platform.

He spotted me, then turned his head and said, "Shamus, come out here."

A tall, heavy man wearing a railroad hat with a shield-shaped badge on the front and an oilskin cape came from inside, a tin cup of coffee in his hand and a scowl on his face.

It was the first time I'd ever seen a railroad bull, those private, strong-arm thugs the rail companies were hiring to stop tramps, vagrants, and other riffraff riding free in the freight cars.

I later learned that the bulls had orders to shoot to kill. Some say they gunned at least a thousand white men in Texas alone. Add Negroes and Chinese and that number triples.

The bull laid his cup on a bench and slowly stepped toward me. The *thud, thud* of his boots on the wooden platform sounded like the drums of doom. He loomed over me. "Git that damn hoss off the platform." He had a round, red, Irish face and small eyes that looked like hard blue marbles.

"I certainly will, sir," I said, getting to my feet.

The bull toed the crumpled, greasy paper sack I'd dropped. "That yours?"

I nodded.

"Pick it up."

I did as he said, then gathered the reins of my horse. "It was nice to meet you."

But the bull wasn't done with me, not yet anyway. "Do you have a ticket?"

"No," I said.

"Why are you here?"

I decided to tell the truth. "Just sheltering from the rain. I meant no harm."

"Sheltering on railroad property?"

"I guess so." I pointed upward. "It has a cover."

Some things I remember vividly about that morning . . . the drip at the end of the bull's nose . . . the whiskey on his breath . . . the rumble of distant thunder and the snare drum rattle of the rain on the roof. I remember all that, but after the bull accused me of trespassing and followed up with a punch to the middle of my face, I recall very little.

I had an instant glance of a fist as big as a ham coming at me, and then my lights went out. I'd never been punched before and wasn't prepared for it.

As far as I can tell, since I was unaware, worse was to happen.

My horse spooked as I dropped, but my

left hand was tangled in his reins and he swung around and dragged me down the ramp. At a frenzied gallop, he hauled me into the muddy street and finally shook me loose after I slammed into a boardwalk, then a hitching rail, and came to rest in a dung-covered puddle.

I mean, I guess all that happened. When I woke with a broken nose and bruised, swollen eyes, the puddle was where I found myself.

Hurting all over, I tried to get to my feet, but my bad leg slipped out from under me and I landed on my back, the furious rain lashing at me.

Two respectable ladies holding umbrellas looked down at me, then one whispered into the other's ear. That lady nodded, reached into her purse and held out her hand. She was holding something I thought was money and reached out to take it.

"Read it and take it to heart, young man," she said.

Then she and the other woman walked away, their noses high and backs stiff.

I looked at the paper in my hand. It was some kind of leaflet. On the front was written DRINK IS A MOCKER. BE NOT DECEIVED. And under that, *Verily, there's a*

serpent in every bottle and he biteth like the
viper!

Suddenly I was angry . . . angry at myself for being a cripple, angry at myself for being poor, and angry at the world for not giving a damn. I struggled to my feet and saw the two respectable ladies gesturing to one another as they stared into a store window.

"Hey!" I yelled. "Go to hell!" I held up the pamphlet and began to tear it into little pieces. "You hear me? Go to hell!"

The women turned their heads, stared at me for a moment, then hurried away, lifting their skirts so their white petticoats and button-up boots showed.

"Go to hell," I said in a whisper, my hurting head bent. "Everybody go to hell."

CHAPTER THIRTY-SEVEN:
THE GOOD IRISHMAN

After a search, I found my horse standing outside a livery stable and led him away. He must have had visions of a dry stall and oats in the bucket, because he was reluctant to leave. But I dragged him after me.

If I was going to rough it, so was he.

I glanced through a bank window and to my surprise the clock on the wall said it was thirty minutes after noon. I'd been unconscious longer than I thought.

It was time to find Manny Clements.

He wasn't hard to track down. He was a well-known character in Austin and a passerby told me he could usually be found at that hour taking lunch at the Scholz Beer Garden on San Jacinto Street.

I led my horse through the rain and somber grayness that drifted like smoke from the north and looped him to the hitching rail outside the restaurant.

The beer garden was a splendid place with

windows on all four walls and a fine gable roof, but I was in little mood to enjoy it. I could barely see anyway. My left eye was completely swollen shut and the right was headed that way.

Fortunately, the rain had washed away the blood from my flattened nose, but before I went inside I scrubbed my hand over my top lip and chin just to make sure.

Can you imagine what I looked like when I stepped inside Mr. Scholz's pride and joy?

I was soaked to the skin and my huge, sodden coat dragged on the floor. I'd found my hat in the street, but it had been run over by a wagon wheel and I'd had to punch it back into shape. It didn't look too good.

Imagine then, my pinched, pale little face, a nose blue and broken, eyes black and swollen shut, and me smelling of mud, and manure, and you'll get some idea why I wasn't exactly welcomed into the beer garden with open arms.

To his credit, the waiter who met me at the door was polite and kept his eyes empty. "Do you wish to be seated, sir?"

"No." I said.

The waiter looked relieved.

"I'm here to see Manny Clements."

"Would that be Mr. Mannen Clements?"

"Yes. That's him."

"Please wait here and I'll see if he's inside," the waiter said. "Whom shall I say wishes to speak with him?"

"Just tell him it's Little Bit."

"Very well, Mr. Bit. I'll find out if Mr. Clements is available."

The waiter left and I stood, hat in hand, dripping onto the polished wood floor. I smelled steak sizzling, possibly corned beef and cabbage bubbling in the pot, definitely frying bacon, and perhaps just a soupcon of grilled German sausage. My stomach rumbled and I fervently hoped that Manny, a great trencherman in his own right, would feed me.

He didn't.

With the waiter leading the way, Manny left the dining room and met me at the door. I smelled sausage and mustard on his breath.

"What the hell happened to you?" Manny asked.

"I ran afoul of a railroad bull," I said.

"Were you trespassing on railroad property?"

"A platform."

Manny nodded. "You're lucky he didn't shoot you."

"Yeah, real lucky, I guess. John Wesley sent me."

"He's in the *juzgado*."

"I know."

"What does he want?"

I told him.

Blood is thicker than water in Texas, and Manny didn't hesitate. "Tell Wes I'll be there. He'll come out of that hellhole naked, so tell him I'll bring him clothes and a gun." He stared at me, obviously not impressed by what he saw. "Can you remember that?"

"Yeah, I can. But I've no money to buy a hacksaw blade."

Manny reached into his jingling pocket and gave me half a dollar. "A blade doesn't cost more than that." He took a step back, looking me up and down. "Little Bit, I'd say you're a sight for sore eyes, but I'd be telling a big windy. You look like crap."

"I feel like crap. And I'm hungry."

"Be outside the jail at midnight tomorrow," Manny said. "You can hold the horses."

He stepped away, back to his lunch, and left me to sadly contemplate my empty, sunken belly.

The hardware store owner sold me a hacksaw blade, slightly rusty, for twenty-five cents. I was overjoyed. That gave me enough change for five beers and allowed me to partake of the free lunch advertised on a chalkboard outside the Star of Erin saloon.

It was good to get out of the rain. I bought a beer and then nonchalantly strolled to the free lunch bar like a well-fed man in the mood for a snack. The menu was fish oriented — pickled herring, sardines in oil, and slabs of yellow, dried cod. But they also had hardboiled eggs in the shell, a massive crock of butter, and a basket of rye bread.

Since crockery tended to walk out the door with the customers, thick brown paper shaped into cones served as plates.

An ominous, chalked sign above the bar read NO SCUM ALLOWED.

Since I was a paying customer, I ignored that. I filled my cone with herring, cod, a couple chunks of bread and butter and sat at a table to enjoy my feast.

Alas, my happiness was short-lived.

The saloon was busy, but one of the four bartenders left his post and stepped over to my table. He was as big as the railroad bull, but not quite as mean. "Take your lunch outside, son," he said, in a strong Irish accent.

I was chewing a mouthful of bread and butter. When I finally swallowed, I said, "Why?"

"Because the patrons say you smell bad."

The bartender smiled, showing teeth like little white pegs.

I always liked white teeth, my own being of that particular shade.

"Son, they're right. You stink like the pigs o' Docherty, so out the door with you. There's a bench outside where you can sit. It's sheltered from the rain."

I'd learned a lesson from my run-in with the bull, and I didn't want to antagonize an Irishman with massive forearms and a head as big as a nail keg. Without a word, I rose and carried my paper poke and beer outside.

"Good lad," the bartender said after he saw me seated on a bench covered by the porch roof. He was a good man, that Irishman.

No sooner was I seated than he returned with a schooner of beer. "This one is on the house. For the inconvenience, like." He stared at me for a long time as though sorting out some sentences in his mind. "You look sick, son, and you've been beaten."

I nodded. I had no sentences of my own, sorted or otherwise.

"Then you take care," he said.

"Thanks for the beer."

I ate my food — the cod and pickled herring were as salty as the sea — and stepped into the rain again.

I knew Wes would be worried about me.

CHAPTER THIRTY-EIGHT:
A TROUBLED EVENING

"Did you bring it?" John Wesley asked me.

"It's down my pants leg."

"Slip it through the grill."

"What about the guards?"

"They're looking in every other direction but this one."

I did as he told me, and Wes said, "You spoke to Manny?"

"He'll have a horse and clothes and a revolver."

"Good. I've got scores to settle." He looked at me, as though seeing me for the first time. "What the hell happened to you?"

"Railroad bull," I said.

"You were trespassing?"

"On the station platform. Me and my horse."

"You're lucky you're still alive."

"I guess."

"Stay out of trouble."

"I will. What about the railroad bull?"

"What about him?"

"Look at my face, Wes."

"Yeah, that's too bad. Don't go near the station again."

"If I could shoot, I'd gun that bull."

"I'm sure you would."

Wes glanced over his shoulder. "I got to go. See you tomorrow night."

"I'll be here."

Wes's face vanished from the door grill and a guard ushered me out of the jail.

That evening I spent my last twenty cents on beer in a saloon with a three-piece orchestra and bummed a whiskey off a puncher who said he'd stand treat if'n I stayed at least ten feet away from him.

Finally, my beer ran out and the bartender's patience wore thin. I was tossed into the rainy street again.

I staked my horse on a patch of bunchgrass behind a Chinese laundry and spent the night in their outhouse.

But come first light, the Chinese chased me away and, damn it all, it was still raining.

I'd taken the precaution of stashing some of the dried cod and bread in my pocket, so I sat on a hotel porch and made a good breakfast.

The outhouse had been uncomfortable, just a narrow, single-holer. I had not rested well. By comparison, the hotel rocker felt like a king's throne. I tipped my hat over my eyes and waited for sleep to take me.

I vaguely remember the sound of a train whistle in the distance . . . the rumble of a freight wagon in the street . . . the *slam-slam-slam* of a screen door opening and closing in the wind . . . the bark of a dog . . .

Then I heard nothing at all.

Something hard poking into my shoulder awakened me. I opened my eyes, tipped back my hat, and saw to my surprise that it was full dark. Reflector lamps had been lit up and down the street.

The beating I'd taken and the bad night in the outhouse had tired me more than I thought. I hurt all over.

"It's time you went home now, young fellow." It was a man's voice, the Deep South accent smooth and unhurried as molasses dripping from a barrel. A tall, slender man with white hair and a trimmed imperial regarded me with mild blue eyes. He held a cane in his hand, but had a soldier's bearing.

"I must have fallen asleep . . . Gen'ral," I said.

The old man smiled. "You've promoted me, sir." He gave a little bow. "Lieutenant Colonel Miles Hannah, late of the Sixty-first Regiment Alabama Infantry."

"Pleased to make your acquaintance, Colonel."

"You must go home now, son," the old soldier said. "The cause is lost, the regiment is disbanded, and I see that you are sorely wounded in the leg as I am."

The rocker creaked as I sat up. "Colonel, do you own this place? I could sure use a glass of whiskey, on the slate, like."

The old man smiled again. "No, I don't own this hotel, but I live here. I'm disabled from battle wounds, you understand. Many battles, many wounds."

"Sorry to hear that, Colonel. But what can you do about the whiskey?"

The old man thought for a few moments, then said, "My daughter and her husband own this hotel. I'll ask them to fill a convivial glass for an old soldier."

I saluted. "That's me, Colonel, an old soldier as ever was."

"We had times, boy, did we not? Fighting for freedom, shoulder to shoulder against the Northern aggressors."

"Sure thing. Good times with Bobby Lee and Longstreet and them."

"But the great cause was lost and now the Bonnie Blue Flag lies trampled in the dust."

"Yeah, that's sad," I said. "Colonel, about the whiskey . . ."

"Ah yes, the whiskey. Stay there. I'll see what I can do directly." Using his cane, the colonel limped to the door. Then he turned to me and said, "What was your rank, son?"

"Sergeant." I hated to deceive this kind and brave old man, but my entire being cried out for whiskey and I'd no other source but him.

He smiled at me. "The most important rank in any army is sergeant." Then he stepped through the open door.

Rain ticked from the porch roof and, illuminated by the lanterns that glowed outside the stores and saloons, fell on the street like a cascade of steel needles. Thunder rolled like dim drums in the distance of the night and lightning flashed gold within the storm clouds.

I sat and waited and worried that the old colonel had fallen down somewhere and couldn't get up again.

After about ten minutes, a woman stepped onto the porch. She was pretty, looked to be in her mid-thirties, but she was much too thin and her eyes were tired. "You're awake."

"Yes," I said. "I hope you don't mind me using your porch."

"People need shelter from the rain. But I think you should move on now."

"Is your father Colonel Hannah?"

"Why do you ask?" She seemed surprised.

"He told me he'd bring me a glass of whiskey," I said, then quickly, "On the slate."

The woman gave me a long look, but I couldn't read her face.

Finally she said, "The colonel has done this before."

I hoped my smile was ingratiating. "He's a fine old soldier."

Without another word, the woman turned on her heel and stepped into the hotel.

But she returned within a couple of minutes with a glass of bourbon. "Drink this. Then please leave."

I said my thankee and took the glass.

The woman stepped away, then stopped and turned to me. The right side of her face was lit by the oil lamp beside the door, the other half in shadow. "My father, Colonel Hannah, died of his wounds two years ago." Then she left me and I heard the quick thud of her boot heels on the timber floor inside.

My hands shook and I held the glass in both as I drank the whiskey like a man dying of thirst.

Whether my tremors were from a lack of booze or my brush with the supernatural I don't know, but I can tell you this. Like most Texans, especially those who'd been around cow camps, I was deathly afraid of ghosts and ha'nts and such. As soon as I downed my whiskey, I got off that porch double quick, collected my horse, and didn't look back.

Some things that are not meant for mortal eyes leave indelible memories, and the specter of the dead old colonel visits me still on thundery midnights, troubling my restless sleep.

CHAPTER THIRTY-NINE: WAR CLOUDS GATHER

I arrived at the jail well before midnight, but stayed back out of sight. Hidden by darkness, I awaited the arrival of Manny Clements. The November night was cold and the thunder that had warned of continuing rain had made good on its promise. It was not a heavy downpour, just a steady drizzle that soaked me to the skin and made it difficult to see anything around me.

After about fifteen minutes, Manny showed up. He was mounted on a rawboned buckskin and led two other animals, a paint mustang and a pack mule. He drew rein beside me and said, "Seen anything yet?"

I shook my head. Realizing it was very dark, I said, "Not a thing. I haven't heard anything, either."

Manny swung out of the saddle and bade me do the same. "Hold onto the horses. I'll go see what's happening." He reached under his slicker, adjusted the lie of his holstered revolver, and walked away from me.

Soon Manny was swallowed by the gloom and I heard nothing but the hiss of the rain and the beat of my own racing heart.

Dreary minutes passed with agonizing slowness . . . then footsteps, squelching in mud, came toward me. The darkness parted and two men appeared, Manny's supporting arm around Wes's waist.

His teeth gritted against pain, Wes wore only ragged long johns and there were bloodstains on the front of the shirt.

Alarmed, I said, "What happened?"

"I had to pull him through the window. The stumps of the iron bars dragged across his wounded belly." Manny helped Wes sit with his back against a tree, then stepped to the pack mule.

I kneeled beside Wes. "Are you all right?"

He looked through me rather than at me. "What do you think?"

I didn't have to answer that because Manny came back, holding a slicker and a bottle of Old Crow. "Here, Wes, before you get some of this whiskey in you we'll put the slicker on you. We'll dress you properly after we light a shuck out of here."

We helped Wes to his feet and got the slicker on him.

Manny passed him the bottle. "Now get

the whiskey down you. It will do you good."

Wes drank from the bottle. "I needed that." He passed it back to Manny who also drank deeply.

He wiped his mustache with the back of his hand and corked the bottle. "Now we'll get you mounted."

"Manny, I could sure use a drink of that whiskey," I said.

The man stared at me for the briefest of moments, then said, "Help get Wes up on his horse."

There would be no whiskey for Little Bit that night.

You may think that Manny Clements was harsh, ignoring me like that, and indeed he was, but he was a product of his time and place, a hard man bred to a hard land where fighting men were esteemed above all others. In Texas in those days such men drank whiskey but in Manny's eyes I was far from being any kind of a man. He would not waste Old Crow on such as me.

No, he was not being cruel.

If you'd asked Manny why there was no whiskey for Little Bit, he would be surprised by your question, just as he was surprised that I'd even made such request in the first place.

I was not worthy. Simple as that.

A crippled little nonentity learns to live with hurts of all kinds, so now I'll drop the matter and say no more about it.

After the jailbreak, Wes decided to remain in Gonzales County among friends, and I rode with him to a tiny burg named Coon Hollow where he met up with his wife again.

Jane, who was heavy with Wes's child at the time, took me aside. "Little Bit, John will be a man with a family soon, and I want you to talk to him."

"About what, Jane?" I was surprised at the request. Mrs. Hardin had always made it clear by word, thought, and deed that she didn't have much time for me.

"About settling down." Her pretty little face creased with worry. "I don't want my husband to get shot again. The next time could be his last." She lightly touched her fingertips to my wrist. "I know he'll listen to you."

I wanted to say, *When did Wes ever listen to me?* but I didn't. Instead I said, "Jane, Wes is talking about splitting his time between Karnes and Gonzales Counties."

"He didn't tell me that," Jane said, her quick temper flaring.

"Wes didn't tell you because he says you've got enough to deal with right now, what with the baby coming and all."

It was a barefaced lie. Wes had said no such thing. But it worked.

Jane's face relaxed and she smiled. "He's a good husband, isn't he?"

"The best," I said. Another lie then a kernel of truth to support my claim to his worth as a husband. "Now that he has responsibilities, Wes plans to buy and sell cattle and rope and brand mavericks. He's even talking about making another drive to Kansas."

Jane just stared into my eyes and said nothing, so I threw in a kicker. "And, of course, he wants to get his Wild West show off the ground and moving. He says it will make us millionaires."

"He's talked to me about that before. Do you think it's possible?"

"More than possible, Jane, probable."

"What about the law? All those men they say John killed?"

"Jane, Wes never killed a man except in defense of himself or others. Of course, the law can make him stand trial, but a Texas jury will never convict him."

"Can I believe you, Little Bit? You're offering me hope."

"Yes, you can believe me," I said, assuming my sincere face. "You and Wes will grow

299

old together and spoil your grandchildren."

So I spun a fairytale that lit up Jane's eyes and if the circumstances had been different it might even have come true. Who knows?

But that very night a grim Manny Clements walked into the house . . . and called in favors. He made war talk with John Wesley . . . and the stage was set for Wes's long, tortuous descent into madness and death.

CHAPTER FORTY:
THE SUTTON-TAYLOR FEUD

John Wesley had tried to stay aloof from the vicious Sutton-Taylor feud that was tearing Texas apart. But with the coming of Manny Clements he could no longer stand aside. Family honor was at stake.

The Suttons were murderous, carpetbagging trash who had already shot down many members of the Taylor clan in cold blood.

William E. Sutton, a former Confederate soldier and turncoat, got himself appointed as a state police force sergeant under Captain Jack Helm. This unholy duo was given command of a detachment of Union troops, and they received but one order from Washington. CRUSH THE REBEL SCUM AND ENFORCE RECONSTRUCTION AT BAYONET POINT.

Pitkin Taylor, a brave man and patriot, brother of a renowned Texas Ranger, could not let this stand. He vowed to resist with fire and sword the Suttons, their Yankee al-

301

lies, and all their evil schemes . . . and thus the feud that in the end would claim two hundred lives was born.

Wes, that gallant Southern cavalier, rode forth with the Clements brothers to stamp out William Sutton, his works, and all his vile brood.

And I tagged along.

Despite the war raging around him, Wes continued to seek additional markets for his cattle and on April 9, 1873, his search put us on the trail to the town of Cuero in De-Witt County. The settlement was prospering, three new hotels were under construction, and Wes assumed there would be a demand for beef.

We were still almost a score of miles south of Cuero when a heavily armed rider appeared on our back trail. Behind him trailed three others, but those looked like respectable cattlemen and I saw no arms on them.

I made the decision right there and then that their leader was either a lawman or a desperado. Because of the feud, he could well be both.

When the man got close and touched his hat, Wes drew rein. "Good morning. A fine day is it not?"

The rider, a tall, thin man with a long,

joyless face and bleak blue eyes did not return the greeting. He wore two Colts at his waist and the stock of a new Henry rifle poked out from under his knee. "Do you live around here?"

"No," Wes said. "I'm heading for Cuero on a business trip."

"Me too," the stranger said. "To find a blacksmith shop. My horse threw a shoe back a ways." The man had the eyes of a buzzard.

I didn't trust him.

I trusted him even less when he said, "Name's Jack Helm. I'm the sheriff of De-Witt County. These men are traveling under my protection."

"You're the sheriff . . . among other things." When he spoke like that, low and flat and unfriendly, John Wesley was the most dangerous man on earth.

Maybe Helm, damn him for a black-hearted Suttonite, sensed this because he managed a slight smile when he said, "And you are?"

Wes gave his name.

"Pleased to meet you after all this time, Mr. Hardin." Helm extended his hand for a howdy-do, which Wes ignored.

"You're not facing a frightened woman or child now, Helm, but a Southern gentleman, face-to-face," Wes said. "I heard you've called me a murderer and a coward and have ordered your deputies to shoot me on sight." Wes opened his coat and revealed his revolvers. "Well, now you've got your chance. Shuck the iron and open the ball."

Helm's face paled and his voice was unsteady. "John Wesley, I'm not your enemy. I'm your friend."

Suddenly Wes's guns were in his hands. "You're no friend of mine. You belong to a band of murdering scum who have killed better men than yourself."

I swear that Wes's eyes glowed like candles in blue ice.

"Your killing days are over, Helm, so shuck the iron and defend yourself or I'll shoot you down like a dog."

The sky was dark blue, the breeze cool and birds sang in the trees. It was not a good day to die.

And Helm knew it. "John Wesley, you're too brave a man to shoot me down in cold blood. I want you to join my vigilante group in ridding our land of rustlers, killers, and all manner of low persons."

"Hear-hear," one of the respectable cattlemen said. "Let us shed our differences and continue to Cuero in peace and good fellowship."

To my surprise, Wes holstered his guns. "Helm, when we reach Cuero, we'll talk of this again."

Now there are them who say that the whole affair was a setup, arranged by Helm and Wes. They say that Wes's dark personality had long since abandoned every shred of honor and loyalty and that he wanted to change sides for his personal gain.

That Helm brought along three witnesses to attest to John Wesley's change of heart meant that they would also be present when the sheriff outlined to Wes what he would gain, legally and financially.

Obviously the supposed bait was a full pardon for past crimes and large donations of money from the Sutton faction, many of them quite wealthy.

But I don't believe a word of it.

Wes wanted to kill Jack Helm, an evil scoundrel, real bad, but at the last moment he decided it shouldn't be done in front of three respectable witnesses whose testimony could hang him.

That is the simple explanation of why Wes lowered his lance and backed down.

And it is the right one . . . as future events would reveal.

Wes and Jack Helm did talk again in Cuero,

at the corner of Hunt Street and Morgan Avenue, but few words passed between them.

All Wes said to me later was, "Helm would have to do a whole lot of work to get me clear of trouble. And I would have to do a whole lot of work for him in return."

I didn't pursue the matter because another dramatic event overtook us in the form of an Irishman bent on suicide, who chose John Wesley as the instrument of his self-destruction.

It was such a pathetic, useless death that it passed largely unnoticed at a time when belted, feuding men were dying violently all over Texas.

CHAPTER FORTY-ONE: "PIMM'S ALL ROUND!"

The suicide death come up after John Wesley spoke to Helm. We stepped into a saloon in Cuero Square where a noisy poker game was in progress. Wes sat at the table, asked for cards, and I stood at the bar and bought whiskey with the dollar he'd given me.

We'd done some long riding recently and my leg was playing hob. My wound had gathered into a head then burst and I felt blood and pus seep down my leg. I felt most unwell and the only medicine that helped was whiskey, the stronger and rawer the better.

I had never been a big eater and the notion that food might boost my strength never entered into my thinking.

It had gone noon but the sun merely smoldered sullenly in the spring sky and the day was cool, fanned by an east wind. It was one of those strange, Texas days when a man could step from winter to summer just by crossing the street from shade into light.

I have always been of the opinion that an east wind drives men mad. I believe Gettysburg was fought in such a wind, and was not that the greatest madness of all?

It seemed that the wind had worked its dark sorcery on the unfortunate Irishman.

Wes had just won a five-dollar pot when the suicidal son of Erin jumped up from the table, did a little jig, and declared that the winner must buy, "Pimm's all round!"

Wes merely smiled. "Perhaps, if I win a few more hands."

The Irishman's ruddy face was covered with broken veins that looked like tributaries of blood. "Now!" he yelled. "Pimm's for everybody or, by Christ, I'll take a stick to ye."

The bartender hammered a glass on the counter. "Here, Morgan, the man doesn't want to buy drinks. Remember that you're a deputy sheriff of this county and act the gentleman."

When Wes heard this, he threw down his cards and stepped outside.

Only later did I learn that J.B. Morgan, a stonemason by trade, was a Suttonite thug who'd been hired by Jack Helm to terrorize the Taylor patriots of DeWitt County.

Wes had entered the poker game under

the alias of Mr. Johnson, but did Morgan know his true identity?

Of course he did.

Everybody in Cuero knew the famous shootist John Wesley Hardin was in town.

Then why did Morgan brace a known mankiller?

Bear this in mind. The hatreds engendered by the Sutton-Taylor feud ran deep and I believe to this day that Morgan threw away his own life to bring down Wes.

In fact, he succeeded all too well.

After a few minutes quiet contemplation, John Wesley stepped into the saloon again.

Morgan, still belligerent, immediately confronted him. "Here you. Are you going heeled?"

"I'm armed, yes." Wes was so polite and quiet you'd have thought he was accepting an invite to tea by old Queen Vic herself.

"Well, then it's time you thought about defending yourself," said Morgan, that willful blackguard. He brushed aside his high-button coat and made a show of reaching into the back pocket of his pants.

"Get your hand away from there," Wes ordered.

"I never carry a gun in my pocket," Morgan said.

Wes drew and fired. A bullet crashed into

Morgan's face, just below his left eye.

The man had time to throw up his hands and scream, "Oh God, he's murdered me!" Then he fell to the sawdust-covered floor, dead as a rotten stump.

Through a gray drift of smoke, Wes looked around the saloon, then said to the bartender, "Pimm's all round."

But no one took him up on his generous offer.

CHAPTER FORTY-TWO:
WES PLANS A MURDER

The killing of Morgan placed John Wesley firmly in the Taylor camp, and me too, of course, not that anybody much cared. Their need was for fighting men, and on that score I didn't qualify.

I did however acquire a notebook and pencil and began to write what would become my first published dime novel, a saga of how Wes stopped a train robbery, saved a virgin in peril of being undone, and tracked down and killed the outlaws.

As I will do throughout this narrative, I'm pleased to give you the title of the novel, so you can pick it up wherever fine books are sold and read it at your leisure. *Captain Hardin to the Rescue,* or *The Maiden On The Train Of Doom.* Wes was newly incarcerated in federal prison when the novel was published, but he read it and liked it so much he declared it, "Crackerjack!"

I've written many more books since, but

that's the one that will always remain in my memory, mostly because of its enthusiastic reception by John Wesley.

As I've said, Wes had thrown in with the Taylors body and soul, but this fact was unknown to Jack Helm who invited him to a parley in the town of Albuquerque, a bustling settlement in western Gonzales County.

In part, the letter Helm sent declared that, "Albuquerque is my town, John, and I am cock o' the walk. Come quickly that we may discuss our urgent business at hand."

Wes had just met members of the Taylor clan, including Jim Taylor, a man with an abiding hatred for Jack Helm and the oppression he stood for. We sat in the front room of his ranch house.

"I say you accept the invite, Wes," Taylor said. "We can get rid of that damned Yankee turncoat once and for all."

For once in his life, Wes was wary. "You read what he said, Jim, that Albuquerque is his town. Helm is an important man and we could face a lynch mob."

Taylor wasn't intimidated in the least. "I'll do the killing, Wes. Just be there to back me up if need be." He jutted his chin in my direction. "And him."

"Little Bit doesn't carry a gun," Wes said.

312

Taylor nodded, his face empty. "No, I don't suppose he does."

"Helm needs killing," Wes said. "Am I right in saying that?"

"Damn right you're right," Taylor said. "Kill him and we'll tear the guts right out of the Suttons." He picked up his whiskey glass, put it to his lips, and said over the rim, "Are you game, Wes?"

John Wesley hesitated for only a moment. "I'm always game. We'll ride up that way at first light tomorrow."

Taylor looked at me. "You?"

I was flattered that a member of the fighting Taylor clan even noticed me. "I'll ride with you."

"Then it's all set," Taylor said. "We'll gun Jack Helm tomorrow."

I was horrified and couldn't just sit there and keep my mouth shut. The whiskey I'd drank helped. "Wes, kill Helm and there can be no going back from it."

"What the hell do you mean?" Taylor asked.

"Helm is a big man in Texas and he has powerful friends, including the army," I said. "I don't think they'd take his death lightly."

"Hell, you can stay behind." Taylor cut me a slit-eyed look. "You wouldn't be much

313

help anyway."

"Helm can die like any other man and no one will mourn him." Wes perched on the edge of his chair like a bird of prey, all his arrogance on show. He shook his head, a slight smile on his lips. "Little Bit, why do I keep you around? You're the gloomiest cuss I ever knew."

Taylor said, "You don't keep him around for the laughs, that's fer sure."

"Wes, I beg you. Don't kill Jack Helm. It will be an ill-done thing." As one last yelp of despair, I said, "Think of your wife and child. Think of the Wild West show."

"The show can wait until the Suttons are all dead," Wes said. "Anyway, I'm thinking of selling the idea, like I'd sell a cow or a horse, except for a sight more money."

"Wes, I heard talk about your Wild West show idea," Taylor said. "I'd surely admire to be in it."

"Well, if I don't sell it, I'll make sure there's a place for you, Jim." Wes turned his attention to me. "Little Bit, you look peaked. I'm leaving you behind tomorrow."

Our eyes locked and I opened my mouth to speak.

Wes shut it for me. "Don't argue. Just do as you're told."

Taylor grinned. "Hell, Wes, pop a cap on

him and put the little feller out of his misery."

"The whiskey will do that soon enough," Wes said.

It was not a thing a friend should say.

CHAPTER FORTY-THREE: THE DEATH OF JACK HELM

"One day, in a playful mood, John Wesley Hardin gave Sheriff Jack Helm a broadside . . . and sunk him."

That's how a Texas Ranger summed up the killing of Helm to his superiors.

He was only half right.

The way John Wesley told it later, him and Jim Taylor rode into Albuquerque and found Helm in the blacksmith's shop, toiling at the anvil. He was part owner of the forge and enjoyed working with iron. He was hammering a glowing knife blade into shape when Wes and Taylor saw him.

Wes said, "Then suddenly I heard Helm scream at Jim, 'Hold up there because I mean to arrest you!' "

Now, since Helm had never met Jim Taylor I don't see how that was possible.

But John Wesley may have misspoken himself. In reality, the vile threat was hurled at him since he'd so steadfastly refused to

316

join the traitorous Suttonite faction.

I do know this. Helm plunged the red hot knife into a barrel of water, and no sooner had it stopped steaming and sizzling than he advanced on Taylor, the *brutish blade* held low for a gutting.

Alarmed, Wes said he watched Helm close on Taylor. "I carried a shotgun because Jack Helm was known to be a dangerous man with a gun and had put many lively Taylor lads into the grave."

To save Taylor's life, Wes cut loose with one barrel of the shotgun. Helm, hit hard, staggered, and Jim Taylor opened up with his revolver.

"Helm fell with twelve buckshot in his chest and several six-shooter balls in his head," Wes recalled in his autobiography. "Thus did the leader of the vigilante committee, the terror of the county whose name was a horror to all law-abiding citizens, meet his death."

So you see why I say the Ranger was only half right.

Wes and Taylor shared the kill, though Wes would later claim it as his thirty-ninth.

Jack Helm was bleeding all over the ground, gasping his last when Wes and Taylor rode out of town.

Nobody tried to stop them.

■ ■ ■ ■

When Wes returned to Gonzales County the word quickly spread that he'd killed the hated Jack Helm. Letters of thanks poured into Wes's ranch from the wives, widows, and mothers of Helm's many victims, and men patted him on the back and said, "John, killing Helm was the finest thing you ever did in your life."

And me, miserable little weasel that I was, once again bathed in the reflected light of John Wesley's glory and convinced myself that I was indeed a man and counted myself lucky to have such a friend.

CHAPTER FORTY-FOUR: TERROR BY NIGHT

I believe that John Wesley wanted to separate himself from the Sutton-Taylor feud and he'd even talked of trying to broker a peace treaty between the two factions. Despite his best intentions, the fighting still raged, and *hooded nightriders* spread terror across south and central Texas, killing, maiming, and burning by the light of the moon.

Others took advantage of the chaos and rode moonlit trails for their own personal gain. The worst of them were the murderous Roche brothers, a trio of killers so fiendish that Wes refused to take any credit for his part in their ultimate destruction.

Now, for all the doubters who say John Wesley was a common killer, the story I'm about to narrate reveals Wes at his best. As I saw him, he was a noble knight in sable armor who sallied forth to right wrong wherever he found it.

My dire predictions about the consequences of Jack Helm's murder had not yet come true, but Wes, wary of the Suttons and their nightriders, had sent his wife and baby daughter to Comanche in Central Texas to live with his younger brother Joe, a successful young lawyer.

It was the midnight hour, a couple days before the eve of Christ's birth. Outside the night was cool and the bright moonlight covered the ground like a frost.

Wes and I sat before a blazing log in his parlor, sharing a bottle of fine port wine. Despite suffering from a severe attack of bronchitis, I felt happy and privileged.

Jane would never allow me to remain long in the house. She said she could smell me and my diseased leg from two rooms away.

Wes, who was drowsing in his chair, woke with a start as hoof beats sounded outside, then a horse whinnied as it was reined to a violent stop. "Nightriders."

He leapt from his chair, grabbed his pistols and stepped to the window. As he pushed the curtain aside to take a look into the darkness, fists pounded on the front door.

"John Wesley!" a man yelled. "It's me, Andy Conlan."

Wes threw me a quick glance. "He's one of ours."

"Or somebody impersonating his voice," I said.

Made wary by my warning, Wes left the parlor and a moment later I heard the door open.

This was followed by a man's squeal of fright. "Wes, don't shoot for God's sake! It's me, old Andy Conlan as ever was."

Wes said something I couldn't hear. The door closed and Conlan stepped into the parlor.

He was a man of late middle years, short and stocky, and he sported a beard that spread over the chest of his wool mackinaw like a gray fan and at some time or other a bullet had clipped an arc out of the top of his left ear. He looked like a man who'd just seen the devil himself and he shivered, from cold or fear I did not know.

Wes put his guns back on the table, then poured whiskey for Conlan. "Drink this. Then tell me why you're disturbing a man's peace in the middle of the night."

Conlan gulped the whiskey. "Wes, a terrible thing has happened. A horrible thing."

Wes waited for a moment, then said, "So horrible you're not going to tell me about it?"

As though he was indeed reluctant to relive the frightening memories that lingered in his mind's eye, Conlan said, "Wes, you know me. I was a mountain man, then an army scout. I fit Injuns and I seen what the Comanche and the Apache can do to a man." He drained his glass. "This was worse, a sight worse than anything I seen."

"Tell it, Andy." Wes glanced at the china clock on the mantle. "It's gone midnight."

Conlan held out his glass. "Fill this first, Wes. Me pipe is dry as a stick, like, and I'm nervous as a whore in church."

Wes poured more whiskey, waited until Conlan drank, then said again, "Tell it, Andy."

"Late this afternoon I rode to the Goodson place —"

"On Dead Deer Creek?" Wes said.

"The very same, though now it's more dry wash than creek."

Wes waited and Conlan said, "When I got there it was already dark, but I figured I could stay the night, the Goodsons being such nice folks."

"What was your business there?" Wes asked.

"Sam Goodson had a Mulefoot sow for sale, and I figured I would buy it if'n the price was right."

"So what happened?"

"You know Sam is ages with me, and he

322

wed that pretty young Walker gal from the Trinity River country," Conlan said. "How old was she . . . fourteen . . . fifteen?" The old mountain man laid down his glass and rubbed the back of his hand across his eyes, banishing images.

Once more, I must implore the ladies, especially those of a nervous disposition, to pass over the next few paragraphs with closed eyes.

"The girl was heavy with child." Conlan hesitated a heartbeat, then said, "Ask me how I know that."

Wes didn't ask, nor did I.

But Conlan told it anyway. "Because the living child was torn out of her belly and thrown in the fire. That's how come I know."

The crackle of the log in the fireplace and the timid tick of the china clock were the only sounds in the room.

"The girl?" It was a silly question, but I needed to break the deafening silence.

"Dead," Conlan said. "Strung by her long hair from a crossbeam. Sam was hanging by his heels since both his hands had been burned to the bone. He was tortured because the three killers wanted something. I would guess his money and the few valuables he possessed."

Ladies, my compliments. You may reenter

the story from here.

Wes frowned. "How do you know there were three of them?"

"I was a scout, remember?"

"Damned Suttons. They'll pay for this, by God."

Conlan shook his head, almost sadly. "It wasn't the Suttons, Wes. Trash they may be, but they wouldn't treat a white woman like that. No man with even a shred of decency would."

"Then who?" I said.

"Wolves in the guise of men," Conlan said. "That's my guess."

"I'm going after them," Wes said. "I'll kill them all for Sam, who was a Taylor man through and through."

"Be careful, Wes, and remember what they say," Conlan said. "Never trust a wolf until it's skun."

"You can remind me of that on the trail, Andy," Wes said. "On account of you're going with me."

Conlan was horrified. "Wes, it will be close work in darkness. I'm not a revolver fighter like you."

"I know, and I'm not a scout like you," Wes said. "Find me those three men, Andy. That's all I ask. I'll do the rest."

"Maybe we should round up a few more

men and pick up their trail in the morning," Conlan said.

"How far ahead of us are they?" Wes said.

"Three, maybe four hours."

"Then we go now. It's cold, and they'll
probably hole up somewhere for the night."

Conlan thought that through then said,
"I'll find them, Wes. But I'll leave the gun
fighting to you."

"Of course you will," Wes said, smiling.
"That's my game."

CHAPTER FORTY-FIVE: DEATH IN THE MEADOW

"Damn it, Little Bit, quit that coughing," John Wesley snapped at me. "I don't know why the hell you insisted on coming along."

I stifled a cough. "Sorry."

"Sorry don't cut it," Andy Conlan said, his voice stressed. "You'll get us all killed."

The three of us rode under a full moon through shallow hills and among pines. The light was cold and white, as though we travelled through an ice cave. The old scout led us to the dry wash that had ceased to be a creek maybe a score of years before, and there were pale skeletons of dead trees on both banks.

Conlan followed the wash's looping course that took us to within twenty yards of the Goodson cabin. The place was dark, ghostly, and achingly lonely now that the people who'd lived there were gone.

"You want to see in there, Wes?" Conlan asked, his face shadowed by his hat.

"No, we'll come back and bury them."

Conlan spoke to himself. "Ground's like iron."

"Pick up their trail, Andy," Wes said.

This time Conlan said it aloud. "Ground's like iron."

"You've tracked men across iron before," Wes said.

The old man nodded. "I'd say I have. Let's go."

For the next two hours, across dark country, we rode in silence, except for my strangled, gurgling coughs.

Andy Conlan broke the quiet twice to tell us he'd seen bad omens. Once a crow that shouldn't have been there flapped over his head and his horse shied at a dead coyote.

He turned to me in the saddle. "The crow is death's scout and the dead coyote means that the grim reaper passed this way and touched the animal."

Wes grinned and his teeth gleamed. "Stand behind me when the shooting starts, Andy. I'll gun ol' death before he lays a bony finger on you."

"Death can't be stilled and he can't be killed." Conlan held a red, coral rosary in his fingers.

Wes laughed. "Hell, man. There ain't nothin' a Colt can't kill."

The sinking moon had spiked itself on a nearby pine when Conlan drew rein, tilted back his head, and tested the wind. "Smoke," he whispered.

"How close?" Wes said, his own voice quiet.

"Close."

The old mountain man made a motion with his hand. "Climb down. We go the rest of the way on foot."

Wes was the greatest pistol fighter who ever lived, but he'd taken the precaution of jamming a shotgun into the rifle boot. He slid the gun free then said, "Let's get it done."

Conlan shook his head. "This is as far as I go, Wes." He indicated with his bladed right hand. "They're camped in that direction, maybe a hundred yards, maybe less."

"Three. You're sure?" Wes asked again.

"Three men riding shod ponies," Conlan said. "Yeah, I'm sure."

Wes pointed a finger at me. "Little Bit, you stay here with Andy. This will be hot work and dangerous."

Without another word, Wes turned and silently vanished into the darkness.

Of course, I girded up my old army great-coat and followed.

I kept my distance from Wes, knowing that if he saw me he'd send me back. My iron leg ensured that I was no Dan'l Boone in the woods, but I stepped as quietly as I could.

The smell of smoke grew stronger and somewhere ahead of me in the gloom I heard men yell and laugh, the whiskey-fueled, false merriment I knew so well from the saloons.

Around me the pines thinned and I walked into a clearing about as big as a hotel room. Moonlight dappled the grass and silvered a boulder to my left. A wind whispered in the trees and a thin mist hovered at the limit of my vision.

I walked on, stepped around the boulder, and froze as a gun muzzle shoved into my left temple, just under my bowler hat.

A muffled curse came as Wes holstered his Colt. He grabbed me by the front of my coat and his fierce, stiff face got close to mine. He didn't speak, but his eyes were burning. Finally, he pushed me violently away from him with so much force I stumbled back and fell on my butt.

Then Wes was gone, moving like a ghost through the pines.

Like a whipped puppy, I picked myself up and humbly followed . . . my master.

It was my ill luck on that star-crossed night that I should stumble over a tree root and lose my footing. I staggered forward and crashed into Wes who was standing at the edge of a small, wildflower meadow.

Off balance, he stumbled forward . . . into a gunfight . . . at a time not of his choosing.

My feeble, sputtering pen cannot do justice to what happened next.

It all came down too fast, one flickering image following rapidly after another, like a demented magic lantern show.

I saw two men sitting by the campfire, tussling over a plain gold ring, yelling and laughing as they pulled each other back and forth.

The third man, standing by the horses saw Wes, cried out and charged at a run, a gun in his hand.

Wes let him have both barrels of the scattergun. Screaming, exploding, blood haloing around him, the man fell.

Wes threw down the shotgun and drew his Colts. The man on his left, a towhead wearing a fur coat, got to his feet and scrabbled for his gun. Wes killed him.

The third man rolled, jumped to his feet, his gun in his hand. He emptied his Colt at

Wes. Missed with all five.

Wes fired. The ball slammed into the corner of the man's left eye. He went down hard, then chewed up the ground with his kicking, booted feet. Another shot from Wes and the scoundrel lay still.

Three men dead . . . in the time it takes a grandfather clock to chime five.

Smoke drifted across the meadow as though the gray souls of the dead men were rising from their corpses.

As I stepped into the meadow, Wes glanced at the three bodies, then said, "White trash." He turned his head slowly in my direction. "They didn't know how to fight."

"Do you recognize any of them, Wes?" I asked.

He shook his head and walked over to one of the dead men.

I went after him.

"Look at that face," he said.

Indeed the man looked strange, small piggy eyes, slack mouth, and lopsided forehead, the temples hollow.

"Know what that is?" Wes didn't wait for my answer. "That's inbreeding. His mother couldn't run fast enough to get away from her brothers." He looked around him. "The other two are just as bad. Andy was right, they're not Suttons, just murdering scum."

Given my stunted body and deformed leg, I figured my own ancestry was nothing to boast of, so I kept my mouth shut.

"Little Bit, keep this between us. I won't take credit for shooting down . . . shooting down —"

"Cretins," I said.

Wes nodded. "Yeah, cretins." He smiled. "I don't know what the hell it means, but it's a top shelf word."

"I'll be silent, but will Andy Conlan keep his mouth shut?"

"If he knows what's good for him he will," Wes said.

As it turned out I needn't have worried about it . . . Conlan's mouth was shut forever. Struck in the head by a stray bullet, we found him dead beside his grazing horse.

Death is a black dog that barks at every man's door and Conlan read the signs and knew it was coming. He could not have avoided the bullet that passed through ten acres of trees and killed him because death had his name marked down in his book.

And there's my explanation for it.

Conlan had a wife and kids, so Wes collected the ponies of the dead men, their guns, and the twenty-seven dollars he found in their pockets and later gave it all to the widow. He told her that Andy had been murdered by Sutton nightriders.

Before I close this chapter of my narrative and move on to other adventures in Wes's life, let me just say that I broke my word to him and told about the three cretins he killed only because John Wesley is dead and it doesn't matter any longer.

We didn't bury the bodies in the Goodson cabin.

Wes said, "Let somebody else do it. The ground is too hard to dig graves and they'll need dynamite."

But he did keep Mrs. Goodson's wedding band, the ring the trash had been squabbling over, and gave it to his wife as a gift.

My hero knight deserved a trophy, did he not?

CHAPTER FORTY-SIX:
THE KILLING OF
CHARLIE WEBB

In late January 1874, John Wesley joined his wife in Comanche and I was reacquainted with his brother Joe, a man I'd always liked. He was a slim young lawyer with a lovely wife and a thriving legal practice. He was well respected in Comanche and owned a large amount of property in the town. Jane was not happy to see me.

Much later, she didn't object when I celebrated the last weekend in May with the Hardin family.

The town fathers had declared the date a festival, and Comanche was going full blast. The saloons, splitting at the seams, roared and throngs of people patronized the racetrack.

Wes entered his American stud, Rondo, in several races and the big horse won easily, earning him three thousand dollars, fifty head of cattle, fifteen saddle horses and a

Studebaker wagon. Naturally, a celebration followed and the rum punches flowed freely.

The day shaded into night and the lamps were lit around the town square. Jane and most of the other friends and family called it a day, but Wes, Jim Taylor, and myself decided to celebrate further. Drunk, we staggered into Jack Wright's saloon where Wes tossed a double eagle onto the counter and ordered drinks all round. We were noisy and boisterous certainly, but not belligerent.

Wes was friendly to everyone and even pressed a second gold coin into the hand of a saloon girl who had a birthday that night.

But trouble soon appeared in the form of Comanche deputy sheriff Frank Wilson, a decent sort, who'd also been drinking. He stepped beside Wes and put his hand on his arm. "John, the people of this town have treated you well, have they not?"

Wes, grinning, admitted that they had and said he had his racetrack winnings to prove it.

"Then don't drink anymore. Go home to your wife and avoid trouble," Wilson said. His eyes narrowing a little, he added, "You know it is a violation of the law to carry a pistol."

For some reason, in my drunken state, I

took exception to this statement and pushed between Wilson and Wes. "Leave us the hell alone. We're not bothering anyone."

Wilson stared at me for a moment as though trying to figure out what species I was, then his balled fist came down like a sledgehammer on the top of my bowler, ramming it down over my eyes.

I staggered around, trying to push the damned thing off my head.

This brought cheers, jeers, and laughter from the crowd and more than a few empty bottles were thrown in my direction.

Finally, I grabbed the brim in both hands and shoved upward with all my strength. My head popped free of the bowler like a cork out of a bottle and I could see again. I caught Wes's look of utter disdain.

He focused on the deputy again. "Frank, my pistols are behind the bar. Out of sight, out of mind, as my ma says." Wes didn't mention that hideout gun he carried under his vest.

"Leave the weapons right here, John," Wilson said. "Pick them up in the morning and stay for breakfast."

Jim Taylor, drunk as a skunk himself, pleaded with Wes to go home. In the end, he agreed, saying that the evening had lost its snap anyhow.

"Remember to let the guns stay behind the bar, John," Wilson said. "Pick them up in the morning and then have breakfast. You haven't lived until you've tasted Jack's biscuits and gravy."

Things might have ended amicably . . . but outside a predator stalked the night, a man with an overinflated ego and a yearning to be known as a *pistola rapida*.

Brown County Deputy Sheriff Charlie Webb was a two-gun man. He carried his new-fangled Single Action Army Colts in crossed gun belts, the holsters finely carved in a flowered pattern. He was said to have killed four white men and a Negro, and his fine mustache and dashing good looks impressed the ladies when he cut a dash.

I believe that Webb was looking for trouble that night and had selected John Wesley as his target. Killing Wes was a way to enhance his reputation and establish himself as a dangerous man with a gun.

How it come up, Webb had been pacing up and down outside the saloon and walked within a few feet of Wes who stood on the boardwalk with me, Jim Taylor, and Bud Dixon, Wes's cousin.

For some reason the sight of Webb irritated Wes. "Have you any papers for my arrest?"

"Easy, Wes," Dixon said. Then to Webb, "That man has friends in this town and won't be arrested."

"Hell, man, I don't know you," Webb said to Wes.

"My name is John Wesley Hardin and I come from good Texas stock."

"Well, now we've been introduced, I remember the name," Webb said. "But I still don't have an arrest warrant."

"You're holding something behind your back." Wes was on edge and sobering rapidly.

"Only a ten-cent stogie." Webb produced the cigar, its tip glowing red in the gloom.

I saw Wes relax. Now he was prepared to be friendly. "Come, join us for a drink, Deputy Webb. A hot gin punch is warming on such a chilly evening."

"By all means," Webb said, smiling.

Wes turned to reenter the saloon — and I saw Webb's hands drop for his guns.

"Look out, Wes!" I shrieked.

John Wesley turned as Webb fired. The lawman's bullet burned across Wes's ribs on his left side, ripping a gash in his coat and his skin.

Wes instantly returned fire and his ball hit

338

Webb in the face, just below his left eye.

Cursing, his mouth running blood, Webb took a step back and fired again.

His bullet splintered wood from the sidewalk between Wes's feet.

Jim Taylor and Bud Dixon cut loose. Their .44 balls tore great holes through Webb's body and he fell dead.

Thus perished an arrogant man whose gun skills fell far short of his ambitions. I shed no tears for him.

Within a couple minutes of Webb's death, all hell broke loose. The news of Webb's death was carried through the town like a fiery cross. Comanche spawned a ravening pack of vigilantes yelling, "Hang the killers!" The bloodthirsty mob rushed Wes and his stalwarts, myself included, only to be driven off by a rattle of pistol fire.

Recently appointed Comanche sheriff John Carnes rushed to the scene, just as the vigilantes launched another attack.

Believing, I'm sure, that a fine man like John Wesley didn't deserve to be the guest of honor at a hemp party, Carnes held off the mob with a scattergun.

Fearlessly, Wes handed his gun to Carnes. "It was not my fault, John. Webb tried to murder me, but I didn't think things would come to such a pass."

"Get the hell into the saloon and stay there. This situation could get out of hand real fast." Carnes turned to me. "You too, Peckerwood, go with them. And if you've got any prayers, this would be a good time to say them."

Scared, my weak bladder betrayed me as I scrambled into the saloon after Wes and the others. I was almost knocked over as the crowd inside stampeded for the door and a saloon girl with yellow hair and big blue eyes pushed me aside and yelled, "Get the hell out of my way, gimp!"

From somewhere inside I heard Wes shout, "The side door!"

The noise in the street had risen to a roar as men demanded Wes's head. I heard Carnes plead with them to calm down and he vowed that he would see *justice done.*

Throwing tables and chairs aside, I limped to the side door in time to see Wes and Jim Taylor in the alley outside, swinging into the saddles of horses they didn't own.

"Wes!" I screamed. "Wait for me!" I was terrified of hanging, and my despairing wail sounded frantic, even to my own ears.

Wes saw me, heard me, ignored me. He galloped out of the alley into the street, but Jim Taylor, a big and strong man, leaned from the saddle, grabbed me by the back of my coat and threw me on a horse. Then he too was gone.

The paint I straddled didn't like the feel of my steel leg and he bucked a few times. But I managed to grab the reins and leave the alley at a dead run.

Bullets split the air around me as I followed Wes's dust, a billowing cloud tinted orange by the street's reflector lamps. I glanced behind and saw John Wesley's wife in the street, a handkerchief to her eyes. Beside her stood his father with his brother Joe, both holding shotguns.

Then I was beyond the town, galloping into the night.

I allowed the paint to pick his way since I don't see real well in darkness. After half an hour I caught up to the others who sat their blown horses outside a burned out cabin.

Wes grinned at me. "You made it, Little Bit."

"No thanks to you," I said, feeling mean and petty as I uttered the words.

"In a situation like that, it's every man for himself," Wes said. "If you didn't know that before, you sure as hell know it now."

"Truer words was never spoke," Jim Taylor said.

A strange thought popped into my head as I sat silent in the saddle after listening to

Wes and Dixon. *How many of his precious cattle would Wes give to save my life?*

No matter how I studied on it, up, down, sideways, I came to the same conclusion.

The answer, that liked to break my heart, was *none.*

CHAPTER FORTY-SEVEN: WES PLANS REVENGE

Anger over the killing of Charlie Webb was out of all proportion to the worth of the man himself.

Wes had shot Webb in self-defense. Everybody knew that except the town fathers of Comanche and their damn, foaming-at-the-mouth citizens. The imbeciles even sent a letter of complaint to Governor Coke demanding a strong force of Texas Rangers to rid their county "of murderers and thieves led by the notorious John Wesley Hardin."

Wes was no murderer and although he lifted stray cattle and horses now and then, he was not a thief. However, he had managed to rope in a couple cousins who supported him in this matter.

The authorities, aided and abetted by vengeful Yankees, thrust Wes into the same category as the Mexican bandits who came up from the Rio Grande to kill and plunder.

It was an outrage.

But worse was to follow.

A force of fifty Rangers arrived in Comanche with orders to hunt down "the John Wesley Hardin gang of murderers who are preying on the citizens of this county."

Wes was enraged. "Call those Rangers what they are. A vigilante band leading a mob composed of the enemies of law and order."

We were living rough in the brush, every man's hand turned against us, when Wes got news that his wife and many of his relatives and friends had been taken into "protective custody" and were locked up in a two story rock house in Comanche.

That was the straw that broke the camel's back.

Wes huddled with Jim Taylor and they made war plans.

After a while, they called the rest of us over and we sat around a spitting fire in a cold, drizzling rain, surrounded by a tangle of scrub oak, thorn briar, and thickets of poison ivy.

"We follow the lead of the great Bloody Bill Anderson and raid into Comanche," Wes said. "We'll free my wife and my father, then teach those turncoats and Yankees a lesson they'll never forget."

"He was a rum one, was Bill," Wes's

344

cousin Ham Anderson said. "He'd kill them all, like he done in Lawrence, Kansas that time."

"And so will we," Wes said. "Except the women and children. We're Southern patriots fighting Yankee tyranny, not the murderers of innocents."

"Hear, hear," Jim Taylor said.

And me, caught up in the moment, exclaimed, "Huzzah!"

Anderson glared at me, the skin of his young face tight to the bone. He didn't like me. "You only get to say that when you bear arms like a man."

Wes smiled. "Let him be, Ham. Little Bit is one of us."

"To the death," I said.

But nobody listened to me or cared.

"When do we hit them, Wes?" Taylor asked.

"In a couple days. We need a few more men."

"Once the word gets around, they'll come in," Taylor said. "I guarantee we'll have two score fighting men soon. When our boys open the ball, they'll play Comanche such a tune they'll remember it forever."

Days passed, but the volunteers never materialized.

Men stayed close to their homes and loved ones as lynch mobs roamed the countryside, hanging or shooting any man they deemed an outlaw or just a damned nuisance.

The Rangers, in their eagerness to root out anyone connected with John Wesley Hardin, seed, breed, and generation, turned a blind eye to the mayhem and the murder of patriots.

Then came the day that Ham Anderson, and Alec Barekman, another young Hardin cousin, weighed the odds against them and decided to cut and run. Their intention was to surrender to the authorities in Comanche, but within twenty-four hours they were both in shallow graves . . . gunned down by the Rangers.

Dead men tell no tales, and when the Ranger fusillade was over, both Anderson and Barekman weighed about five pounds heavier deceased than they did when they were alive. Those poor boys took a lot of Ranger lead, and their deaths plunged Wes into a deep depression.

All talk of a raid on Comanche ceased and Wes took to compulsively reading a Bible that someone had brought to camp.

"Wes," I said to him, "we have to ride north and live among the savage Canadians for a spell. With no Yankee law chasing us, we can sit back and make plans for the Wild West show, big plans."

Wes looked up from the Good Book and regarded me with lusterless eyes.

"And there's gold up there," I said, talking into his silence. "Nuggets big as a man's fist just lying on the ground for the taking." I smiled. "Within a few months, maybe just weeks, we'll have enough gold to fund the show and have plenty to spare. Hell, you could ride back into Comanche in a carriage and pair. A rich man can thumb his nose at everybody, including the Yankee law."

"Who told you there's gold for the taking?" Wes asked.

"I read it in a book."

"There's only one book a man should read — the holy book I'm holding in my hand."

"At least let's get out of Texas," I said. "We'll head to the New Mexico Territory. No one will find us there."

Wes stared at me with quizzical eyes. "What's this 'we' and 'us' business? There's only me and you. There's no 'we' and 'us.' If I decide to leave Texas, I'll go by myself. A cripple would only slow me down."

Wes dropped his eyes to the Bible again and read, his lips moving. Without looking up, he said, "Get away from me, Little Bit. Leave me the hell alone." After a pause, he added, "And take a bath sometime, huh?"

Wes was worried about his wife and kinfolk, and I forgave his harsh words. Besides, later that day he gave me whiskey and a cigar and said I was "a stout fellow."

CHAPTER FORTY-EIGHT:
MEN WITHOUT MERCY

Since I talked about John Wesley's new interest in the Bible, it's somehow appropriate that terrible news reached our camp carried by a rider on a pale horse . . . *and his name was death and hell followed close behind him.*

The rancher Long Tom Lee swung off his lathered gray and walked directly to Wes. "John Wesley" — he breathed hard like a man in pain — "I don't have the words."

Wes's face took on a stricken, blotched look. "Jane? Is it Jane?"

Long Tom held his battered Stetson in his hands. "Jane is fine and so is your daughter."

"Then find the words, Tom," Wes said. "And find them damn quick."

"They're harsh, John."

"Damn it, say them," Wes said.

Long Tom, a veteran of Stonewall's brigade, was a tall beanpole of a man with a bloodhound's face and the tired, seen-it-all eyes of an Inquisition executioner. "Your brother Joe is dead, John Wesley, and with him Bud Dixon and his brother Tom."

"How?"

"Hung."

That was a punch in the guts.

Wes rose to his feet, his face drained of color. He loved his brother Joe, the quiet one of the family, and the news of his death devastated him. "Tell it, Long Tom. Every last word of it."

"Hung is hung, John," the rancher said. "There ain't no more to tell. Let it go. Pick at it, and you make the wound worse."

Wes's jaw muscles bunched and his teeth gritted. "Tell it all, Long Tom."

"All right, I'll say what I know." His hat crushing in his twisting hands, Long Tom told how it had been. "Twenty nightriders, all of them masked, rode into Comanche about the one o'clock hour. There was a full moon and the town looked like it was lit by silver lanterns." Long Tom flushed. "I mean, that's how I saw it."

"Go on," Wes said.

"The vigilantes rode to the rock building where your wife and family were held, and overcame the guards."

"Name them," Wes said.

"Does it matter?"

"Name them."

"John James and the county clerk, a man called Bonner," Long Tom said. "They're not lawmen, John."

"Names to remember," Wes said. "But I know Bonner. He and Joe were brother Masons."

"Well, the way it was told to me, Bonner did nothing to save Joe," Long Tom said. "And he should've. Joe was a mighty shady lawyer all right, everybody knew that, but he did nothing that deserved getting hung."

"Joe did nothing that other lawyers don't do," I said. "He was hung only because he was John Wesley's brother."

"That's a natural fact," Long Tom said. "I can't argue with that."

"The vigilantes overcame the guards, or so they say. Then what happened?" Wes said.

"John . . ."

"What happened?"

"Joe and the Dixons were drug to a tree and hung," Long Tom said.

Wes lifted his head and for long moments stared at the clear blue bowl of the sky where a few crows wheeled like charred pieces of paper. Finally, without looking at Long Tom, he said, "Did . . . did Joe . . . was it quick?"

The rancher's face was grim. "I'm not a

lie-telling man, John."

"Then say it."

"Joe died hard. He pleaded for his life as he strangled to death and he kicked for a long time. An awful long time."

At first Wes showed no reaction and stood as still as a statue. Then he drove his fists into his belly and doubled over, screaming. His mouth agape, he fell to his knees, but the screaming did not stop.

I feared it never would.

Long Tom replaced his hat then looked at me. "Is there anything I can do?"

I shook my head.

"Then I'll leave." He cast a final look at Wes in a paroxysm of grief, swung into the saddle, and galloped away.

Jim Taylor stepped beside Wes, put his hand on his shoulder, and whispered, "Wes, don't go to that dark place. Come back, now."

The screaming stopped, and Wes kneeled with his head on his knees and made no sound, no movement. He stayed in that position until night fell.

None of the vigilantes were ever identified or brought to trial.

The Texas Rangers wrote the murders off as a necessary evil, unworthy of their notice.

As their captain said, "Why all the fuss? Often violence is the only way to get rid of undesirables."

CHAPTER FORTY-NINE: REVENGE OF THE WHITE KNIGHTS

Now begins what I call the "wandering time," when John Wesley was cast out and forced to flee Texas, his ancestral home.

"And he will be a wild man; and his hand will be against every man and every man's hand against him; he shall live to the east of all his brethren." Thus the Bible speaks of Ishmael the Wanderer, and I use those same words to speak of John Wesley, since he too was an outcast condemned to wander the earth.

Jim Taylor was dead, murdered by Suttonite vigilantes, and I was the only one to join Wes in his bitter exile.

After a brief reunion with his wife and daughter in New Orleans in the late summer of 1874, Wes fled to Gainesville in Florida, a rough and tumble settlement in the middle of the state.

Wes was appalled at the number of blacks in the town, brought in to harvest the cotton crop. He soon joined the local branch of the Young Men's Democratic Club, a Ku Klux Klan organization, and pledged to uphold white supremacy and the American way.

Wes bought a saloon that just about wiped out all of his money, and he lived in a room at the back. I worked as swamper and slept on the billiard table at night.

He'd become John H. Swain by then, adopting the last name of Jane's kin. His intention was to earn enough money from the saloon to establish his Wild West show in Great Britain where he could live in peace, unmolested by Yankee law.

"I bet old Queen Vic will come and watch," I said one night as we sat at a table sharing a bottle after closing. "She's real interested in wild Injuns and such."

"How do you know that?" Wes asked.

"Read it in a book. This one," I said, pulling the book out of my pocket. "It's called *The Visitors Guide to Great Britain,* and tells us everything we need to know about living over there."

"We'll need a special box for the queen and her court," Wes said. "She can sit beside Jane."

"And me," I said.

Wes shook his head. "Queen Vic won't want to sit beside you, Little Bit. You're low class and you smell."

I took exception to that. "I'll have a bath before I sit with Jane and the queen."

"You'll still be low class."

"Maybe she'll surprise you and make me a knight like Quentin Durward," I said.

Wes nodded. "Maybe, if she likes the show enough."

I was about to say more, but Wes raised a silencing hand.

"An argument going on out there. It sounds like them uppity blacks from around here." He rose to his feet and got a long-barreled revolver from behind the bar, one of those new cartridge Colts that were becoming all the rage.

The saloon door slammed open and a young man wearing a star on his vest stepped inside. "Mr. Swain, I need help. Luke Wilson, remember me?"

Wes recognized the sheriff as a fellow member of the Democratic Club. "The blacks rioting?"

"Arguing with me," Wilson said. "They want to come inside and drink more alcohol and I said no."

"Don't they know better than to give a white man sass and backtalk?"

"Not the blacks around here," Wilson said. "The Yankees got them uppity, telling them that they rule the roost."

"Not in my saloon, they don't," Wes said. "And not in my town."

"Good," Wilson said. "I now appoint you as my deputy."

I followed Wes and the sheriff outside into the humid, tropical heat of the Florida night. Cicadas and frogs carried on an endless, chattering, croaking argument and out in the swamps alligators bellowed their opinion.

Five black men stood outside the saloon, illuminated by the lanterns that hung on each side of the saloon door. They looked angry and one of them wore an old Union army blue jacket with a sergeant's chevrons on the sleeves.

"You men go about your business," Wes said. "The saloon is closed."

"The hell it is," the man in the coat said. "The door is open and we're going inside."

"Eli, go home," Sheriff Wilson said. "You're drunk enough already."

"I'll tell you when I'm drunk enough." The black strode straight at Wes who stood still and let him come.

At the last second, Wes sidestepped and swung the Colt. The barrel crashed into the side of the Negro's head and the man dropped like a felled ox.

Another tall, thin man uttered a vile curse, born of the savage heart of darkest Africa, and drew a wicked knife of the largest size. He charged and then fell stone dead a moment after Wes's bullet tore his heart apart.

The three remaining Negros decided that they wanted no part of Mr. Swain that night. In the most abject fashion, they threw themselves on their knees, raised their hands in prayerful supplication, and begged for mercy.

"Lock them up, Sheriff." Wes glanced at the dead man. "Then throw that to the alligators."

Wilson, young and impressionable, raised an eyebrow. "Quick to shoot, aren't you, Mr. Swain?"

"And so should you be, Sheriff, if you hope to live long."

But we were not yet finished with the Negro who wore the blue coat. His name was Eli Brown and he had dreams of one day standing for public office. The blow to his head from Wes's gun enraged him and inflamed his already ferocious hatred of the white race.

What better way to express his loathing than to rape a white woman, a Southern belle of good breeding and fine family who resided in Gainesville town?

Thankfully, the girl's cries were heard before she was cruelly undone, and the cursing, struggling Brown was thrust into jail.

That night there was a gathering of brave and resolute men in John Wesley's saloon, Sheriff Wilson among them. Each man, including Wes, wore a dazzling white robe like a holy Crusader knight ready to do battle with the Infidel.

I was not one of them, but my heart swelled with pride as I beheld such a glorious scene and I felt honored that I was of their race.

"I've got a rope," one stalwart said. "I say we string him up from the nearest telegraph pole."

But Wes would have none of it. "The jail is old and the wood is as dry as tinder. Set fire to the place and we can watch the black demon roast in hell."

This brought a round of applause and cheers for Mr. Swain.

"Drink up, boys," Sheriff Wilson said. "It's almost midnight and time to get it done. I don't want that damn black breathing the same air as us for a moment longer."

This brought another round of huzzahs, then the white knights drained their glasses, donned snowy hoods, and sallied forth into the darkness.

Eli Brown died horribly. He burned to death even as he stood at a window, his sizzling arms reaching through the bars, pathetically begging for his life.

It was a fate the Negro richly deserved.

Later, we all repaired to the saloon and enjoyed champagne cocktails. Mr. Swain, who had a fine voice, sang "When This Cruel War Is Over," to much applause and many a manly tear.

It was a happy time.

CHAPTER FIFTY:
A CHILLING WARNING

Four thousand dollars. That was the sum the vindictive Texas legislature placed on John Wesley's noble head . . . *dead or alive.*

The happy times had been short and they were about to end.

Wes had long since sold his saloon, kept one step ahead of the law and trusted no one.

The reward was enough to interest the Texas Rangers, especially that redheaded scoundrel J. Lee Hall and his able lieutenant John Barclay Armstrong.

You remember Armstrong. As a Ranger sergeant he arrested, shot, and hung a score of the survivors of the Sutton-Taylor war, and he's the man who took King Fisher into custody.

According to the Yankee authorities, Fisher, a friend of Wes's, was the second worst man in Texas.

We all know who was first.

What worried Wes most was Governor Hubbard's appointment of Jack Duncan, the famous detective, to help in the hunt. "Look at that," Wes said, tossing a newspaper on the table in front of me. "This time they mean business."

The front-page headlines said it all.

JOHN WESLEY HARDIN SCOOTS
FAMOUS SLEUTH ON HIS TRAIL
Ordered to Capture — or Kill!
'Hardin will hang,' vow Texas Rangers

We were residing in Pollard, Alabama, with the Bowen family, relatives of John Wesley's wife, but the news about Duncan had Wes on edge. "Damn it, I've heard of the man. He's a bloodhound and once he's got the scent, he never gives up the trail."

Wes had taken to wearing his guns in the house, something he'd never done before, and his eyes had a hollow, hunted look, as though he felt the very walls were closing in on him. He sat at the breakfast table and crumbled a piece of dry toast in his fingers, lost in thought.

Then his nose wrinkled. "Little Bit, hell, you're stinking up the place."

"My leg is bad, Wes. It's so rotten it hardly supports me any longer." I managed a weak smile. "And the brace is rusting."

"Seen you walking with a limp recent." Wes nodded to himself. "I sure enough have."

"It has to be amputated," I said.

"Pensacola," Wes said, sitting up straight as he snapped his fingers.

"Huh?"

"That's the place for me." Wes lifted his eyes to mine. He had cold eyes and I swear they'd gotten colder with every killing.

"Hell, it's just across the Alabama border and Chance Rawlins — you know him?"

"The gambler."

"Yeah, him. Chance says Pensacola is a gambling town because of the fortunes being made in cotton and lumber. Hell, I could make a big score there."

"Seems like."

"If the Florida law gets too close, all I have to do is skip back across the border into Alabama again."

"Seems like," I said again.

"Then it's done. I'll see Jane settled, and head east."

"Maybe you'll win enough to stake the Wild West show."

Wes nodded. "Yeah, maybe so. Head for England like I planned."

"I'd need to get a wooden leg first. I

mean, before I met the queen."

"Sure, a wooden leg would do the trick." Wes grinned at me. "Then them royal folks won't call you the gimp with the limp, huh?"

"No, I guess not."

My leg was indeed odorous and nobody knew that better than me.

The Bowens would not allow me to sleep in the house and I was banished to the barn, where I shared my quarters with the horses and mules, the occasional pig, and a nightly horde of mosquitoes.

I was not then very familiar with women of the respectable sort, though a few had treated me well, as they would a bird with a broken wing or a wounded puppy. Alice Flood, a distant Bowen cousin, fell into that category.

An orphan, Alice depended on Bowen charity. They provided her with food and board and in exchange, they demanded she act as a skivvy, cleaning out the fireplaces, scrubbing floors, washing clothes with the harsh lye soap that chafed her hands red, and whatever else they needed.

The Bowens called Alice a housemaid, but it was slavery under a different name.

I guess it was inevitable that we should be drawn together, two pathetic, miserable creatures who found solace in each other's company.

Alice was neither pretty nor smart, neither joyful nor sad. She had no past, no present and no future. She just existed from day to day . . . like me.

Ah, my self-pity is showing, is it not?

Alice lifted me out of that pit of despair. As fate would have it, I had her for only a few short years, but those were the best years of my life.

The evening after Wes made his decision about Pensacola, Alice visited me in the barn as she did every evening. As always, she brought me little treats from the kitchen, usually a piece of cake or some cookies.

As I recall, it was cookies with shredded coconut in them that evening, though I was fairly drunk and set them aside for breakfast.

Alice removed the brace and bathed my leg. She frowned. "It's getting much worse, William." She refused to call me Little Bit, saying it was a disrespectful name for a man.

"Not much of it left, is there?"

"You're limping terribly."

I smiled. "I can still ride a horse."

"But not for much longer, I fear." She had unremarkable brown eyes, brown hair and a brown skin, but I thought her beautiful that night.

"It has to come off," I said. "Then I can get a wooden one."

"I think modern artificial limbs are made of metal, and some can bend at the knee."

"How do you know that?"

"I met Dr. Dinwiddie in town and asked him. He says great strides —"

"Ha-ha." I laughed. "Great strides. I like that."

Alice smiled. "Anyway, artificial limbs improved very quickly because of the war. So many boys lost arms or legs."

"Well, that gives me hope." Then as romantic as Quentin Durward, I said, "You give me hope, Alice."

She took my hand and kissed it. "You and me are fated to be together."

A moment later our bodies joined.

Shall I draw you a word picture of two singularly unattractive people making love on straw in a barn among farm animals to the music of yipping coyotes?

I think not.

But after it was over and I lay back exhausted, Alice seemed troubled.

"I'm sorry," I said.

"For what?"

"I disappointed you."

366

Alice smiled. "You didn't disappoint me, William. Nothing about you disappoints me."

A silence stretched between us, then she said, "About your friend, John Wesley."

"What about him?"

"He talks too much and too loudly."

"I don't understand."

"In front of Brown Bowen."

I felt a stab of alarm. Bowen was Jane's brother, a truly vile creature without a trace of loyalty or manhood. He was a rapist, murderer, and robber.

Ultimately, he dangled from a noose. When he was cut down, no one shed a tear for him or claimed his carcass.

"Do you think Brown might betray Wes?" I asked.

"He's betrayed everyone else." Alice smiled and picked a piece of straw out of my hair. "Maybe I worry unnecessarily."

"You like Wes, don't you?"

"He's a fine man and a true patriot."

"He's both of those things, and much more," I said.

"Will you talk to him? About Brown Bowen, I mean?"

"Yes I will. First thing in the morning." I took Alice in my arms. "But in the meantime . . ."

CHAPTER FIFTY-ONE: THE MIGHTY ARE FALLEN

John Wesley would not hear a bad word about Brown Bowen. "He's kin. And in Texas, kin don't betray each other."

"Wes, he's vermin and the only reason you put up with him is because he's your brother-in-law," I said.

Wes's temper was always an uncertain thing, and it flared. "And you? What about you? Why the hell do I put up with you?"

"I don't know."

"Neither do I. All you're good for is stinking up the place and sticking it to that Flood gal whose face would scare a cur off a gut wagon."

"Wes, don't say things like that about Alice," I said, my own anger rising.

"Then take back what you said about Brown. I won't have the likes of you ragging on my kinfolk."

I shook my head. "Wes, he's a yellow-belly and sly as a fox. He'll sell you down the river to save his own worthless neck."

"The hell with you, Little Bit." Wes's lip curled. "Go back to your two-dollar whore."

I hit him then.

I mean, I hit him on the chin with all the power of my eighty pounds and little bony fist.

Wes wore his guns and he'd killed men for less. But for a moment he looked shocked, and then mildly amused, the red welt on his chin no bigger than a mosquito bite.

"Don't ever talk about Alice like that again." I was breathing hard, angry as hell, and more than a little scared.

To my surprise — and considerable relief — Wes didn't utter another word. He just turned on his heel and walked away.

He never again mentioned Alice's name in my presence, even when we got married while he was in jail.

He could have killed me that day, but didn't.

That says something about him that's all to the good, doesn't it?

For the next few days, the relationship between Wes and me was frosty and we exchanged few words.

But he made no objection when I asked if

I could join him on his gambling trip to Pensacola, saying only, "You're on your own, so just don't ask me for money."

Later, I branded the date of our trip into my memory. August 24, 1877.

The day that John Wesley Hardin's long martyrdom began.

In addition to myself, Wes travelled with fellow gamblers Shep Hardy, Neal Campbell, and Jim Mann, a nice young fellow who'd just celebrated his twenty-first birthday. Notably absent was Brown Bowen who was supposed to make the journey with us.

When the train pulled into the Pensacola depot, Wes decided to linger in the smoking car to finish his pipe and sprawled on a seat alongside the aisle. Mann and I stayed with him, while Hardy and Campbell got off to stretch their legs.

We'd shared a bottle on the trip from Alabama and I was tipsy. I'd say Wes was relaxed and young Mann, who wasn't a drinker, coughed around the black cheroot between his teeth.

No sooner had the locomotive clanked and steamed to a halt, than a man who walked with a limp sat in the aisle seat opposite Wes.

I later learned this was the famous John B.

Armstrong, who'd accidentally shot himself in the crotch a few weeks earlier. Unfortunately, he'd missed his balls.

Something about the man made me uneasy, especially when he moved in his seat and I saw the handle of a Colt sticking out of his waistband.

A few moments later, two big, muscular men barged down the aisle, throwing off drunks and laggards, and I knew that the law was about to open the ball.

"Wes! Look out!" I yelled.

John Wesley moved with the reaction of a panther. "Texas, by God!" he yelled as he rose halfway out of his seat.

You're too late, Wes!

The pair of lawmen jumped on top of him, even as Wes tried to draw his Colt from his waistband. But the hammer stuck in his suspenders and one of the lawmen wrenched it from his hand.

Then it became a free for all.

Wes punched and bit, but the big lawmen pounded him into his seat. His face was soon covered with blood and saliva.

Armstrong sprang to his feet, a long-barreled Colt in his hand.

Young Jim Mann didn't recognize Wes's assailants as lawmen. "Assassins!" he yelled, drawing his gun.

Armstrong fired and Mann slammed back into his seat, his chest pumping blood from a dead-center bullet wound. He died within seconds.

I rushed at Armstrong, my puny fists flying, but he pushed me away and I fell on my back on the carriage floor.

The Ranger ignored me and joined his fellow lawmen. He didn't take part in the struggle, but waited his opportunity with his clubbed pistol raised.

He didn't have to tarry long.

As soon as he got a clear shot at Wes, he crashed the barrel of his Colt into Wes's skull.

Wes didn't cry out. He just went limp. Within seconds, they shackled him hand and foot. His hair was matted with blood, his face a vivid, scarlet mask. His head lolled on his shoulders when they dragged him to his feet, no fight left in him.

My God, my knight had fallen!

Enraged, I scrambled to a standing position and was greeted by the muzzle of Armstrong's revolver ramming into my forehead.

"Call it," The Ranger thumbed back the hammer of the Colt and its triple click sounded like my death knell.

"Call it." he said again. His eyes were

bloodshot and wild. Flecks of saliva foamed on his lips.

I am not cut from heroic cloth. "I'm out of it."

"Then get the hell away of here," Armstrong said.

After one last glimpse at the unconscious John Wesley, blinded by salt tears, I stampeded from the car.

Behind me I heard Armstrong yell, "And take a bath!"

Men laughed as I stumbled onto the platform and into . . . I knew not what.

CHAPTER FIFTY-TWO: "HE'LL DANCE AT OUR WEDDING"

That evening I got drunk on somebody else's money. I had to since I had no funds of my own. I rolled a drunk in an alley. I'm not proud of what I did, but desperate times required desperate measures.

The man was taking a piss against the wall of the Penitent Pelican saloon and I crept up behind him and hit him over the head with a bottle. After he dropped, I went through his pockets and found twenty-three dollars, a nickel railroad watch, and a small Roman Catholic medal with an image of the Virgin Mary that, never being inclined to popery, I stuffed back into his vest.

The man started to groan and attempted to rise, and I scampered.

I bought a bottle of Old Crow, and, since the stores were still open, a necklace for Alice — a small, enameled bluebird on a silver chain.

I thought the necklace was pretty, but

before I could give it to my sweetheart, I lost it.

I drank myself into oblivion and spent the night on a park bench. No one troubled me because in those days Pensacola was full of homeless vagrants like me.

Come first light, I breakfasted on the last inch of whiskey in the bottle, then went in search of Wes.

I didn't get far. After but a few steps, I collapsed in the street, overtaken by the stress of my friend's capture and the liquor I'd drunk.

I recall the disgusted faces of women looking down at me, then, after I returned from unconsciousness again, the jolting misery of a wagon and a clear blue sky passing above me.

After that, I knew nothing until I woke in darkness. For a few minutes, I lay still and listened to the chatter of insects and the rustles and gibbering cries of forest animals.

Where the hell was I?

I rose to a sitting position and my head reeled. It took a while before the darkness ceased to cartwheel around me. Then came the slow, terrible dawning that I was alone in a vast wilderness. Dusky moonlight revealed a forest of scrub pine, live oak, and tangles of bushes with wide, leathery leaves.

It also shone on the sheet of white paper pinned to the front of my coat.

I tore the paper free, then, after much squinting, read

STAY OUT OF PENSACOLA. RETURN AND I'LL HANG YOU FOR VAGRANCY.
— *Wm. H. Hutchinson, Sheriff*

It was easy to put together what had happened. I'd been loaded into a wagon and dumped outside the city limits — well outside, if the backcountry where I found myself was any indication.

Had they gotten rid of me because of vagrancy, or was it that I'd been identified as a friend of John Wesley?

I decided on the former. I wasn't significant enough to be taken seriously as a Hardin associate. I'd just been dumped like so much garbage littering the street.

A goblin gets used to that.

I still had fifteen dollars and change in my pocket — enough, I hoped, to see me across the border into Alabama and my darling Alice. She would have news of Wes.

I'd ridden the cushions to Pensacola, but I'd have to walk at least part of the way. I figured some long miles across rough country on a bad leg until I found another town with a railroad depot. I may have well thought about walking to the moon.

I had no option but to try.

Come morning, I padded my leg with the big green leaves of the plant that grew everywhere, then set out, pointing my nose to the east.

I was a hundred and fifty miles from Alice . . . and my long journey had begun.

The fine readers of this narrative are interested in the life and times of my friend and hero John Wesley Hardin, not Little Bit. So let me just say that my odyssey was a long and painful one, but after two weeks (Yes, that long. Such was my hobbling gait and occasional drunks until my money wore out) I arrived at the Bowen farm.

Alice welcomed me with a glad smile and open arms, but the Bowens did not. Brown had been arrested and was facing the hangman's noose. That cast a pall over the family.

I was once again relegated to the barn, told I could stay only a few days, and would have to work for my keep, helping Alice with her chores mostly. Again, this is all beside the point, because I did learn that Wes had been taken to Austin to stand trial for the murder of Charlie Webb.

My worst fear had finally caught up to me.

The night I arrived, Alice joined me in the barn, and she was worried. "You'll go to Austin, won't you?"

"I reckon Wes needs me more than ever now."

"He won't be imprisoned, the public would never stand for it."

I shook my head. "Alice, Wes has friends, but he's got some mighty powerful enemies who'd like to see him hang."

Her eyes took on a dazed look, as though trying to understand the implications of what I'd just told her. Finally she said, "If you go to Austin, I'm going with you."

"I'll have to walk, unless I can hitch the freight cars." I remembered the railroad bull. "It's dangerous and I don't think you'd like that."

"I have a little money. Enough to get us to Austin."

"I don't want to take your money, Alice."

"You said that John needs you. I don't think you can refuse my offer. How could you live with yourself if you desert him now because of masculine pride?"

I smiled. "I don't have any pride, masculine or otherwise."

"Then we'll go to Austin together. I'll take pride in you."

"You're a wonderful girl, Alice." Then, because I had nothing to offer her, I said, "I bought you a present in Pensacola, but I lost it somewhere. It was a necklace, a bluebird on a chain."

Women are full of surprises . . . and Alice surprised me then.

She reached into the pocket of her dress and brought out a little paper package. She opened it carefully, almost lovingly, and held up what it contained . . . a plain gold wedding band. She smiled. "This was my mother's wedding ring." She laid her hand on mine. "William, the only present I want from you is the right to wear this ring on my left hand."

"You mean —"

"Marry me in Austin."

My words got tangled up in my throat and the only sound I could make was a strangled croak, like a bullfrog with a hernia.

Alice took her hand from mine and wrapped up the ring before returning it to her pocket. "You don't want to marry me," she said, her eyes bruised.

"Of course I do," I said, my voice coming back.

"Then why are you so hesitant?"

"After I check on Wes, we'll get hitched, I promise."

"Do you really mean that? Can I trust you?"

"Yes I mean it, and yes you can." I held out my open hand. "Give me the ring." I placed the slim band on her wedding finger. "We'll make it official in Austin. Right after I see Wes." I smiled. "I'm dying to tell him about us."

Alice kissed me. "He was very good to you, wasn't he?"

"The only friend I ever had."

"Then he'll dance at our wedding, William. I just know he will."

Chapter Fifty-Three:
Twenty-Five Years
at Hard Labor

The Travis County Courthouse in Austin was a brand new, three-story limestone building of breathtaking size, built in what was then called the Second Empire style.

Alice and I stood outside for a while, at the corner of Eleventh Street and Congress Avenue, and stared up at its ornate iron-work, palatial dormers, and lofty Mansard roof. We looked exactly what we were, a pair of open-mouthed rubes fresh in from the country with dung on our shoes.

The monumental, elegant courthouse dwarfed us into puny insignificance. For the first time in my life, I realized just how colossal was the edifice of the law and how effortlessly it could crush even a giant of a man like John Wesley Hardin.

In a small, nervous voice, Alice asked, "William, are you sure we can we go in there?"

"Of course we can," I said with more

confidence than I felt. "It's a big place, but remember that it belongs to the people of Texas."

"People like me and you?"

"Yup, just like us."

The *us* that morning was a less than imposing sight.

Lacking a portmanteau, Alice had tied up her few belongings in a sheet that she slung over her back. I still wore the huge army greatcoat and battered bowler hat. Underneath were pants, shirt, and shoes much the worse for wear.

When we walked into the echoing, marble magnificence of the building and asked for the clerk of court, the uniformed doorman looked as though someone was holding a dead fish under his nose. "What do you people want? Court is not in session today."

"We're here to see a friend." I dropped the name. "Mr. John Wesley Hardin."

"All sorts of scoundrels" — the man looked hard at me — "are dragged through those doors. I can't be expected to remember their names. Come back tomorrow and talk to the clerk of court."

Alice said in a tremulous whisper, "William, we can come back tomorrow."

"Indeed," the doorman said, "when court is in session."

A tall young man in a dark gray suit, some sort of lawman's shield on his vest, walked past with a sheaf of papers in his hand. He stopped when he saw Alice and me.

"Everything all right, Mr. Murdoch?" he said to the doorman.

Before the man could answer, I said, "Sir, we're here to visit with our friend John Wesley Hardin."

"I told you court is not in session today," Murdoch said. "Now be off with you."

"It's all right, Mr. Murdoch." Then the young man spoke directly to Alice, perhaps because she was so nervous. "Mr. Hardin has already been tried and convicted of murder in the second degree. I'm afraid he was sentenced to twenty-five years at hard labor."

I felt as though I'd been stabbed in the heart and Alice's face was as pale as an oyster.

"I'm sorry I have no better news for you." The young man gave a little bow. "Good day to you both."

"All right you two, out you go." The doorman surprised me. "Hardin has appealed his sentence. Try the county jail behind us at Eleventh and Brazos."

He slammed the door on our heels and for a few minutes we stood, struck dumb, at the corner.

The young man's words kept spearing through my mind . . . twenty-five years at hard labor . . . twenty-five years at hard labor. . . .

For a freedom-loving knight errant like Wes, it was a death sentence.

CHAPTER FIFTY-FOUR:
JAILBIRD

John Wesley was to spend a year in the Travis County Jail as his appeal progressed, so I will describe at some little length, that grim bastion as it was the first day I ever set eyes on it.

Imagine if you will, a massive building fifty feet wide by sixty long with walls of solid stone two feet thick. It contained twenty-four dank, dark cells only eight feet by ten, their ceilings two stories high. A lever arrangement meant that all the doors could be opened and closed at the same time, without the jailors coming in contact with the prisoners.

There could be no escape from such a bastille and Wes was well aware of that fact.

After we left the courthouse, Alice and I walked down Eleventh Street to the jail. Gas lamps lined the shady avenue. We drew many stares, some highly amused, others openly hostile. A couple of ragged country bumpkins were a rare sight — one to see and talk of later.

The coming of the Houston and Central Texas Railway had attracted many wealthy, sophisticated residents to the city. The beautiful Austin belles in watered silk fascinated Alice, their huge bustles and tiny hats perched atop masses of glossy, piled up hair in stark contrast to her own threadbare, homespun dress and shabby leather shoes.

As we walked, I vowed there and then that Alice would one day wear silk.

Foolish Little Bit, again building his rickety castles in the air.

We were ushered into a tiny visiting room partitioned by an iron grill. The prisoner stood on one side, the visitors on the other. There were no chairs or benches and no window, the gloomy interior lit by an oil lamp hanging from the ceiling.

When Wes was ushered inside, a prison guard cradling a shotgun stood against the door. He made it perfectly clear when he stared at Alice and me, he didn't like what he saw.

The feeling was mutual.

Wes looked really good. His hair was neatly combed and brushed straight back from his forehead and his mustache was trimmed. He seemed to be in good spirits.

"So what brings you here to Austin?"

I smiled. "You, of course. How are you getting along?"

"Real good. My lawyers say I'll be out of this hellhole within the week."

"I'm glad to hear that, Wes. Have you made plans?"

"Of course I've made plans. And the most important of them is to get even with them as put me here. Beginning with that damned traitorous dog Brown Bowen."

I wanted to say *I told you so,* but I didn't.

"Take it easy, John," the jailor said. "Keep it light."

"Sorry," Wes said. "But Bowen tried to pin all his foul and disgraceful crimes on me."

"I know that, John," the jailor said. "But you'll be a free man when you see him hang."

For some reason I've never been able to fathom, law enforcement officers of every stripe liked John Wesley. The big jailor was no exception. Maybe they saw something of themselves in him — Wes's regard for law and order and his grit, determination, and coolness under fire. Whatever it was, he received respect and admiration from lawmen all his life.

In fact, Wes also liked peace officers. He

proved that to me when he said, "Little Bit, if you see Ranger John Armstrong, tell him I've got no hard feelings. He treated me fair and square and he's a credit to Texas."

"I sure will, Wes," I said, although I'd no intention of ever talking to Armstrong again. My one brush with him on the train was enough. To bolster Wes's spirits, I told him a little lie. "I've been working on the business proposal for the Wild West show."

Wes smiled. "How much funding do we need?"

I picked a number out of the air. "I'd say twenty thousand." To soften the blow, I added, "But maybe a lot less."

"Hell, twenty thousand is nothing," Wes said, grinning. "I can make that at the gambling tables in a good year." He thought for a moment, then said, "Or I can talk to Sam Luck again."

"Either way, we can raise it, Wes."

"Good. Then bring the proposal to me and I'll read it." He slammed his right fist into the open palm of his left. "Damn it, Little Bit, we're off and running."

"I'll let you read it in a few days, once I add a few finishing touches."

"Yeah, take some time and get it right. I might even be out of here the day after tomorrow."

"I sure hope so." I believed him, every word. I really believed Wes's lawyers could work a miracle.

Out of the blue, Wes asked, "Where is my gun, Little Bit?"

I shook my head. "Wes, I have no idea."

"Then talk to the Rangers, get it back for me. It's my property, not theirs, and I'll need it when I'm freed."

Rather than suggest that asking for his gun might not be such a good idea, I said, "Hell, Wes, you can buy a new one."

"No. I want my own Colt back. I've never used a revolver that balanced as well as that one."

"I'll see what I can do."

"I'll see what I can do," Wes repeated in a high, sarcastic tone. "Don't see. Do it!"

"Of course, Wes. I'll get it for you."

"Time's up, John," the prison bull said.

I talked fast. "Wes, say howdy to Alice. You remember her."

Wes gave my intended a stiff little bow, his face empty.

"We're getting hitched," I said. "Right here in Austin."

"Don't forget the gun." Wes turned on his heel and the iron door clanged shut behind him.

Alice spoke into the ringing echoes of the

389

door. "He doesn't like me."

I smiled at her. "You're Bowen kin and he's upset about Brown telling all those lies on him."

"It's not that."

"Then what is it?"

"You're showing some independence, William, and John doesn't like that. He has nothing but contempt for you, but he enjoys the idea that you count on him for everything, even your self-esteem."

I laughed then. "Alice, I don't have any self-esteem."

"I know, because John Wesley Hardin took it away from you. But I'm going to give it back to you, William."

"Well, Wes told me that he wanted his gun is all."

"Damn him and his gun!" Alice yelled. She stomped out of the room, her back stiff.

I stood openmouthed with shock. I'd never heard sweet little Alice cuss like that before.

CHAPTER FIFTY-FIVE:
A GRIM REALITY

John Wesley's appeal dragged on for a year and kept him behind bars.

During that time, his family — he now had three children — descended into poverty. Jane, already dying from cancer, moved them in with Wes's mother. The Reverend Hardin had passed away in 1876 while his son was on the scout in Florida.

I can't say that Wes's spirits were high.

I believed that in his heart of hearts he knew his appeal would founder and that twenty-five years in state prison was close to becoming a grim reality.

Alice and I were married by then. She restricted my visits to the jail, but one day after he'd spent five months in his cell, I found Wes elated, beside himself with joy.

"Good news! Hot dang, Little Bit, I'll be out of here soon."

Happiness is contagious, and I eagerly awaited the good tidings.

"Read this!" Wes yelled. His face fell. "You can read, can't you?"

"Wes, you know I can read."

His face brightened. "Oh, yeah, that's right. You can."

The jail rules dictated that nothing could be passed from prisoner to visitor, so Wes held a letter up to the iron grill. "Read it!" he shouted, or I should say *roared.*

The prison guard stirred uneasily and gripped his scattergun tighter, his eyes never leaving Wes for a moment.

I moved closer to the grill, and saw that the letter was from Elizabeth, Wes's ma. After telling her son to praise the Lord and look to Heaven for guidance, she wrote:

I am willing to speak with the lawyers about your case, dearest boy. Your pa wrote a true statement of the killing of Charlie Webb, but died before he could publish it. I am willing to do so now.

Your father said that there was a plot to murder you on the day Webb was killed and that you only defended yourself from a hired assassin.

My loving, dutiful son, your pa's death-bed testament will set you free!

After I indicated that I'd read the letter,

Wes said, "Well, what do you think? Don't Ma milk a good cow?"

Since his attorneys had used this same argument before the jury that found Wes guilty, I figured his ma was milking a dry cow.

As it happened, indeed she was. The reverend's statement never saw the light of day.

But I withheld my gloomy misgivings. "Wes, that's wonderful. Just wonderful."

"Damn right it is. Everybody believes a reverend, don't they?" Wes carefully folded up the letter and put it in his pocket. "You get my Colt back?"

I lied my way out of that question. "I sure did. Ranger Armstrong gave it to me and it looks as good as new."

"They hung Brown Bowen," Wes said. "They say he died pretty well."

I nodded. "Heard that."

"There will be others like him when the reckoning comes."

I didn't know the guard and he looked mean. I changed the subject. "I'm still working on the business proposal for the show."

"Yeah, good," Wes said, with little enthusiasm. He looked me over. "You look like hell, even skinnier. That woman not taking care of you?"

"She takes care of me just fine."

"How's the leg?"

"Bad as ever."

"All right, that's enough. Move it, Hardin." This from the guard.

Then this from Wes, "Sure thing, boss."

After he was gone, I felt oddly depressed about two things. The first was that Wes didn't remember that I was a reader, the second that he was losing the respect of his jailors.

Later, I read in the newspaper that Wes had beaten an old trusty to within an inch of his life for being late with his dinner. This might explain the change in attitude of the guards.

But his memory slip troubled me. It was the first indication I had that Wes's mind was going. It would be a long, destructive process, spanning decades, but in the end it would contribute to his death.

CHAPTER FIFTY-SIX:
I TURN A NEW PAGE

Alice found work as a kitchen maid while I stayed at home to write what I knew best — dime novel tales of the West, its heroes, bad men, and beautiful maidens in every stage of distress.

After a few tries, I got the hang of the thing, and was soon selling on a regular basis.

From this happy time in my life, I'm sure you recall that my best sale was for a book I wrote in less than a week. *Hands Up! Or John Wesley Rides The Vengeance Trail.*

Sadly, the day the novel came out, Wes's appeal being denied, he was transferred to the Huntsville Penitentiary in June of 1879 to east Texas to begin his quarter-century of confinement.

I wrote him and gave him my address, *Mr. & Mrs. William Bates, 27 Sunnycourt Crescent, Austin, Texas,* and asked how he was faring in that dreadful prison.

Several months later, Wes replied. He addressed the envelope to *Little Bit, Esq.* He said he'd already made two attempts at escape, and both were foiled. After the second one . . .

They threw me into a cell and spread-eagled me on a concrete floor, then gave me forty lashes, less one, with a bullwhip. Little Bit, my back and sides were torn up something awful, but I was taken from there and thrown into a solitary cell. I was there for three days without food or water. After a week, I was tossed into yet another cell and now I have a high fever and I'm too weak to walk.

My health is not good, but I'll beat them in the end, Little Bit. They may kick me, flog me, and starve me, but I won't let the scum win. I'll keep on trying to escape until I am successful. In the meantime, I will bear my persecution with Christian fortitude.

Wes's letter depressed me and may have been the cause of my bad leg finally giving out on me two days after Christmas. Cancerous, it was amputated in my own bedroom. The surgeon used chloroform so I felt little at the time, but the stump pained me considerably and my drinking worsened.

I experienced even greater pain when Alice, who'd been failing for some time, died of what a doctor said was, "consumption and a mighty hard life." She passed away in the spring of 1881, not yet twenty years of age.

I was lost. The happiness I'd known had been abruptly snatched away from me, and I turned more and more to the whiskey bottle for solace. Yet through it all I continued to write, thanks to the urging of my editor, Frank Starr, a fine man who never gave up on me. I was, I believe, the first drunken writer in Texas, though others have since followed my path.

My novels sold very well, and, despite myself, I began to prosper.

I was fitted with a fine artificial leg that helped me walk better than I ever had before, and I gradually reduced the amount of whiskey I drank. By 1884, the Little Bit of old was gone forever. My old leg brace, bowler hat and filthy army greatcoat I burned . . . and with them the name, Little Bit.

I was a fairly rich man and I dressed the part, favoring three-piece ditto suits of somber shade and winged collars with an ascot tie and diamond stickpin.

■ ■ ■ ■

"Bill, you owe that man nothing," Frank Starr said. "What did he ever do for you but turn you into a drunk and a fugitive?"

We sat in my parlor while Cassie, my housemaid, served us afternoon tea, Frank being a temperate man.

"I owe him a great deal. Wes helped me survive. What chance did a crippled little runt like me have in Texas after the war? Wes was my protector and my inspiration. I wanted to be like him."

"If you'd turned out like him, you'd be serving time in Huntsville right now."

"Maybe, but without John Wesley, I'd probably be dead."

Cassie poured the tea and I said, "Earl Grey. I hope you like it. I understand it's a favorite of old Queen Vic. And please make a trial of the sponge cake."

After Frank declared the tea good and the cake better, I reached into my inside coat pocket and produced a letter and a newspaper clipping. I passed the clip to Frank, but he declined.

"I left my spectacles on the train from New York," he said. "I'm afraid you'll have to read it to me."

"It's short. The newspaper is dated September 12, 1884, and it says, 'The health of the notorious John Wesley Hardin is very bad and has taken a turn for the worse. He is not expected to survive much longer. He has served out five of his twenty-five year sentence.' "

"Well, I guess I'm sorry to hear that," Frank said. "But what has it got to do with you?"

I opened Wes's letter. "This may explain why."

I read aloud, " 'The shotgun wounds I got from Phil Sublett and the pistol ball injury that Charlie Webb inflicted on me became first inflamed and then abscessed. Little Bit, they did not allow me in the prison hospital but confined me to my cell where I lay in great pain for eight months. When they thought I was recovered, they told me I must work in the rock quarry, but I spit in their eye. I was lashed and after two weeks on a bread and water diet, was sent to make quilts in the tailor shop.' "

I looked at Frank and said, "And then this. 'No one comes to visit anymore. Manny came a few times but not for the past couple years. Has the world forgotten me, Little Bit?' "

Frank flicked the letter with his forefinger

and smiled. "No, Mr. Hardin. The world's moved on and you've been left behind."

"I've not left Wes behind," I said. "I'm going to visit him."

"Bill, you just signed a contract for four more novels."

"And I'll meet my deadlines. I'll only be gone for a week at most."

Frank drew a deep breath. "I hope you know what you're doing. Hardin has always been a baleful influence on you and I'd hate to see you go back to what you were."

"What was I?"

"I can tell you what you were *not*. You were not a successful, respected author who makes enough money to live comfortably for the rest of his life."

I smiled at that. "Trust me, Frank, I won't stumble and fall."

"Then I'll take you at your word," Frank Starr said. "I don't want to bury you in a pauper's grave like I did Edgar Allan Poe."

CHAPTER FIFTY-SEVEN:
THAT SCOUNDREL
BUFFALO BILL

A penitentiary is a wheel within a wheel and together they grind slowly . . . inexorably . . . a motion that's unrelenting, unalterable and pitiless. The purpose of a penal institution is to crush a man between the turning wheels, pulverize his soul, his mind, his being, while keeping his useless carcass alive so that he can remain only healthy enough to suffer his just punishment in full measure.

The man I met in Huntsville was no longer the John Wesley Hardin I knew.

A man can't be whipped, beaten, and starved into submission without it leaving a mark on him. Wes had served less than six years of his sentence, but already, he was broken by the wheels.

We met in a Huntsville Penitentiary visiting room during a thunderstorm, my affluent appearance and the hired carriage at the gates allowing me immediate access. The room was furnished with a table and two wooden chairs. A barred window high in one rock wall glimmered with lightning and allowed inside the sullen roar of the thunder.

Clanking iron shackles bound Wes hand and foot.

The prison guard pushed him into a chair. "Ten minutes," he said to me. "And make no physical contact with the prisoner."

The guard carried only a billy club. Judging by Wes's bruises, he had made its acquaintance recently.

I smiled at him, prepared for the usual polite *how-are-you?* exchange.

But Wes grabbed my wrist. "Did you hear?"

"Hear what?" I asked.

"A damned scoundrel by the name of Buffalo Bill Cody has started a Wild West show on the North Platte, up Nebraska way."

"I'm sorry to hear that, Wes."

"He stole my idea, and, by God, he'll pay for it." Wes leaned closer to me and dropped his voice to a conspiratorial whisper. "As soon as I get out of here, and it could be any day now, you and me will ride up to the North Platte and shoot that thief." He leaned back in his chair, his shackle chains chiming. "And then we'll take over his show and get rich, just like we planned."

I didn't like Wes's eyes, the odd way he stared at me. In the flickering light of the thunderstorm, he seemed much older. The bright, inner glow of his golden youth was gone. He was a man old before his time.

Every time I looked at him I died a little death.

Out of nowhere, he said, "Did you hear about Jane?"

"Yes I did. She was a fine woman and you have my deepest sympathy. Alice also passed away."

Wes ignored what I said. "Why are you all dressed up like a dude?" It was as though he saw me for the first time.

I smiled. "Why, to meet you of course."

"Are you a spy?"

"I don't understand."

"You ain't Little Bit."

"I was Little Bit."

"He wasn't much."

"He was your friend."

"I don't have any friends. Nobody comes to visit me."

"I've come," I said.

"Have you brought tobacco?"

"No. But I'll bring some next time."

"Get Passing Clouds Navy Cut. Accept no substitute."

"I'll remember that."

403

Then, as he'd so often done in the past, Wes surprised me. "Little Bit, I can't take another twenty years of this hell."

He'd finally remembered who I was and I took that as a good sign.

"Wes, I'll do everything in my power to get you out of here," I said.

"Make it soon."

"It may take a little while. In the meantime, just don't kick against the system any more or it will destroy you. Play their game, Wes. Toe the line."

"I don't want to be whipped again."

"Then don't try to escape again or refuse to work. I'll see you're freed. Trust me on that."

"Bear it with Christian fortitude," Wes said.

"Yeah, that's the ticket." I almost said *And the years will fly by,* but I bit my tongue.

After my visit, Wes took my advice and became a model prisoner. He managed the library and led Sunday devotions for his fellow cons and, as far as I am aware, was never punished again. In addition, he studied law and by all accounts became very learned in all its twists and turns.

Thank God, I didn't know then that, despite all my efforts on his behalf, John Wesley would spend a total of fifteen years, eight months, and twelve days in Huntsville.

Finally, at my urging and that of other prominent citizens, his lawyer W.S. Fly met with newly appointed Texas governor James B. Hogg. He was said to be, "All for the underdog when the underdog has a grievance."

I ask you, who was more sinned against than John Wesley?

Fly met with Hogg and declared, "I can get a thousand men in Gonzales County who will sign an application demanding that John Wesley Hardin get a full pardon. I have faith in his integrity and manhood and believe it is not misplaced."

Petitions soon poured into the governor's office from all over Texas, signed by judges, businessmen, politicians, and twenty-six sheriffs. In addition, a flood, nay, a deluge, a torrent, a cascade of letters came from private citizens.

"Parole granted!" a delighted Hogg declared on February 7, 1894.

John Wesley walked out of Huntsville, a free man, ten days later. He was forty years old.

I had a carriage and pair waiting for him at the gates.

When Wes was released, the frontier he had

known no longer existed . . . except in isolated communities like the wild border town of El Paso. Even so close to the beginning of the twentieth century it still had more than its share of resident gunmen.

Of course, the town would eventually attract Wes like a moth to a flame.

Chapter Fifty-Eight:
Beginning of the End

"Gentlemen, I now declare to you that my future life will be one of peace and goodwill toward all men."

Thus, on July 21, 1894, did Wes address the District Court of Gonzales County after it allowed him to practice law in any of the state's district and lower courts.

W.S. Fly was so moved, he jumped up and in a loud, stentorian voice, addressed the court. "You have all read Victor Hugo's masterpiece, *Les Miserables*. It paints in graphic terms the life of a man so like Mr. John Wesley Hardin, a man who tasted the bitterest dregs of life's cup, but whose Christian manhood rose, godlike, above it all and left behind a path luminous with good deeds."

The audience cheered and no huzzahs were louder than my own.

I didn't realize it then, but it was the last time I'd ever feel proud of Wes and bask in the dazzling radiance of his glory.

Restless as ever, Wes ran for sheriff of Gonzales County, lost by a mere eight votes, then closed up his law practice and relocated to Kerrville in the hill country around the Guadalupe River. Before he left, he sent me a letter explaining the move. He said that one of his kin, Jim Miller, needed help with a legal wrangle.

But what really drew him west was a woman.

Callie Lewis was a flighty fifteen-year-old who'd fallen in love with the Hardin legend. She apparently admired desperadoes and their deeds of derring-do and thought it would be a hoot to wed and bed one.

What she didn't realize was Wes was a man old beyond his years, his bullet-scarred body stiff and not easy to get going in the morning.

But he wanted her. She was a flashing, vibrant, beautiful girl who reminded him of his own reckless youth. He hoped he could recapture all those lost Huntsville years if he made Callie his wife.

And so vivacious Callie played Catherine Howard to John Wesley's stooping, stumbling, aging Henry VIII and the end result was just as tragic.

The happy couple wed in London, Texas, on January 9, 1895, and parted forever early the next morning, a few hours after they'd exchanged their vows.

Callie never said what caused the split, but to me it was obvious — the sickly, middle-aged man she married fell far short of the legend.

To me later in the day, he tried to make light of what had happened. "She took one look at me, standing nekkid as a jaybird by the bed, and promptly fainted. Hell, every time I tried to wake her up, she took one look at me and fainted again. Come morning, she threw on her duds and skedaddled out of there."

"Sorry to hear that, Wes," I said, though I had no liking for Callie. She was air-headed as they come and not very intelligent.

We were seated at a table in the Black Bull saloon. My artificial leg became intolerable if I stood at the bar for too long. I poured us both whiskey from the bottle we shared and glanced around me. The saloon was busy since evening was coming down, but no one paid us any heed.

Once well-wishers would have crowded around Wes and slapped his back, told him what a fine fellow he was, and the saloon girls would have vied for his attention.

But that night . . . nothing.

I felt a pang of sadness, almost painful in its intensity, and a deep sense of loss. *John Wesley you are a man of your time and that time is over.*

"Maybe it's just as well," Wes said.

I was shocked. Had he read my mind? "What's just as well?"

"When I go after Bill Cody, Cassie would just slow me down." Wes leaned across the table, his face within inches of mine. "I think she was in on it. That's why she left me. She was scared I'd find out."

I frowned. "Wes, I don't think that's the case. I don't think Cassie even knew about the Wild West show."

"How the hell do you know that, Little Bit? You know nothing and you never did."

"Buffalo Bill is an important man," I said, refusing to take offense. "You can't gun him."

"Yeah I can, because I'm an important man myself. Watch this."

Wes turned in his chair and yelled, "Which one of you rubes will buy John Wesley Hardin a drink?"

He got blank stares and no takers.

I watched anger flare in him. "Take it easy, Wes."

He ignored me and rose to his feet, staggering a little. He yanked a blue Colt from his waistband and yelled, "Do I have to leave men dead on the floor to get a drink?"

Standing there, half drunk, he did not look the heroic figure of old.

He was what he was — a sickly, rapidly aging man whose day was past. The owl-hoot trails he once rode were scarred by the slender shadows of telephone wires and the tracks of horseless carriages.

Then I witnessed the start of John Wesley's terrible downfall.

The bartender, a massive brute with a bullet head and hairy forearms the size of rum kegs, stepped from behind the bar, strode up to Wes, and wrenched his revolver from him so roughly I heard Wes's trigger finger break.

Yes, it was that swift and that easy.

The brute tossed the gun to me. "Get him the hell out of here before he gets hurt."

Twenty years before, the bartender would have been dead on the floor and Wes would have ordered a round of rum punches for the house. Now, he clutched his broken finger to his chest and meekly allowed me to guide him into the pale blue light of the gas-lit street.

I had discovered two truths that night. The first was that my knight in shining armor was no more. The second was that I was finally free of him.

CHAPTER FIFTY-NINE:
THIS WAS ONCE A MAN

I returned to Austin and resumed my writing career. I'd always been an admirer of Poe, and in later years I kept up a lively correspondence with Bram Stoker of *Dracula* fame. With Frank Starr's blessing I wrote my first horror novel in June 1895.

I'm sure you've read the work. *The Phantom of Yellow Fork, A tale of Western terror.* If you haven't, I believe it's still available . . . after thirteen printings.

In July I got a letter from John Wesley. He stated that he'd hung his shingle in El Paso and was walking out with a married lady and sometimes prostitute named Beulah M'Rose.

Two weeks later, I received a second missive. Wes said that his lady's husband, Martin M'Rose, had just been murdered under mysterious circumstances and that he was the prime suspect. He wrote:

But I didn't shoot the dirty dog. Though God knows he deserved killing. By holding true to my Christian faith and by dint of much prayer, I know I will triumph in the end.

Then a postscript that deeply troubled me:

Little Bit, send me $5. I am in dire financial straits right now.

There is no witness so dreadful, no accuser so terrible, as the conscience that dwells in the heart of every man. I had abandoned John Wesley to his fate and turned my back on him when he needed me most. Our years of friendship were *gone for nothing.*

I could not live with that.

Whatever slender claim to manhood I possessed would be forever crushed under the jackboot of treachery and I would never be the same again.

This I knew, even as I lied to myself that a trip to El Paso would be an excellent opportunity to do some research for my next book. Almost without thinking about it, I found myself hurriedly throwing my things into a valise, including the Colt revolver that the London bartender had taken from Wes.

Why I packed the weapon I'll never know. Its blue, oily sheen and cold black eye told me nothing.

But I did, and there's an end . . . and a beginning . . . to it.

I arrived in El Paso on the morning of August 19, 1895. It was a hot, dusty town surrounded by the Chihuahuan Desert with a distant view of purple mountains against a sky that stayed blue almost the entire year. The place was booming. Ten thousand people crowded its streets.

During my short walk from the train station to my hotel, I rubbed shoulders with priests and prostitutes, gamblers and gunmen, businessmen and beggars, and more Mexicans than I'd ever seen in one place in my life.

The throngs made the town noisy. Rumbling drays and spindly carriages vied for road space. Their drivers cursed each other and street vendors hawked their wares in loud, raucous roars from the boardwalks.

The town smelled of dust, beer, smoke, Mexican spices, and sweaty people.

But, by God, it had snap.

After I checked into my room, I came back downstairs and asked the desk clerk to direct me to the law office of Mr. J.W. Hardin.

The man looked at me as if I was an insane person. "What law office? Hardin hasn't set foot in the place for months."

"Then where can I find him?"

The clerk smiled. "Mister, there are a dozen saloons in El Paso and the same number across the border in Juarez. He could be in any one of them."

"This early?" I said, more from shock than curiosity.

"Hell, man. He's the town drunk. Where else would he be this early?" The voice came from my right side.

I turned and saw a stocky man of medium height with hard gray eyes glaring at me. He wore a holstered revolver, supported himself on a cane, and had a lawman's shield pinned to the front of his vest. "You a friend of his? Kin of his maybe?"

"I'm John Wesley's friend," I said.

The man nodded. "When you find him, give him a message from me. Tell him the only curly wolf in El Paso is me. Nobody else. You got that?"

I felt a spike of anger. "And who are you?"

"Constable John Selman. Your friend Hardin has been messing with me and mine for too long."

I said nothing.

Selman said, "Watched you walk here. You some kind of gimp or something?"

"Or something," I said.

"Don't forget what I told you." Selman limped to the door, then turned to me and said, "If Hardin doesn't leave El Paso, I'll kill him."

After Selman left, the clerk gave me a worried look. "If Hardin is your friend, I'd get him out of El Paso. Selman is a hardcase and he's put more in the grave than I can count on one hand."

"He'd like to be known as the man who killed John Wesley Hardin. That's what I think."

"Mister, you need to catch up with the times. Hardin might have been somebody once, but that was a long while back. Now he's a drunk and a laughing-stock. To prove how good he is with a gun, he shoots holes in playing cards at five paces and sells them to folks for whiskey money. He misses a lot more than he hits." The clerk shook his head. "Get him out of El Paso or take the next train to anywhere yourself."

"I'll find him." I stepped toward the door.

The clerk said to my back, "Try the Wigwam first. He's usually there this early. And another thing —"

"You sure are a talking man," I said.

"Maybe so, but listen to this — Selman has you marked. If I was you, I'd be looking over my shoulder" — he spun the register and glanced at the last entry — "Mr. Bates."

As the desk clerk had predicted, Wes was at the Wigwam saloon. He wasn't mean drunk, or silly drunk . . . just drunk.

Unnoticed, I stood inside the doorway and studied him for a few moments.

He sat at a table with his back to the wall. His face was red-veined and bloated and he looked every day of his hard, forty-two years. I'd seen his like many times before, men who were used up, had a past, but no present and less future.

All that's left for men like that is to die with as little fuss, bother, and inconvenience as possible.

When Wes looked up and saw me step toward him, his hand dropped from inside his coat. "Little Bit, you again. You keep showing up like a bad penny."

"Just passing through, Wes. I thought I'd stop and see my old friend."

"I don't have any friends, old or new," Wes said.

"That's a hell of a thing to say to me, Wes."

He motioned to a chair. "Sit down."

After I did, Wes said, "I didn't mean that. I guess I've got old friends, just no new ones." His voice dropped. "A lot of men want to kill me."

"You're square with the law. Those killing days are over."

"Maybe. But wouldn't you like to be the man who killed John Wesley Hardin?"

I shook my head. "No, I wouldn't like that one bit."

"Well, there are them who'd revel in it."

"Are you talking about John Selman?"

Wes stiffened. "You heard about him?"

"He talked to me at the hotel. He said you've got to leave El Paso."

Wes rubbed a trembling hand across his mouth. "I'm scared, Little Bit. I'm real scared."

His words hit me like a shotgun blast to the belly. "No! John Wesley, you're afraid of no man."

"I'm afraid of John Selman. I think he can shade me." Wes grabbed my hand. "Little Bit, I want out of this town. Take me with you."

"Sure, Wes, you can come with me. But you'll have to leave the bottle behind."

"I will, Little Bit. We'll leave tomorrow."

"No, Wes. We'll leave on the next train out of El Paso."

That should have ended it, but it seemed there was no end to Wes's humiliation. He called for more whiskey.

Instead the bartender brought a ledger bound with black leather. "Hardin, I'm getting mighty sick and tired of this." He pointed a thick finger to an underlined entry. "Pay the thirty-eight dollars and ten cents bar bill you owe or you'll get no more whiskey in this house."

"Damn you, Matt," Wes said. "I'm part owner of this establishment."

"The hell you are. You drank away your share a long time ago."

A second man stepped up to the table. He looked big enough and mean enough to be a bouncer. "Got some trouble here, Matt?" He rested a huge, clenched fist on the table in front of Wes.

It was an aggressive play, but Wes didn't seem to recognize it as such.

"No trouble. I'll pay Mr. Hardin's bill," I said.

The bartender had huge side-whiskers that curled around his cheeks like billy goat horns. I was dressed well, looked prosperous, but it seemed that being in the presence of John Wesley did not engender trust.

"Show me your shilling, mister," the bartender said.

I reached into my coat for my wallet and gave him two twenty-dollar bills. "Now, coffee for two."

"The hell with that," Wes said. "Bring me whiskey. We're in the money!"

CHAPTER SIXTY:
FOUR SIXES TO BEAT

I returned to my hotel room sick at heart. The man I'd known and adored as John Wesley Hardin was gone forever, in his place a scared, drunken imposter.

And only I could help him.

El Paso was a rickety skip in the middle of a vast, desert sea. By late afternoon, a strong east wind drove sand along the street outside and drove people to the boardwalks where the sting was less severe.

As he had for most of the day, John Selman was at his post under the awning of the New York Hat Shop, his eyes fixed on the window of my room.

Well, I thought, let him stand there all he wants. In a few hours, Wes will be clear of this burg forever.

We'd agreed to meet that evening at the Southern Pacific Railroad Station to board a sleeper train leaving at seven-thirty for San Antonio with a connection to Austin.

In the meantime, I sat in an easy chair, a box of good cigars and a bottle of brandy at my elbow, rising occasionally to check on Selman.

Despite the windblown sand, he stood at his post like a good soldier, ever watchful.

That puzzled me. Why this interest in me? Did he suspect something and didn't want Wes to escape his clutches?

Only time would answer that question.

I rose and retrieved the Colt revolver from my valise.

During all my western adventures I'd never carried a gun, never fired at another human being. That was about to change. I prayed for one good shot, just one straight aim . . . one unerring bullet.

Yes, I said I prayed, but not to God. I prayed to the devil.

I arrived at the station fifteen minutes before the appointed time.

The train arrived twenty minutes late. I watched it pull in, load up with passengers, and depart. I did not see John Wesley.

A Southern Pacific slumber car was to be the start of my redemption plan for Wes, but it had failed. I knew there could be no other unless I made it happen.

I returned to my room, dropped off my

bag, and shoved the Colt into my waistband as I'd so often seen Wes do.

Though the town lights were lit and the wind had grown stronger, John Selman had returned to his post on the boardwalk. I suspected that he'd followed me to the station and back.

That was all to the good. He was where I wanted him.

I walked . . . I should say *hobbled,* since my stump was paining me . . . down the stairs. The same desk clerk was on duty.

He saw me and smiled slightly. "The Acme. This time of night." He told me where the saloon was.

"Do you have a back entrance?"

"Of course," the clerk said. "Just turn right and follow the hallway. Good luck, Mr. Bates."

Surprised, I looked at the clerk, but he'd turned his back to me and I couldn't see his face.

The back entrance took me out onto Overland Street. Despite the driving sand, it was busy with people and wheeled traffic.

My head bent against the wind. Constantly checking the position of the revolver, I turned left and walked along a street lined on both sides with boarding houses and commercial buildings. I can't remember its name.

Then I turned right onto San Antonio Street. The desk clerk had told me the Alamo would be on my left, opposite the Clifford Brothers grocery store.

I hadn't caught a glimpse of Selman, but I was sure if he intended to follow me he'd have picked up my trail by now. My legs dragged as I drew closer to the Alamo and faced the harsh reality of what I planned.

People passed, heads bowed, without sparing me a glance.

A windblown leaf hit my face, then fluttered away, and I found myself listening to the *thump-thump-thump* of my artificial leg on the walk, like a bass drum at a funeral.

The Alamo was lit by electric lights and glowed in the darkness. I walked closer and heard the voices of men inside the saloon. I was sure I recognized John Wesley's drunken laugh.

Despite the wind, the night was warm. The door of the saloon was ajar. I heard footsteps behind me and looked around, but they'd suddenly stopped and I saw nothing.

I pulled the Colt and stepped closer to the door. My heart thumped in my chest and my mouth was dry, the brandy I'd drunk sour in my stomach.

I stopped at the door and looked inside. Wes stood at the bar, his back to me, playing dice with a man I didn't know.

I swallowed hard. Dear God, was I doing the right thing?

Then the thought, like a whisper in my ear. *Take the shot, Little Bit. It's an act of mercy, the first and only noble thing you've ever done for your friend.*

I pushed the Colt through the doorway and took aim.

"Brown, you've got four sixes to beat," Wes said.

I pulled the trigger.

Before you ask, yes, I saw the bullet hit.

I saw it crash into the back of Wes's head, saw the sudden eruption of blood and skull — and then John Selman was on me like a rabid wolf.

He shoved me aside and I fell on my back in a heap.

Selman rushed inside and I heard two shots, then a yell of triumph. "I killed him, by God," he shrieked. "I'm the man who killed John Wesley Hardin."

You know, after that yell, I heard a few scattered cheers.

I didn't wait to hear more.

Sick to my stomach, I got to my feet and lurched into the night. My long torment of grief and guilt had begun.

Chapter Sixty-One:
Afterward

John Selman, his hand on his gun, saw me off at the train station.

I remember his words to me plainly. "I knew you would kill him the first time I ever saw you. You had to do it, didn't you?"

"Yes, I had to do it. Once, John Wesley was a great man and my friend. I could not let him suffer any longer."

"Well, you keep your damn trap shut about what really happened, understand?" Selman said.

"I will never boast of it."

"See you don't, or I'll come looking for you." Selman's eyes were ugly.

"No you won't, Mr. Selman." I smiled at him. "You are the man who killed John Wesley Hardin, remember? You will be killed very soon."

And he was.

Without John Wesley, the end of my story is

of no importance.

I resumed my writing career, but was stricken with a virulent blood cancer and given months to live.

Fearing to die alone and unmourned, in the spring of 1914 I bestowed my fortune on the Sisters of Charity on the condition that I be allowed to spend my last days in one of their hospices.

The good sisters readily agreed, and now, as it snows outside, my last hours are at hand and the sisters stand around my bed.

Putting pen to paper is very difficult for me, but I am at peace with God. I know he's forgiven my most grievous sin.

~~I will meet~~

~~I will see~~

I know Wes has forgiven me and will meet me at the gates of Paradise.

Oh wondrous sight!

Golden revolvers will be strapped to his chest and he'll hold the reins of two milk-white horses. And he'll be as he was in his shining youth.

He'll grin at me as he did so often of old and say, "Mount up, Little Bit. We've got riding to do."

I'll run to him then, wearing my old army greatcoat and bowler hat, but on two sturdy legs.

And we'll

William Bates died before he could quite finish this account of the famous outlaw John Wesley Hardin. Mr. Bates had converted to Catholicism before his death and was fortified by the Last Rites of Holy Mother Church. He asked that this narrative not be published until a hundred years after his death. We will honor his wishes.

— Sister Mary Frances Walters.
Written this day, November 8, 1914.

J. A. JOHNSTONE ON WILLIAM W. JOHNSTONE
"WHEN THE TRUTH BECOMES LEGEND"

William W. Johnstone was born in southern Missouri, the youngest of four children. He was raised with strong moral and family values by his minister father, and tutored by his schoolteacher mother. Despite this, he quit school at age fifteen.

"I have the highest respect for education," he says, "but such is the folly of youth, and wanting to see the world beyond the four walls and the blackboard."

True to this vow, Bill attempted to enlist in the French Foreign Legion ("I saw Gary Cooper in *Beau Geste* when I was a kid and I thought the French Foreign Legion would be fun") but was rejected, thankfully, for being underage. Instead, he joined a traveling carnival and did all kinds of odd jobs. It was listening to the veteran carny folk, some of whom had been on the circuit since the late 1800s, telling amazing tales about their experiences, that planted the storytelling

431

seed in Bill's imagination.

"They were mostly honest people, despite the bad reputation traveling carny shows had back then," Bill remembers. "Of course, there were exceptions. There was one guy named Picky, who got that name because he was a master pickpocket. He could steal a man's socks right off his feet without him knowing. Believe me, Picky got us chased out of more than a few towns."

After a few months of this grueling existence, Bill returned home and finished high school. Next came stints as a deputy sheriff in the Tallulah, Louisiana, Sheriff's Department, followed by a hitch in the U.S. Army. Then he began a career in radio broadcasting at KTLD in Tallulah, which would last sixteen years. It was there that he fine-tuned his storytelling skills. He turned to writing in 1970, but it wouldn't be until 1979 that his first novel, *The Devil's Kiss,* was published. Thus began the full-time writing career of William W. Johnstone. He wrote horror (*The Uninvited*), thrillers (*The Last of the Dog Team*), even a romance novel or two. Then, in February 1983, *Out of the Ashes* was published. Searching for his missing family in a post-apocalyptic America, rebel mercenary and patriot Ben Raines is united with the civilians of the

Resistance forces and moves to the forefront of a revolution for the nation's future.

Out of the Ashes was a smash. The series would continue for the next twenty years, winning Bill three generations of fans all over the world. The series was often imitated but never duplicated. "We all tried to copy the Ashes series," said one publishing executive, "but Bill's uncanny ability, both then and now, to predict in which direction the political winds were blowing brought a certain immediacy to the table no one else could capture." The Ashes series would end its run with more than thirty-four books and twenty million copies in print, making it one of the most successful men's action series in American book publishing. (The Ashes series also, Bill notes with a touch of pride, got him on the FBI's Watch List for its less than flattering portrayal of spineless politicians and the growing power of big government over our lives, among other things. In that respect, I often find myself saying, "Bill was years ahead of his time.")

Always steps ahead of the political curve, Bill's recent thrillers, written with myself, include *Vengeance Is Mine, Invasion USA, Border War, Jackknife, Remember the Alamo, Home Invasion, Phoenix Rising, The Blood of Patriots, The Bleeding Edge,* and the upcoming *Suicide Mission.*

It is with the western, though, that Bill found his greatest success. His westerns propelled him onto both the *USA Today* and the *New York Times* bestseller lists.

Bill's western series include *The Mountain Man, Matt Jensen, the Last Mountain Man, Preacher, The Family Jensen, Luke Jensen, Bounty Hunter, Eagles, MacCallister* (an Eagles spin-off), *Sidewinders, The Brothers O'Brien, Sixkiller, Blood Bond, The Last Gunfighter,* and the upcoming new series *Flintlock* and *The Trail West.* May 2013 saw the hardcover western *Butch Cassidy, The Lost Years.*

"The Western," Bill says, "is one of the few true art forms that is one hundred percent American. I liken the Western as America's version of England's Arthurian legends, like the Knights of the Round Table, or Robin Hood and his Merry Men. Starting with the 1902 publication of *The Virginian* by Owen Wister, and followed by the greats like Zane Grey, Max Brand, Ernest Haycox, and of course Louis L'Amour, the Western has helped to shape the cultural landscape of America.

"I'm no goggle-eyed college academic, so when my fans ask me why the Western is as popular now as it was a century ago, I don't offer a 200-page thesis. Instead, I can only offer this: The Western is honest. In this great country, which is suffering under the yoke of political correctness, the Western harks back to an era when justice was sure and swift. Steal a man's horse, rustle his cattle, rob a bank, a stagecoach, or a train, you were hunted down and fitted with a hangman's noose. One size fit all.

"Sure, we westerners are prone to a little embellishment and exaggeration and, I admit it, occasionally play a little fast and loose with the facts. But we do so for a very good reason — to enhance the enjoyment of readers.

"It was Owen Wister, in *The Virginian* who first coined the phrase *'When you call me that, smile.'* Legend has it that Wister actually heard those words spoken by a deputy sheriff in Medicine Bow, Wyoming, when another poker player called him a son of a bitch.

"Did it really happen, or is it one of those myths that have passed down from one generation to the next? I honestly don't know. But there's a line in one of my favorite Westerns of all time, *The Man Who Shot Liberty Valance,* where the newspaper editor tells the young reporter, 'When the

truth becomes legend, print the legend.'
"These are the words I live by."

The employees of Thorndike Press hope you have enjoyed this Large Print book. All our Thorndike, Wheeler, and Kennebec Large Print titles are designed for easy reading, and all our books are made to last. Other Thorndike Press Large Print books are available at your library, through selected bookstores, or directly from us.

For information about titles, please call:
(800) 223-1244

or visit our Web site at:
http://gale.cengage.com/thorndike

To share your comments, please write:
Publisher
Thorndike Press
10 Water St., Suite 310
Waterville, ME 04901

CPSIA information can be obtained
at www.ICGtesting.com
Printed in the USA
FFOW04n0312040914
7205FF

9 781410 471840